LIAR LIAR

LIAR LIAR

L.G. DAVIS

bookouture

Published by Bookouture in 2022

An imprint of Storyfire Ltd.
Carmelite House
50 Victoria Embankment
London EC4Y 0DZ

www.bookouture.com

ISBN: 978-1-80314-669-0
eBook ISBN: 978-1-80314-668-3

I dedicate this book to the memory of my aunt Ella who, by following her own dreams, inspired me to do the same.

PROLOGUE

It's pitch-black outside with just a few feeble stars breaking through the clouds, and the cold is as sharp as needles as it seeps into my skin. I'm crouching down with my hood up, hidden in the bushes, watching her through the window as she tidies away their plates and makes her modern kitchen sparkle. He finishes the washing-up and kisses her, and I feel my insides clench with anger. She really has it all; a perfect wife with a perfect life.

But she doesn't know that when the time is right, I'm going to take everything away from her. The life she has stolen is nothing more than a tight knot ready to unravel, and I know exactly which pieces to pull, where to rip, and when to let go of the damaged strands. I have it all planned out.

She straightens her back and peers out of the kitchen window, so I step back and hide deeper within the shadows of the bushes. When she looks away again, I light a cigarette and savor the burn of the smoke in my throat, then I wait for a while, until the lights go out and I'm certain they have gone to bed.

Finally, I toss the cigarette to the ground, crushing it with the bottom of my shoe before I emerge from my hiding place, my knees creaking as I walk softly up to the backdoor. The key turns slowly in the lock, and with my ears attuned to every sound, I enter the house I know like the back of my hand. Enjoying the thrill of creeping around in the dark, I listen hard for the sound of someone coming down the stairs and quietly make myself a cup of coffee. It's that expensive coffee that she always buys, because of course she always has to have the best. Gradually, my invasion of her space soothes my anger, just as the coffee melts away the cold that has now reached my bones. Then I leave her silly little terracotta and cream mug in the pristine sink for her to find.

A little reminder that she is far from safe. Her days are numbered.

I have come for her.

CHAPTER ONE

PRESENT

The past has eyes. Like a jealous lover, it watches me dance with the present, waiting in the shadows, ready to spring up on me. If I stop to listen, I'll hear it whispering in the leaves outside my kitchen window.

"I know what you did," it whispers. "I'm coming for you."

Not today. Today, I choose to pretend it does not exist. The kitchen is warm and humid, the air laced with the smells of the outdoors and roasting lobster. I'm removing the casserole from the oven when Oliver walks in, dressed in his gray and black workout clothes, having stopped by the gym on his way from work. His dark-brown hair is cropped close to the scalp, and his chin is clean-shaven. A year ago he had long hair, often worn in a low ponytail at the back of his neck, and a full beard, but, like me, he now has a brand-new look to match his new life, our life. While he opted for shorter hair, I grew my toffee-brown, bob-length hair out until it reached the middle of my back. Then I dyed it inky black and that was all it took to make me look and feel like a different person.

"You didn't have to do that." Oliver points to the casserole in my hands before kissing my cheek. He smells like cologne and sweat, and some of his sweat clings to my skin, but I don't mind. I savor these moments still, the sweet domestic normality I once thought could never be mine.

"What?" I ask my husband. "Cooking, you mean?"

"Yeah. I know you've been tired lately, darling, and we haven't ordered in for a while. I'm sure Mason would love some pizza."

I lower the casserole to the counter and remove the red and white terry cloth oven gloves. "It's okay. Cooking keeps me calm. But if you prefer pizza, I could take this with me to the book club. I'm sure they'll appreciate a hot meal."

Oliver works very hard as a real estate broker with his own company, and I know he feels guilty that I do so much around the home. Even though we can afford to hire help, and home-schooling our son Mason keeps me very busy, I relish every opportunity I have to show Oliver how grateful I am for what he did for me, and to make our life together as happy as possible. Because, sometimes, it feels like I'm living on borrowed time. And after everything Mason has been through in his seven years, I'm determined to make the rest of his life as comfortable as I possibly can.

"Don't you dare," he says, with a low chuckle, a rumble from deep within his chest. "I'm not complaining. You know I can't resist your lobster casserole." He sits down at the marble kitchen island and watches as I toss the salad.

"How was your day, honey?" I ask. "Did you sell any houses?"

"You bet. Luck was with me. I sold two properties, one of which closed escrow today."

"That's great, baby. I'm so proud of you."

"Yeah, it is pretty awesome." He clears his throat. "So what time is your book club meeting?"

"In about an hour, so I have enough time to give Mason a quick bath and feed him before I leave."

"I can do it, you know. How about we try again tonight?"

I sigh. "You know how he got last time you wanted to bath him. It took forever to calm him down."

"I know." Oliver smiles gently, but I know he's hurt by Mason's constant rejection of him. "And you're right. I guess it is a step forward that he didn't throw a tantrum when you told him he's staying home with me tonight."

The truth is, Mason *did* get upset when I told him, I just didn't tell Oliver about it. When it's not too late in the day, I like bringing him with me to our meetings. The others don't mind: in fact, they have accepted him as a member of the club. I move behind Oliver and wrap my arms around him, melting into him. His scent of sweat and musk fills me with a sense of belonging. I instantly feel my stress dissolve away and I can feel his body relax in my arms. Being held by him always makes me drift into a state of euphoria.

"Baby, I know this is hard for you, and I appreciate that you keep trying to bond with him. But you have to understand that he went through a lot, and he's just trying to handle it the best way he knows how. We all are. Baby steps, remember?"

"Yeah." He scratches the back of his head. "Baby steps. I'll keep reminding myself of that. It's just that I really try, you know?"

"I know." I release him and get back to the stove. "It will be weird being at the book club without him, though."

Oliver clasps his hands under his chin. "I know we already talked about this, but do you really think you should be part of that book club? I mean, you guys probably talk about a lot of things. I'm just worried that one day you might slip and say something you shouldn't. Not much time has passed; it's all still so raw."

The Cherry Lane Book Club was founded almost six months ago by my friend Carmen Hill, who lives just down the road from us and arrived in Westledge, North Carolina, two months after we did. She'd walked by our house one lazy Friday night and saw me reading on the cushioned front porch swing, surrounded by flickering candlelight with a glass of red wine next to me. I'd just put Mason to bed and needed something to occupy my churning mind.

After a few minutes of conversation about the weather, she'd introduced herself, and I'd invited her to join me for a glass of wine. Before long, she'd pulled up a rocking chair beside me and we'd got into a wonderful discussion about books. And for the first time in months, I'd forgotten my ever-present fear that my guilt was written across my eyes, that something I said would give everything away. Although we had just met, I'd felt an instant connection with Carmen. I could immediately see her open and genuine personality and she'd made me genuinely laugh out loud, something that hadn't happened in a long time. Her laughter was so contagious it had been impossible not to participate. She'd sounded like a little kid, really laughing with her whole body, and I'd found it adorable. We'd talked about everything and nothing as if we'd known each other all our lives. I'd felt like I could tell her anything and I'd wanted to, even though I couldn't. Even so, that did not stop me from bonding with her, and a week later she'd mentioned that she wanted to start a neighborhood book club.

"You must join us, Tess! It would be a great opportunity for us newbies to get to know the neighbors," she'd said, brimming with excitement. "They say the easiest way to bond quickly with other people is through sports and books."

Oliver had not thought it a good idea. He'd refused to join and urged me not to either. "I don't mean to deprive you of the opportunity to make friends, but we just arrived in town not long ago, and we have got to be careful about who we associate with. You can never really know who to trust."

So, over the next two weeks, I'd pestered him about it until he'd given in. Determined to make the book club a big success,

Carmen had gone from house to house, recruiting people easily with her irresistible energy and warmth. Six of us, including myself, had joined—all women, except for Dan. And a week later, Carmen had hosted a meeting in her cozy, cushion-filled living room with its warm shades of deep red and brown, and I'd stayed with her afterwards to help her clear up. As we'd got to know each other, I learned that a year before moving to Westledge, she had lost her husband to a heart attack and had been in search of a friendly place to start over. She'd chosen Westledge because it is close to Lumberton, where her mother is in a nursing home with Alzheimer's.

The book club has really kept me sane over the last few months. It's an opportunity to lose myself in a different world and feel like an ordinary neighbor. While many of the group members often choose true crime books or thrillers, I always go for something much further away from my own reality. It's truly a delight to find a book that makes me laugh and smile, something I once thought I'd never do again. I also deeply appreciate the company of other people, the easy friendships I'm building there with Carmen, and with Dan—kind-hearted, thoughtful Dan who re-awakened my love for writing.

Meeting up with my new friends makes me feel like a real person, instead of somebody who is fading away and just going through the motions of my ordinary daily life. So even though Oliver gets nervous at the thought of me getting close to people, and I know he is probably right, the book club isn't something I'm prepared to sacrifice.

I blow out a sigh and shake my head. "Honey, it's only our neighbors and I've been a member for months now. Nothing has happened. I'm very careful about what I say."

"I know." He runs a hand over his hair. "But I do worry about you putting yourself out there. You know I don't think they'll ever give up looking."

I smile at him, saddened by the worry in his eyes. He

didn't deserve any of this, this life of fear burrowing into our happiness. He sacrificed a lot for my freedom, and I owe everything I have to him. I don't want to make his anxiety worse, and that's why I hardly ever go out. But the book club is my only escape, and it's just a little weekly community meeting at a chosen member's home. I'm sure we can trust all our neighbors, and I'm always careful never to do anything to suggest there might be more to my little family than first meets the eye.

Mason and I rarely leave the house unless I'm taking him to his doctor's appointments. So, it's important to me that our home is a pleasant place to be. I've loved it here since the moment we first moved in, and I've really made it our own. With Mason being in a wheelchair, it's only one level and the interior is painted a clean light gray and white, with dark hardwood floors. Huge sliding glass doors open up to a wraparound porch. The back of the house has a huge garden that's always lively and full of the sounds of nature: the birds, the insects buzzing, the rustling of the leaves. But my favorite part of the house has to be the kitchen with its sleek and modern stainless steel and black glass appliances. The entire length of one wall is made of glass that extends out to the porch, so it's the perfect place to sit and watch the sunset while I'm cooking. Of course, it also gives anyone standing in the back garden a perfect view of me through the glass, but I try not to think about that right now.

"Okay, fine," Oliver says when I don't respond. "I know how much it means to you. But please, Tess, just make sure you continue being careful about what you say. Don't drink too much; we both know how much looser tongues can be after alcohol. And just for my peace of mind, please leave as soon as it's over."

"I promise. I'll go and give Mason a bath now before I get ready to leave. You go ahead and eat."

"With all this sweat on me?" He grimaces. "I'll jump into the shower first."

"Sounds like a plan." I blow him a kiss and leave the kitchen.

Twenty minutes later, Mason giggles when I accidentally brush his armpits as I lift him from the rose-scented bubbles in our deep bathtub, scooping him into my arms. Since it's not often that I get to hear his laughter, it gives me a warm, fuzzy feeling deep inside, and I hold him for a few moments to relish it before lowering him into his wheelchair. The chair is white, with dark gray wheels and a metal frame, and it's decorated with moon and star stickers.

Today, he seems smaller than ever, as if he's slipping away from me. His legs are thin and formless, with only the faintest suggestion of muscles showing through the freckled skin. The accident left scars on more than his body. He is seven now, but thanks to the physical and mental trauma he has endured in his short years, Mason seems to have regressed back to toddlerhood. As I drape another worn and faded blue towel to dry him before he gets cold, I remember the time when he was a happy and active little boy, when his accident had not robbed him of the ability to control his movements. But I choose to be grateful for the fact that even with a thoracic spinal cord injury, he still has normal hand and arm function that enables him to eat, hold a cup, and turn the pages of a book. Whatever Mason can't do, I do for him so he can live a life that's as close to normal as possible.

As I do often at bath time, I hum "Jingle Bells" as I finish drying his body, and I smile when he hums along with me. It's spring, but he loves listening to and singing Christmas carols all year round. I guess he finds it comforting, and so do I. Having dressed him in his planet-print pajamas, I sit on his bed with him in my lap, holding him close and feeling my heart swell with my love for him.

"I'm going to the book club, okay? When I get back it will be late, so we need to say goodnight now."

The brief moment of joy he exuded earlier evaporates and he hangs his head, rocking back and forth. "I don't want you to go," he murmurs. "Stay here with me."

Since we spend so much time together, Mason hates it when I go out and don't take him along. But, sometimes, I do crave a little time to myself even though I always feel guilty being away from him.

"You won't be alone. Daddy will be here with you." I cup his chin with my hand. "Look at me, sweetie." When our eyes meet, I give him a smile. "If there are cupcakes, I'll save some for you."

The corners of his mouth turn up into an almost-smile. His eyes, once wide and innocent, now always carry a shadow of pain behind them. The happy little boy I used to know is still haunted by the past; he has lost so much of his childhood joy. And I would do anything to get it back.

"It's time for dinner. Do you want to eat? I made a lobster casserole."

He shakes his head, looking miserable. "I want to sleep."

"You can't sleep without dinner, Mason! You'll wake up hungry in the night."

He shrugs. "I'm not hungry."

I try to convince him that he should eat, but he doesn't budge. After discussing it for a few minutes, I give up, hoping he will change his mind on his own soon. "If you get hungry later, shout for Daddy, okay?"

I bend down and place a gentle kiss on his warm head, guilt tying my stomach in knots. "I'll see you later, sweetheart. I love you so much."

When I return to the bedroom, I don't find Oliver in the

shower. He's in his office with the door almost shut, even though he usually keeps it wide open to let trapped air out of the room. Peering through the crack in the door, I watch him sitting on the leather couch, talking on the phone in a low voice.

When I walk in he stops mid-sentence, lifts his head and our eyes meet. As I take in his pale face and dilated pupils, my stomach twists with anxiety. What is going on? His gaze still on mine, he tells the person on the other end that he has to go and quickly ends the call. I'm about to ask him if everything is okay and who he was talking to, when he comes to me and wraps his arms around me.

"Have I told you today how much I love you?" he asks, pressing his lips to mine.

"I love you too," I say against his lips, still feeling uneasy but knowing he would tell me if it was something serious. It's probably just stress at work.

"I know you do." He breaks our kiss. "Before you leave for your book club, I have something for you. Come with me."

He takes my hand and leads me to our bedroom, where he hands me a little box, wrapped in silver-colored foil.

"What's this?" I ask, taking the box from him.

"Open it," he says.

When I remove the wrapping paper, I find a beautiful jewelry box, blue with a silver lid. I lift the lid, and gasp. A diamond ring with a large round center stone sits on a gray velvet cushion.

"Oh my God, Oliver. It looks just like the old one."

"I know." Oliver plucks the ring from its velvet bed. "I know you've been feeling terrible about losing your engagement ring, so I got you a new one. I wanted to surprise you with it when you came home from the book club tonight, but I couldn't wait."

Three months ago, I was out for a walk with Mason and when I got back home, my ring was not on my finger. I had no idea where I had dropped it. I retraced my steps but could not locate it, and since then every time I looked at my finger, I felt terrible.

"I love it!" I say as warmth spreads through my chest. It never ceases to amaze me how he finds so many ways to show me how special I am to him. He grins as he slides it onto my finger, but as I look in his eyes I see an unfamiliar shadow there and it drives ice into the pit of my stomach.

* * *

When I return home around eleven, Oliver is sitting on the back porch outside the kitchen, bathed in the soft light from the outdoor lamp. His head is bent and his shoulders are slouched inside the thick black sweater. Since I'm in the kitchen and he has his back turned to me, he cannot see me, and I'm about to go outside to join him when his head tips back to face the sky. Then a plume of smoke billows out of his mouth and surrounds his face. I watch as he takes one more puff, then stubs out the cigarette before rubbing the side of his face. I've never seen him smoke before, and as I step outside, the same unease I felt earlier returns. Who had he been talking to on the phone, and why did he end the call when I walked in?

As soon as he sees me, he pops a gum into his mouth. "I didn't hear you come in." Even though he's smiling, his face looks drawn and tired.

"Are you okay?" I ask, taking a step toward him and placing my hand on his arm.

"Yeah, I'm fine. I just have a lot on my mind and work is..." He shakes his head. "You know what, let's not talk about work. My wife is home and that's all I care about. It's late. Let's go to bed."

I'm tempted to ask him about the smoking, but I don't want to add to his stress. But I notice that, before he says goodnight, he switches his phone off before plugging it in to charge. As I snuggle up to him, my mind is racing. What could be on his mind besides work? Has he heard something from *them*, and not told me? Why would he switch his phone off?

Before I fall asleep, my phone beeps to signal a new message in the Cherry Lane Book Club WhatsApp group. It's from Lillian, and she's praising a book she's just finished reading called *My Father's Lies*.

It was so good, you guys, and deliciously disturbing. If anyone is looking for a great true crime thriller, give it a try. It's about a sperm donor who murders the women who are pregnant with his kids. I think there's going to be a movie about it.

Before I finish reading, Dan responds.

I read that book last year. It's really great, but also creepy. I could not get it out of my head for weeks. Here's the link.

Even though thrillers are very much not my thing at the moment, I find myself clicking on the link to read the book description.

Secrets rarely stay hidden. No matter how fast you run, the truth always comes out.

The words are like a bullet hitting me right in the center of my chest. I inhale sharply and, with my hands shaking, I get out of the page and switch off the phone.

CHAPTER TWO

It's been three days since I caught Oliver smoking, and I'm standing in the doorway watching Mason and Randy Jones performing a series of stretches in the den. Once a week, Randy, a physical therapist, works with Mason to improve his lower body's strength and mobility. He's in his twenties with gray eyes, black hair, and a muscular build, and he has a positive attitude and cheerful disposition. I really appreciate that while working with Mason, he likes to feed his mind with positive thoughts like "Your body can do more than you think. You have to believe that." And he's good at tickling laughter out of my son. When we interviewed him a year ago, one of the things that impressed us most was his determined, positive outlook on life.

I watch from the doorway as he and Mason move from using the standing frame with handles and foot supports to working out on the floor. Randy is now showing Mason how to roll over from his back to his side and then onto his stomach. Mason laughs at something Randy says as he tries to master the movements and, even though he isn't complaining, it's clear that the exercises are challenging for him.

"Are you sure you don't want anything to drink, Randy?" I ask.

He shakes his head, concentrating on his work. "I'm good for now, thanks."

"Okay, well, if you change your mind, just call. I'll be in the living room."

I glance at my watch. 11:30 a.m. The therapy session will last for another hour and a half, and I'll use the time to work on my novel. Mason's weekly sessions are also my writing sessions. I take my laptop and a glass of water out to the living room and settle down on the couch. For a moment I just sit and listen to Mason's laughter floating into the room from the den, followed by the sound of Randy making horse noises. I smile, feeling a sense of peace wash over me, and I'm just about to start writing when the doorbell rings. To my surprise, Oliver is standing on the doorstep.

"Hello there, gorgeous," he says, bending down to kiss me.

"Hey, aren't you supposed to be at the office?"

"I am actually, but, as the boss, I decided that I wanted to come home early today to have a date with my wife." He's holding a bulging plastic bag. "I brought lunch. Chinese takeaway."

My heart swells with affection. "A date? And lunch at eleven thirty in the morning?"

"Why not? Who made the rules anyway?"

I grin up at him. "Well, since Randy is here and he's going to be with Mason for a while, why not?"

"Exactly, that's why I came now. And I brought something else with me." He's holding one hand behind his back and brings it forward to reveal an exquisite bouquet of white calla lilies.

"Are those for me?" I ask, my eyes wide.

"Of course they are, sweetheart." He hands them to me and I hold them up to my face.

"You really know how to sweep a girl off her feet, don't you?"

"I try." He holds out his hand to me. "Shall we, my lady?"

I follow him into the dining room where he sets up the table as if we're having a dinner party, placing our best plates, utensils, and wine glasses on the table.

We sit down to talk while we eat, and I reach for a fish ball and raise an eyebrow. "What's the occasion?"

"I wanted to spoil you a little. I know I've been a little distant the past few days, and I apologize for that. Today is about you."

Oliver has always been good at surprises, and it turns out to be the perfect date. Once we've finished eating, we sit in the rocking chair on the porch, feeling the sun warming our faces. The moment should be serene, but it isn't completely. I feel slightly on edge, with the familiar sinking feeling that someone is out there watching me. So instead of relaxing in my husband's arms, I'm tense. I scan the street, the neighboring houses, and the cars that drive by, but I don't notice anything out of the ordinary. And yet, my skin continues to crawl.

Oliver doesn't return to work and the rest of the afternoon is spent playing games with Mason and catching up on our favorite television shows. When night falls, after I tuck Mason in and he kisses my forehead to wish me goodnight, I go to our bedroom to have a shower but Oliver is already in there. I'm about to leave the room again to use Mason's bathroom when a vibrating sound stops me. Oliver's phone is on his side of the bed and it's dangerously close to the edge. Before it falls to the wooden floor, I step around the bed and grab it. The Caller ID is flashing on the screen: *Her*.

"Tess?"

Just as my fingers are curling around the device, Oliver appears at my side and snatches it from my hand. I watch him in confusion as he takes a step back. A towel is wrapped around his waist and shiny beads of water are clinging to his short hair.

"Hey." I frown. "What was that about?"

His Adam's apple bobs with a swallow. "What do you mean?" His already dark eyes are almost black now, his lashes thick, as if under a coat of mascara. The phone continues to vibrate in his hand, and I gesture at it. "Aren't you going to answer that?"

"Yep." He walks away, disappearing back into the bathroom.

When the door closes behind him and I hear the hushed sound of his deep voice, I sink onto our bed, pulling our knitted gray throw over my knees a hard knot forms in the pit of my stomach. Who is *Her*? And why is he having secret conversations? I rake my fingers through the curls in my hair and tug them at the roots, the sharp pain on my scalp numbing the hurt spreading through my heart. Tears sting my eyes, and I wipe my face with my forearm. After only seven months of being married, is my husband having an affair? My temple throbs as I sigh, and I rub my forehead. I shouldn't let myself think these thoughts, just because of my previous experience. Oliver wouldn't do that to me. He wouldn't do that to Mason.

I gaze out the window and watch the leaves on the oak tree sway in the evening breeze, trying to focus on my breathing. In, out. In, out. But it doesn't help me clear my head. I'm not sure how much time has passed when Oliver joins me on the bed, his phone forgotten for a moment. He sits next to me, so close that our thighs touch. It's as if he wants to tell me something but can't find the courage.

"Who were you talking to?" I ask to break the silence and end the misery.

"A client," he says and pushes to his feet.

I'm not stupid, and I can tell he is lying to me. I thought his secretive calls behind his closed office door were about work, but who am I fooling? Just hours ago, I was enjoying spending time with my husband, and one phone call ruined everything.

After falling asleep with a heavy feeling in my chest, I wake up in the middle of the night from a horrible dream. Oliver said that he no longer loved me, and he was leaving.

There's no way I can go back to sleep now. Not when I've just found out my husband is keeping a secret from me that could ruin everything.

After everything I went through to get here, I won't let him destroy my life.

CHAPTER THREE

Silence can be powerful. Some people find it peaceful, a chance to recharge. Not me. Growing up, silence in our house was the calm before the storm, an opportunity for my abusive father to think up the next hurtful word or way to break me. By filling it with words, I protected myself.

My stomach churns as I fight down the urge to tell Oliver exactly what's on my mind. Sitting across from me as we eat breakfast, I can see that he knows something is wrong and he's trying hard to work out what it is, to read my mind. Two more weekly book club meetings have come and gone and I'm still tormented by the thought that my husband could be having an affair. Haunted by thoughts of another woman in his life. I can't sleep, can barely eat, and every time Oliver is on the phone, I can't help thinking he's speaking to her.

Before that night, I trusted him and believed in the solidity of our marriage. But that day shook me enough to realize there had been signs all along. He had already been sneaking away for private calls and, for a month now, he's been traveling much more than usual. He arrived from one of his trips four days ago, announcing that he closed on a condo he had been trying to sell for months in Stamford, which is no more than two hours from Westledge. He could have driven there and back the same day, but he chose to spend two nights away from us. Why wouldn't I be suspicious? I used to believe him when he told me his real estate business had picked up and clients were flooding in, and I celebrated every win. But now I can't help wondering if his trips were both for business and pleasure.

I need to get on his phone. For the past few days, whenever I've had the opportunity, I have been tempted to pick it up, unlock it, and find the proof I need. It wouldn't be hard to get in, his password is my birth day and month, and the last two digits of the year I was born. Zero. Three. Sixteen. Eighty-three. But as much as I want to unveil the truth, I also want it to stay buried. The fear of what would come next is what always stops me from going on the search for answers.

"Sweetheart, you're awfully quiet this morning," Oliver says through a mouthful of toast. "And you're not eating."

I peel my gaze from his and busy myself with refilling Mason's mug with hot chocolate. Maybe I should tell Oliver outright that I suspect he's cheating. But I want evidence first, and I can't do it in front of Mason.

"I'm a little tired, that's all."

"You didn't tell me about your book club yesterday," he says, ignoring the iciness I can't hide in my voice. "How was it?"

I shrug. "Fine. We celebrated Dan's birthday."

"Is he still the only guy?"

"I don't get it," I snap. "Why does it bother you that Dan is the only male?"

"It doesn't bother me." Oliver frowns. "I find it strange, that's all."

I say nothing as I push my chair back. His biggest concern is not that Dan is at the book club, but rather that he has become a good friend of mine whom I occasionally meet up with for writing sessions. I have a feeling that makes him jealous, but, unlike him, I'd never be unfaithful. As for Dan, I know he loves his wife and baby son and would never hurt them.

"I need to start a load of laundry before Mason's lessons," I say and get to my feet.

When we arrived in Westledge, we both agreed that Mason should be homeschooled as the two schools in town are not adapted to children with special needs, and I'd much prefer that he learn at his own pace. He's struggling with so much already and, honestly, I wouldn't want anyone out there to make him feel small. After being bullied in school myself, I know how cruel kids can be.

"Tess," Oliver says when I walk to the door.

I take a breath before turning to face him, a tight smile pasted to my face.

"I know it's hard for you sometimes, but we'll get through this together."

Together. That's what I used to think, that we're a team.

"Sure," I say. "It's just that some days are harder than others."

Mason looks up and one corner of his lips twitches. I could really use one of his rare smiles right about now, but he just picks up his little mug and brings it to his lips. No smile today. I busy myself in the laundry room until shortly before Oliver leaves to go to his office, located less than twenty minutes from the house. Although we have set up a home office for him, he prefers to have a dedicated place outside to work. He feels more professional and productive that way. Today, as he kisses me, pats Mason on the head, and gets into our wheelchair-adapted Citroën Berlingo, I worry that he might be making a stop somewhere else. It's not as if I can trail him, not when he has the only car we own, and I need to care for Mason. I guess the fact that I'm pretty much immobile must make it easy for him if he wants to have an affair.

As the hours drag by, I suddenly feel claustrophobic in the

house. To keep from going crazy, I throw myself into my daily tasks, from homeschooling Mason, to ironing Oliver's shirts—even though I hate ironing—to scrubbing the tiled kitchen floor until it's spotless and wiping down the counters and cabinets. I even manage to write a few chapters of my novel. Now I'm sitting on the couch, watching Mason laughing at his favorite cartoon, *The Fart-a-lot Family*. This time, his laughter only manages to lighten my heart a little, as my mind keeps thinking about Oliver's affair and what it might do to us and our secret. The secret that brought us together and made us a family.

By the time Oliver returns home after 6 p.m., I'm ready to crash. As he always does, he comes straight over to kiss me, but I can't help wondering if his lips have just been on someone else's. I can't do this any longer. I need to know the truth.

"I need to have a shower before dinner," he says, loosening his tie.

When I first met him, he was not a suit and tie kind of guy, but always opted for jeans and t-shirts. There are times I miss the old Oliver, the free-spirited soul I used to know. Though I do catch glimpses of him from time to time, such as the day he showed up for our surprise date, the new Oliver is usually more rigid and less carefree. But the truth is, I'm to blame for his loss of self. Almost overnight, he had to step up and become a husband, a father, and the sole breadwinner after handling something unspeakable. I know that it's quite a burden on him.

"That's alright," I say, my tone injected with fake cheer. "Go ahead. Dinner will be ready when you are."

Once I hear the sound of the shower running, I sneak into our bedroom. His phone is charging on his side of the bed and I lower myself next to his pillow, taking deep breaths before I do something I might regret. I never thought I would be the kind of wife who goes through her husband's phone, but then I never thought Oliver was the cheating type. People change, I guess. A hard, painful part of me knows that if Oliver has changed so much, it's all because of me and what I did, what I made him do. Nobody recovers from that.

As I stare at his phone, I think of *her*. The fact that he didn't use her name makes it that much harder. It could suggest that he thinks this woman is *the one* for him, rather than me. Or maybe I'm being paranoid. *Her* could be an acronym for something else, a company perhaps? These thoughts are torturing me. I need to find out the truth so I can fix it, and then focus on Mason again. I've been so absent lately and he seems to be mirroring my mood.

I wipe my sweaty hands on my skirt and pick up the warm phone, taking another deep breath and praying I won't chicken out. The screen lights up, and my finger trembles as I swipe upwards. I'm prompted to enter the six-digit password and when the phone lets me in, I sigh with both relief and anxiety. I look through his call log and see that there have been several calls made to *her* in the last forty-eight hours. He called her last night at 11 p.m., well after we'd gone to bed. He must have snuck out while I was sleeping. He also called her this morning at 7 a.m., when I was preparing breakfast. Some calls lasted as long as half an hour, some were shorter than five seconds. My gut twists with jealousy as I tap on his messages icon. The last message was sent to her thirty minutes before he arrived home.

Oliver: *I'll call you when I get a moment. I'm about to leave the office.*

Her response is short, but it says everything.

Her: *I look forward to it. I miss you already. My new bed misses you even more.*

Tears blur my eyes as I read his response.

Oliver: *I'll try to get away next week. What are you wearing?*

Her: *Your favorite perfume.*

I need to stop reading. It hurts too much, but I can't stop picking at the scab. I read her next message.

Her: *I really need to hear your voice or I'll go crazy.*

Oliver: *Alright. Give me a moment.*

A tear slides down my cheek and I press my lips together, trying to hold back the waves of pain crashing over me. I scroll through earlier messages, drowning myself in the pain, feeling sick to my stomach but unable to stop. I pause when I come across a photo. Perfect breasts wrapped in peach lace and silk, a push-up bra with a little golden clover in the center. *Thank you for my present. It arrived a few hours ago.*

When the water in the shower is switched off, I turn off the phone and leave the room. I keep my emotions in check until I reach the pantry, which is separated from the rest of the kitchen by a door, filled floor to ceiling with tidy shelves of jars and canned goods. I shut myself inside, not bothering to switch on the light. Then I allow the pain to break me.

I hate my husband for doing this to us. I hate that I still love him even though he's causing me so much pain. I hate that he'd never have done something like this if it wasn't for the hurt he carries around inside him, because of me. I hate that, even if I wanted to, I could never pack my bags and leave because there's too much binding us together, and I need him.

Crouching down on the floor, my head on my knees, I'm overcome by fear. I thought that I would confront him if I had real proof that he's been having an affair. But now that I've seen just how serious it is, I'm terrified. What if by confronting him, I push him into leaving me? Oliver has already broken a promise and betrayed our marriage vows. How can I trust that he will not break the other promise he made to me, if he's not even by my side? How can I trust that he won't tell this other woman my secret?

If he betrays me, I will lose everything, and so will Mason. Every decision I've made in the past twelve months has revolved around Mason, providing him with a safe and loving environment, offering him security. But if Oliver leaves me and my secret comes to light, our lives will fall apart around us and I will lose the little boy I've come to love as my son.

He is my son in every way that matters.

I can't allow Oliver to destroy our marriage; there's too much at stake. Clearly, this other woman must go. But how can I make him stay?

CHAPTER FOUR

As soon as I wake up in the morning, I know I need to talk to someone otherwise my stomach will eat itself alive all day, so the moment Oliver leaves to go to the office, I message Dan and Carmen on WhatsApp and they both offer to come over.

Carmen is the first to arrive. She's tall, lithe, and slightly curvy, with copper hair that cascades to the small of her back and gray eyes that twinkle above high cheekbones. Today, she's dressed perfectly for the unusually warm April temperature in a loose, white cotton shirt and khaki shorts with bare feet and her toenails painted bright pink. She looks like she's just returned from a tropical vacation. She's three years younger than me, but I feel old and frumpy in a teal-colored tank top and black jeans. I can never bring myself to be jealous of her though, because there's something inherently kind about her and she's always made me feel instantly at ease.

When Carmen hugs me, she leaves behind the sweet, clean scent of her homemade apple and flowers perfume. Since she's wary of the ingredients in store-bought hair and beauty products, she makes her own. The products are also available in her online store, *Fleurs de Vie*, which is gaining quite a reputation as a trustworthy retailer of natural beauty products.

"Is Dan already here?" Carmen asks, peering over my shoulder.

"Not yet. He'll be here a little later. He took Noah to the doctor for his checkup."

The squeak of Mason's electric wheelchair appearing from down the corridor lets us both know he heard Carmen's voice. He wheels himself into the living room and stops in front of her, and his rare smile lights up his face and warms my heart. The two really get along well. A few months ago, Carmen even joked about Mason calling her Aunty and he jumped on it; he's been doing it ever since. The way his body relaxes in her presence shows me that he feels comfortable around her, and whenever I need to run last-minute errands, she always steps in to look after him. She keeps urging me to take some time for myself, promising that she would be there for Mason, but as much as I appreciate her offers, I rarely take her up on them. Mason requires a lot of care and I wouldn't want to put that on someone else's shoulders.

"Hi, Mason," Carmen says, patting the top of his head.

"Hi, Aunty Carmen. I have to do math."

"Really? How fun. If you need help, I'm your person. In school, they used to call me Math Girl."

"I love math," he continues. Then he wheels himself around again and disappears.

"It's his favorite subject," I say to Carmen.

Mason is so good at math that sometimes he figures things out before I do.

While Mason is completing the work I gave him, I take Carmen to the kitchen. She glances at the door before eyeing me with concern. "Are you okay? You said you needed to talk, is everything alright?"

I open the fridge. "Do you want something to drink? Tea, juice, wine? Or if you haven't had breakfast yet, I could make you something."

Even though I called Carmen over, a part of me is still debating whether to bring the news of my husband's infidelity out in the open, to make it real. But I do need advice on how to handle this situation before it gets out of hand.

"What I need is for you to sit down, sweetie. Tell me what's going on."

I sigh and sit down opposite her. "I think... I know... Oliver is having an affair." Shame, anger, and pain mix into a bitter cocktail that fills my stomach.

A soft gasp escapes Carmen's lips. "What? Are you sure?"

I nod, biting back tears. "I have proof. Well, I saw it."

"But how? You two are perfect for each other. I'm so sorry, Tess."

I wipe my eyes on my arm. "What's perfect on the outside isn't always perfect on the inside."

Sometimes you can do everything right and still get it wrong. I know that thanks to me, Oliver's life was ruined. But I did my best to make it up to him, to be the perfect wife and create the perfect home. Even though Mason requires constant care, I still give Oliver as much of my attention as I can. And now the tainted, delicate little life we created is slipping from between my fingers and I don't know how to hold on to it.

"I loved him," I whisper more to myself than to Carmen. "I love him."

From somewhere in the house, I hear a loud "YES." It has to be Mason, proud of himself for getting something right.

"But exactly how do you know?" Carmen asks.

"I saw text messages." I feel my shoulders slump as I let out a harsh breath. "To be honest, looking back, I probably suspected something was going on and ignored my gut feeling."

Carmen bobs her head. "Yep, I know that feeling all too well."

"Wait." I straighten up in my chair. "Your husband cheated on you?"

I expect her to say no because I can't imagine any man cheating on a woman like her.

"You got that right. Miles seriously messed up at one point. We made it through, but we almost didn't."

"How do you get over something like that?"

She shrugs. "When you think he's the one and he just stepped out of line, you swallow your pride and make it work, I guess. I did everything possible to work through it, but, honestly, the pain was so bad I wouldn't wish it on anyone, and if I could go back in time, I'd tell myself to leave him. I don't think I'd be able to go through that with any other man. That's why I don't date." She massages the bridge of her nose. "Sorry, Tess, this is not about me. It's about you and Oliver. Do you know the woman he's cheating with?"

I shake my head. "She has many faces inside my head. I saw her boobs, though. She sent him a photo on his phone. Her name is Her."

"What kind of name is that?"

I swallow down the tears lingering in my throat. "It's not; he either wants to keep her anonymous or he believes she's the only *her* there is. The one for him, you know."

Carmen's face is a mask of pity, but she doesn't say anything more. She wants me to get everything off my chest and it's exactly what I need.

"He's been sneaking off for calls, traveling a lot, and writing texts or whatever in the middle of the night when he thought I was sleeping." Tears are flowing faster now, and I know my face must be a smudgy mess but I don't care anymore.

"Sweetie, I'm so sorry. This is horrible."

Carmen gets up and holds me for a while as I cry until I have no more tears left. When I look up, Mason is in the kitchen doorway, his brow furrowed. Embarrassed, I give him a watery smile.

"Are you done, darling?" I ask, forcing a smile onto my face.

"I think so." His voice is low.

"Okay. I'll be right back," I say to Carmen and I hurry over to him. Together, we return to his room and when I'm done correcting his work, he reaches up his hand and wipes my cheek.

"I'm sorry you have to take care of me," he whispers. "I make you sad."

I drop to my knees in front of him and cup his face with both hands. "Never ever say that. You can never make me sad. You are the best thing that's ever happened to me."

He nods. "I want to take photos."

"That's a great idea." I hand him his iPad and wheel him to the window, and he holds it up and starts snapping away.

"I'll be back soon so we can continue."

I find Carmen in the living room, flipping through our family album that's a permanent fixture on the coffee table. She puts it down and stands up when I enter and enfolds me again in her arms until I pull away, but the doorbell rings before I can take my seat next to her. Dan has arrived, with Noah in a baby carrier attached to him. He lives in the house across the street from us. An attractive man, he stands about six feet tall and has tousled mahogany hair, a straight nose, and a cleft chin. Noah is a miniature version of his dad, with the same color hair and dark-brown eyes. While Dan is a stay-at-home dad, his wife, Amanda, who is a successful architect, makes up the difference in their income.

"Hello," Dan says, hugging me with one arm. "I'm sorry I couldn't come earlier."

"That's fine," I say, opening the door wide for them to enter. "You didn't miss much. Come on in."

After joining the book club, Dan and I bonded over the same book we were reading. Our discussions then moved beyond what was on the pages. As both of us are aspiring writers, we mostly talk about literature and writing. Dan has self-published a book of poetry, but his dream, like mine, is to write a novel. Noah was not yet born at the time, but when we met he also talked about wanting to be a father. He said once he was, he would drop everything to be there for his child because his father died when he was five and he never got to spend much time with him. Noah was born six months ago, and Carmen and I were both surprised and impressed by Dan's commitment to staying at home with him. I hardly see his wife, so I never really got to know her. Like Oliver, she's a workaholic and didn't want to join the book club.

Once Noah is sitting on a playmat that Dan brought along with him, Dan asks, "So, what did I miss?"

"Oliver is cheating on Tess," Carmen blurts out before I can find the words.

"You can't be serious." Dan looks at me for confirmation.

With a bitter smile, I nod and stand. "I think I need a drink. Does anyone else?"

At that moment Noah starts to fuss and Dan picks him up and bounces him on his hip. He tries to sing a lullaby, but the baby will not listen. I ask Dan if I can try, and he hands him over to me. Suddenly I wonder what it would feel like to hold my own baby, but I quickly dismiss the thought. I follow Dan's lead, trying to sing the song he sang while rocking Noah to calm him. A short while later, I look down at him, and he's staring at me, transfixed by my face. The feeling of warmth in my heart surges as he smiles, and I think he's trying to tell me something in a secret language that only he and I understand. As I inhale the sweet scent of shampoo and powder, my heart swells with emotion.

"Hold on a second," Dan says and reaches for the jeans diaper bag he brought with him. He pulls out a bottle and hands it to me. "Here, feed him."

Noah takes the bottle without hesitation and begins to suckle contentedly. His eyes close shortly after that, but he continues to suck on the bottle and after the milk is gone, he opens his eyes, but doesn't cry. He just studies my face until I hand him to Dan in case he needs burping.

"Do you know who the woman is?" Dan asks gently as he massages Noah's back.

"No. I wish I did, but to be honest, I'm not sure what I would do if I did know."

Pulling her feet up on the couch, Carmen dips her head to one side. "How will you handle Oliver?" she asks. "I assume you're leaving him? If you need help tossing his clothes out of the window, I'm your girl."

I sit back down and try to think of how to answer her question. Infidelity is a deal-breaker to most people, but I do not have the luxury of leaving. My connection with Oliver extends beyond just love.

"Want to hear my opinion?" Dan asks as he puts Noah back in the carrier. "I think you should leave, even if it's just to think about what to do. If you stay, it'll be like you're saying he can do whatever he wants and you'll just be waiting for him to do it again. Most cheaters don't stop at one time. You don't deserve this."

"Dan is right," Carmen adds, twirling a red lock of hair around one of her fingers. "You deserve way better than this."

Sighing, I rest my head on the back of our dark gray couch, pulling a cream cushion to my stomach and wrapping my arms around it. "I've considered that option, but I just can't. I love him. I need him."

Right now, I wish I could tell my friends just how much my life depends on staying in my marriage, how dangerous it could be if I left, what I stand to lose. But that's the one thing I can't talk to them about. If they knew the truth, they would never want to be in the same room as me, let alone be my friends.

CHAPTER FIVE

Even though we're at Jocelyn Summer's house for this week's book club meeting, it's Carmen who opens the door, wearing a flowing yellow caftan and a huge tortoiseshell comb in her hair.

"Welcome, Tess. Welcome, Mason. Come on in." She gives me a quick hug and kisses Mason on the top of his head.

"You smell like apples," Carmen says to him. "Did you use the apple shampoo I made for you?"

Mason nods and reaches up to touch his curls. "You're a super smeller." His voice is tinged with awe, but his face remains stoic.

"Hello, lovelies," Jocelyn shrills as she enters the spacious entrance hall of her home. "It's nice to see you both again." She smiles broadly and bends down to give Mason a quick hug, but he looks away, clutching his book so tight I can see his knuckles getting white. Jocelyn has an easy-going nature that makes everyone feel comfortable around her, but I guess Mason is not in the mood today. Unperturbed, Jocelyn straightens up again. As she air-kisses me, I notice a thinness in her smile and suddenly I wonder if the woman Mason is having an affair with is in Westledge. It could be anyone, really; any woman could be a threat to my marriage. Could it be Jocelyn?

As she ushers us into the lounge with its walls covered with expensive art, I study her closer than I ever did before. And even though I don't know if it's her, I feel a familiar sensation of anger uncurling inside me. A feeling that I've experienced before and thought I had long buried.

She's dressed in a clinging black dress that leaves little to the imagination and her thick hair, almost as black as her dress, is pulled straight back and held in place by a rhinestone barrette. Her makeup is heavily done and her green eyes are lined in black with mascara. She's in her early thirties, but too much makeup makes her look a few years older.

Jocelyn doesn't attend the club meetings very often since she travels a lot. New York, where she studied interior design, is one of her favorite places to visit. Despite dropping out of college before she graduated to live off her parents' wealth, the city must have left a lasting impression on her.

Oliver and her being away at the same time wouldn't be unusual.

Stop it, I tell myself. *You're driving yourself mad.*

When we join the others, I keep a light smile plastered on my face. Oliver is not stupid. If he had an affair, it would not be with someone who comes to my book club. A woman out of town would be an easier secret to hide, someone far away from me.

I try not to suspect everyone else.

Lillian Brooker, who recently traveled to Hawaii with her boyfriend, Darius, and came back married, smiles and picks up her chick lit book from the uncomfortable cream leather sofa to make space for me.

"Thank you," I say and wheel Mason's wheelchair next to me.

Unlike the others, Lillian has never warmed to Mason.

She's friendly enough, but the look she often gives him is both pitying and sad, and she has a way of staring at him that makes me uncomfortable, like he's some animal in a circus.

Monica Cross, a former beauty pageant queen turned financial broker, is sitting on the other side of Lillian. She leans forward to flash Mason a smile. "I was hoping you'd come, Mason. I baked your favorite peanut butter cookies."

Probably five feet ten, Monica has an athletic build, a beautiful heart-shaped face, and skin the color of coffee mixed with cream. Three years shy of fifty, she has a few silver strands in her hair that she wears with pride. Wearing white slacks, a loose blue top, and matching flip-flops, she looks fresh-faced and youthful. Among the people in the room, she is the one I admire the most aside from Carmen. She exudes such confidence and grace that I wish I were more like her. When I'm alone, I sometimes imitate her body language, posture, smile, and laugh, just so I can feel more poised and at ease in my own skin.

"Cool beans." Mason rubs his hands together as if about to tear into a delicious gourmet meal. That's his favorite phrase lately; I have no idea where he picked it up. His expression has softened, and his lips are no longer pursed. For now, he's at peace.

"That's so sweet of you, Monica." I smile at her. "I'm sure they are delicious." I gesture in Mason's direction. "As you can see, he can't wait to have one."

"Shall we get started, ladies and gents?" Jocelyn glances at Dan and Mason in turn.

"We shall," Dan says, smoothing his gray trousers. His hands are holding a glossy hardcover as he sits in a peach-colored armchair next to an unlit fireplace. Noah is sleeping in his bouncy chair next to him, the toy bar hanging above it swinging in time with his movement.

Settling into the comfiest-looking armchair full of throw cushions, Jocelyn smiles at all of us.

"Hello, book lovers," she says. "As many of you probably know, today marks the sixth-month anniversary of our book club. I feel, however, that we could still get to know each other a little better. So, I thought it would be fun if we took turns telling each other something interesting about ourselves and asking each other questions. Then we can move on to the books."

As I listen to her, I can feel my stomach churning. The best part of the book club was that no one asked questions beyond books. Now she has to spoil everything.

"Let's start with me," Jocelyn says, even though no one agreed to play her game. "I was once married to a celebrity I met at a concert in New York." She pauses for dramatic effect and smiles when she sees our stunned expressions. "Even though we were only married for one month, our time together boosted his career and gave me a large following on Instagram. We both got something out of it, so I have no regrets."

I swallow, my mind racing as I try to think of something to say. What she revealed was so private, and she might expect us all to do the same. As my heart thrashes inside my chest, I tell Mason to listen to an audiobook. I don't want him to hear anything inappropriate. As soon as his headphones are on and I hear the muffled sound of the woman reading to him, I turn my attention to Lillian, who is lifting her hand as if she's in class waiting for her turn to speak.

"What's your ex-husband's name?" she asks Jocelyn. "Do we know him?"

A smile spreads across Jocelyn's face and her green eyes crinkle at the corners. "Sorry, dears. I don't like to kiss and tell."

Monica leans toward Jocelyn as she clears her throat. "Okay, but why did you bring this up if you weren't going to tell us everything?" She winks.

Jocelyn dismissively waves her hand. "He was a rock star, that's all I'll say. Who knows, I might mention his name at our next meeting."

Lillian pulls out her phone and waves it in the air. "I'll go next," she says. "One interesting fact about me is that I used to write for a gossip magazine and I am very good at digging up dirt on people. Ask me anything, and I will do my best to answer."

I have googled myself before without finding out anything, but it still frightens me to think that someone could discover my secrets.

"Go on," Lillian continues while she types on her phone. "Ask me anything."

Monica folds both arms across her chest. "It would be nice if you told us Jocelyn's ex-husband's name."

"Come on, guys," Jocelyn cuts in. "My time is up. Let's move on to the next person."

"It's Jason Daniels," Lillian says, but her eyes remain fixed on the phone. "That's who Jocelyn was married to. It states here that he was married to another woman at that time, so the marriage was annulled."

Silence falls like a curtain dropping after a play. Carmen covers her mouth with a hand, Monica's long lashes flutter in surprise, and panic riots through me. Dan tries to say something, but no words come out. The only sounds are the cooing of the baby and the thundering of my heart. Jocelyn has done it before. She stole someone else's husband. What would stop her from doing it again?

As everyone stares at her, she suddenly appears smaller in the massive armchair. After a few moments, she pushes her shoulders back and tilts her chin up. "There it is, my dirty little secret. But does anyone here know that Dan was in jail?" She turns to him with a triumphant smile. "A little bird told me that he was behind bars for two years. I'm sure everyone would love to know why."

The vein on Dan's forehead pulses as he glares at Jocelyn. He didn't tell me that about himself, but I also know it's not my business. The fact that the man I know is a good friend, a loyal husband, and an amazing father is enough. His past is irrelevant to me. I have things to hide too.

Finally, Dan stands up to Jocelyn. "What gave you the right to—?"

"That's enough." Carmen flashes a warning glance at Jocelyn. "I started this book club to create a safe environment for book discussion without bringing in the outside world."

Jocelyn shrugs. "I'm not judging anyone. All I'm saying is that we should be honest and open with each other. After all, we are friends, right?"

"We all have a past we don't want to share, Jocelyn," Carmen continues, her voice firmer. "I think it's inappropriate to talk about it when we're trying to have fun. This is a book club, not a gossip club."

The room agrees, except for Jocelyn, who turns her gaze to me. Her expression bothers me. She isn't glaring, but she isn't smiling either, and when she speaks, her eyes are still on me. "That's a pity. I would have wanted to know more about Tess. I bet she has some juicy stories to tell."

Is it possible that she knows something? I feel paralyzed and powerless, and it feels like I'm in slow motion as I turn to look at the others. I'm the center of attention, and I've always hated that.

"Lay off, Jocelyn," Dan snaps. "You heard what Carmen said. This is a book club, not a gossip party."

I mouth a thank-you to him and he gives me a light nod. Jocelyn claps her hands together and smiles like someone who hasn't just lit a match in a room dripping with fuel. "Fine, then. Get out those books and let's get started. As always, eat, drink, and feel free to raid my library if you're into romance novels."

The Cherry Lane Book Club is not the kind of reading group most people are familiar with. Instead of the club members reading the same book, then discussing it with the others, we all pick our own individual copies at the beginning of each month, week, or in between. The main reason for getting together is to be surrounded by people who share the same passion for reading and to take some time away from our busy lives. We chat about what we're reading in the first half of the meeting, and the second half is dedicated to reading together.

My love for reading started when I was a child, and it was an escape of sorts. Having grown up in an abusive home, and later in a children's home and in and out of care, I never had long-term family members let alone a stable friendship group, and I gravitated toward books that featured close friends getting up to adventures together, or a loving family environment. Now I always want to read something that will make me laugh. Reading has gotten me through the tough times and I always come back to it. I wonder if it can get me through this.

Once everyone shares what they're reading, Jocelyn's housekeeper, Silvia, sets two silver platters of food on the coffee table. The shrimp are swimming in a pool of butter adorned with crushed red chilis and garlic cloves. She disappears back into the kitchen, returning with coffee and a jar of red juice.

"This is just a taste," Jocelyn says. "There are more treats laid out for you in the dining room."

Carmen leans forward and grabs a small plate, filling it with shrimp before getting up and walking over to me.

"Should we read in the garden? I can't resist this gorgeous weather."

I glance out the open sliding doors into the extensive garden, which is bathed in soft evening light. Jocelyn's hobby is gardening, and it shows. Her garden is a spectacular explosion of spring colors, with flowers surrounding its lush green lawn, a perfect carpet spread out under the sun. Vibrant pinks and yellows work their way through daffodils, tulips, and flowers I've never seen before. Even from inside, the delicate scents beckon me to step outside.

"Sure," I say. "It's a nice day out."

If my thoughts distract me from reading, I can just enjoy the view. To be honest, I didn't really feel like coming today, but I wanted to talk to Carmen and Dan after the meeting. They're the only people who know what I'm going through and, right now, over a month after I found the evidence of Oliver's infidelity, things are getting worse. My anger and fear are growing inside me every day, and I'm struggling to hold it together.

While I wheel Mason out and park his wheelchair close to a fishpond studded with lily pads, Carmen brings out our books and drinks.

"Do you want some juice or anything to eat?" I ask Mason.

"I want shrimp, peanut butter cookies, and juice, please," he says, and I set him up.

I ruffle his hair and kiss the top of his head. "Eat the shrimp before the cookies and let me know when you want more."

I'm grateful when Dan exits the house and sits next to Mason. Carmen and I sit at a metal garden table not too far away, but with enough distance for a private conversation. We briefly touch on what went on inside, and I'm relieved when we both agree that we're not going to ask Dan about his time behind bars, that it's not our business.

"How are things going with Oliver?" Carmen asks.

"Not great." I bite into a shrimp and don't even taste it. "In the last few weeks, he's becoming increasingly distant from me and hardly touches me anymore. When he *does*, it feels like a chore."

"So you think he's still seeing someone else?"

"Yes, I think he's still seeing her." I pinch the bridge of my nose. "I mean, I know he is. I read more messages and he continues tapping away on his phone till late into the night."

Lying next to him and knowing he's communicating with another woman is unbearable.

"You should stop reading them," Carmen warns, licking

butter off her index finger. "You can't keep hurting yourself like that."

"I know, but it's like an addiction. I want to stop but can't."

Carmen lays a perfectly manicured hand on mine. "I'm so sorry you're going through this. It really sucks. Have you thought about what you'll do? This can't go on, it's tearing you apart."

"I totally agree."

Turning around, I see Dan standing behind me with Noah in one arm and a cup of tea in his other hand. Before answering Carmen, I glance at Mason to make sure he's okay by himself. But he's not alone. Monica is quietly talking to him and he's pointing to something in the bushes, probably a bird.

"I still haven't decided what to do," I say to them. "I think I need a little time."

"It is a difficult decision," Carmen says. "You should do whatever your heart tells you to do, whatever is kindest to yourself."

Dan leans in and lowers his voice. "Look, it's easy for us to give you advice. But I know it must be really hard to leave someone you love. So if you can't leave, you have to find a way to fix what's broken and save your marriage."

"You're right." I smile and open my arms for Noah. He hands me the baby, and I hold him close, the warmth of his body soothing my frazzled nerves. "And yeah, I don't want to lose my husband, so I choose the fix-it approach."

Carmen sighs and shakes her head, but Dan takes another sip of green tea as he continues thoughtfully. "Some say a baby can heal a marriage although, honestly, I don't think that's the best idea for everyone since babies are a lot of work and require a lot of attention. My sister and her husband tried for years to have a baby, and when they finally did, I assumed it would bring them closer together, but that wasn't the case. They split up two months before my nephew turned one."

"Excuse me for a moment," Carmen interrupts. "I need to get more of that delicious shrimp. I'll be back right away."

Watching her leave, I reflect on what Dan just said. A baby. Could that be the solution?

I look down at Noah, and his big brown eyes blink at me as if he agrees.

The mere thought of having a baby right now is overwhelming. With Mason in my life, I never really felt the need to have a biological child. He has filled that maternal void. But this is not just about me. Oliver may be straying because something is missing in our marriage, and perhaps it's a child of our own? He said to me before we were married that he always pictured himself as having two or three children. After everything we've been through, was he worried that if he asked me about trying for a baby, I would feel overwhelmed?

During the rest of the book club meeting, I ponder what Oliver is doing alone at home. Is he talking to the other woman freely on the phone? Is he buying her gifts online and having them sent to her place? Is he even thinking about what he's doing to me?

So long as this ends soon, I think I will forgive him. At least I'll try. What he's doing is terrible, but I'm capable of far worse, and the only way to guarantee my safety and freedom is to keep this marriage intact.

CHAPTER SIX

Mason and I are among the last people to leave. We're heading out the door when Jocelyn pulls me aside and gives me a pie covered in a red and white checkered towel.

"Wow, what's this for?" I ask.

"My famous apple pie, a little gift from me to thank your husband for fixing my kitchen faucet. It wouldn't stop dripping and he fixed it in a flash."

I can feel myself bristling immediately. "He did? He never mentioned it. When was that?"

"Yesterday evening after work. I'm sure it was a great inconvenience to him, but he was kind enough to do it."

The familiar snake of jealousy slithers in and wraps itself around my heart. Oliver can fix a leaking faucet? I had no idea; he doesn't fix anything at home. As my fingers clench around the pie dish, I want to throw it back at her.

"I'm sure you thanked him for his help. You don't have to give him a pie."

"Oh, of course I thanked him in a way, but when he tried my pie he just could not stop raving about it, so I figured I would bake one more."

Despite my discomfort, I force a smile and try to act unfazed. "Thank you. I'm sure Oliver will enjoy it."

On the way home, as I replay my short conversation with Jocelyn, something bothers me. She said she thanked Oliver "in a way." Exactly what did she mean by that?

I can't allow her or anyone else to come between me and Oliver. There is much more to my marriage than love and romance. It's a shield between me and my dark past, and I must do whatever it takes to keep it in place. Whatever the cost.

* * *

Later that night I feel tempted to speak with Oliver about expanding our family, hoping that this could bring us back together again, but something inside keeps me from doing so. Truth be told, I am afraid he will reject the idea and that would be too much for me to handle at this time. How would he react if I didn't tell him and just surprised him with a positive pregnancy test?

Long after he has fallen asleep, the idea still spins around in my head. Though it would be frightening if it backfired, the more I think about it, the more comfortable I feel about it. Without thinking, I slip out of bed and go to the bathroom, locking myself inside.

Our white and gray marble bathroom is modeled after a spa. The shower features dual rainheads, and a deep free-standing tub with claw feet stands to the side. A bench against one wall allows us to relax and admire the view from the window. Walking into our bathroom is a relaxing experience for me most days. Today, however, I am feeling anxious. From behind one of the mirrors, I take my unfinished pack of pills from the medicine cabinet and, in a moment of desperation, pop them out of their foil bubbles one by one. Then, I watch them sink to the bottom of the toilet bowl.

My first step toward saving my marriage has been taken, but something just doesn't feel right. I feel that uncanny sensation of being watched again and I cross over to the window, but I only see the bright full moon and stars, and my pale reflection and frightened eyes in the glass. While I know I'm probably just being paranoid, for months now I always feel as if someone is watching me, like they know what I'm doing.

I return to bed and as I lay there, unable to sleep, I grab my phone and search social media for Jocelyn Summer. Her Instagram account displays pictures of luxury hotel rooms and fancy meals along with photos of her in bikinis posing on beaches or in hotel rooms. Some may find the photos harmless, but I don't. Since some of her getaways coincided with times when my husband was on business trips, he could have been with Jocelyn during those times. Was it him behind the camera?

In a photo posted two weeks ago, the same weekend Oliver was out of town at a conference in Phoenix, Jocelyn is wearing an evening gown with a plunging neckline in a shade that complements her green eyes. In this picture, her dark hair is up in a sleek ponytail with a few loose strands framing her face.

The caption reads: *Dinner with a special someone. #guesswho #makingmemories*

CHAPTER SEVEN

THREE YEARS AGO

As a child, when someone asked me what I wanted to be when I grew up, I always said I wanted to live in a big house with a swimming pool. Thinking of the details was too far-fetched for a girl who grew up in care, often in trailer parks, never staying in one place long enough to call it a home. It was a castle in the sky and, while I escaped there often when times got tough, as I got older I came to see that it was not realistic—at least for me.

So when Doris Granger from the Little Treasures Nanny Agency first presents me with a chance to work for Henry Baldwin, one of the wealthiest men in Greenwich, Connecticut, and the entire country, I turn it down. The child in me feels a lot of bitterness toward families like his, people who have everything I never will, and I can't imagine myself being their staff and then returning home to my little flat every evening. I prefer to work for more ordinary families, people I can relate to. But Doris says that after going through the online profiles of available candidates at the nanny agency, Henry specifically requested an interview with me, and that he keeps insisting even when I refuse to be interviewed. So I hop online and do some research.

Henry is a single father, and the CEO of Baldwin &

Associates, one of the largest hedge funds in the country. The forty-three-year-old businessman is also handsome, in an intimidating kind of way and, even from a picture, it feels as though his piercing blue eyes are staring straight through me. My first thought is, why is he so determined to have me, a nanny with minimal experience, looking after his child?

"Who cares why?" Doris snaps. "He wants you and we want him as a client."

"I just don't understand why he's picked me out?"

"Why not you?" She lets out a frustrated breath. "One more thing, Tess: if you nail the interview, he would want you to move into their home."

I blink at her. "As a live-in nanny? In his house?"

House is the wrong way to describe where he lives, actually. Mansion is more accurate. I've seen pictures online, and it looks very similar to the place I imagined growing up. There is even a swimming pool outside, and impressive gardens stretching out to the edge of a forest.

But, even though I now have the opportunity to live in the home I once dreamed of, even just as a nanny, a fearful part of me won't let me accept the offer. Not because it isn't an amazing opportunity; it is. Not because I don't need the large amount of money Henry Baldwin is willing to pay; God knows I have mountains of bills. But after the research I've done into Henry, something deep in my belly just doesn't sit right. He has a reputation for being a litigious and formidable man, from an influential family that nobody would want to cross. I don't want to be around a man like that; I know all too well what men can be capable of when their power and ego take over.

So I push back again, until the call comes in. Two days ago, he requested my phone number from Doris and, with my permission, she gave it to him.

"We need to talk," he says now, as soon as we get the greetings out of the way. "I have cleared my schedule for Monday, May eighth at eight a.m. I'll send a car to pick you up."

His request is non-negotiable and I don't even have time to speak before he puts the phone down. Despite myself, after hearing his voice, I find myself intrigued. What harm could it do just to go to the interview? It's Friday, and I have the weekend to prepare.

In the end, I am far too nervous to prepare. But I want to meet the man in person, and I tell myself that my instincts have always been right so far. If I get a bad vibe from him and he offers me the job, I can just turn him down.

* * *

Monday arrives quickly and before I know it, an actual limousine pulls up in front of the agency and I am whisked away like a princess in a fairy tale. Except I'm not a princess, and this isn't a fairy tale.

The Baldwin estate is over thirty minutes by car from downtown Greenwich. During the drive I stare out the window, begging the scenery to calm me. The evergreens, rolling hills, and a clear blue sky paint a picture reminiscent of a New England postcard. The road winds through the picturesque landscape until the property looms into view and, shifting in my seat, I smooth down my gray pencil skirt and simple white blouse. I look professional, but I don't feel like it. Deep down, as excited as I am to see his beautiful home, I almost hope he won't like me, that the interview will be a disaster and he won't want me to look after his child.

I've seen photos of the stone mansion online, but they did not do it justice. It is three or four times the size of most houses I know. The landscaping is a riot of color, a sea of flowering shrubs and lush trees, and beautifully pruned foliage. It is surrounded by woods, as if for protection, and has a long, private road leading up to the circular driveway. The house is three-stories high and the limestone exterior looks like it has been around for centuries. It is beautiful but also overwhelming in a way, like the man who lives in its walls.

Instead of turning into the long driveway, the limo drives to the front of the house with its grand entrance, which is framed by two bold pillars. To my surprise, Henry Baldwin is already waiting, wearing a suit that probably cost more than my annual rent, with a clean-shaven jaw, and his brown hair styled to make it look as slick and clean-cut as his attire. The driver opens the door and I take my time getting out. It feels almost as if I am stepping into one of my own childhood dreams. The spring air is warm, and smells of wildflowers and freshly cut grass. Henry Baldwin smiles at me, his teeth gleaming pearly white, and I can't deny that the sparkle in his eyes causes a flutter in my stomach.

"Miss Rivers," he says, extending his hand. "Thank you for coming. Please, let's go inside."

I swallow hard and force a smile. "Okay."

Okay? That is all I can say? It's as if my brain has been fried by just the sight of this man. But Henry Baldwin doesn't seem to mind that I am nervous, or maybe he hasn't noticed. On shaky knees, I follow him inside to the long hallway of the main floor leading to what I assume is the living room. He leaves behind a trace of his cologne, and it is subtle and masculine, the scent of spice and leather.

The interior of the house looks even more magnificent than the outside. Rich fabrics, high ceilings, chandeliers, antique furniture, and the soothing sound of a fountain in the background. The walls are a creamy white, adorned with abstract paintings. Despite myself, as I walk around, I find myself thinking about what I would do, if it were my home. As I am not a fan of abstract art, I would replace them with landscape paintings to liven up the space. The antique furniture would also be replaced by contemporary pieces with clean lines, and I would have a large library with a fireplace and comfortable couches and ottomans.

A three- or four-year-old boy in shorts and a bright-yellow t-shirt stands in a doorway, a frown on his freckled face. In his hands he holds a picture book, but he isn't reading it. He is just staring at me with wide, curious, smoky-gray eyes and a shock of red hair that sticks up and out like a porcupine's quills. He is quite simply the most adorable kid I have ever seen.

"What's your name?" he asks confidently, scratching one of his feet with the other.

"Miss Rivers," Henry answers before me, "this is my son, Mason." Then he turns to Mason and smiles. "Mason, meet your new nanny."

"She doesn't look like a nanny, Daddy," Mason says as I stand there in shock. My mind reels with confusion. What is going on here?

"Mr. Baldwin... I... I didn't—" I try to keep the panic out of my voice. "What about the other candidates for the job?" I ask finally.

We haven't even had a conversation, let alone an interview.

"What about them?" His tone is as firm as it is smooth.

"Aren't you interviewing more people?"

"I don't need to," he says. "I trust my intuition completely and it's telling me you're the perfect person for the job." He extends his hand toward me. "Congratulations, Miss Rivers. You are hired. You'll be moving in next week Monday, May fifteenth."

"Moving in?"

"Yes. I will pay for any moving costs, of course."

"You haven't even interviewed me. How do you know I'm the right person?"

He chuckles. "Miss Rivers, I know what I want, and I want

you. We can go over the details when you arrive on Monday. The rest, I'll discuss with Doris."

I open my mouth to protest one more time, but he is already walking away, gesturing at me to follow him. I'm taken to the kitchen, where he introduces me to Becca, the housekeeper, who seems just as enthusiastic to meet me as he was, her honey-colored eyes sparkling with kindness. She's wearing a pink apron over a black pullover, and beige sweatpants, and her salt and pepper hair is slicked into a topknot on top of her head. I'm surprised she wasn't the one to answer the door, but I guess Henry wanted a more personal touch.

"Excellent," Henry says. "Now that we have introductions out of the way, let's have breakfast so we can all get to know each other better."

The breakfast spread out on the dining table includes a wide selection of pastries, fruit, cheese, and everything one would expect from a typical continental breakfast, including loose tea in a variety of flavors and a cafetière of hot coffee. Henry, Mason, and Becca all seem happy to have me in their midst, and I can't help but feel a little bit more at ease about this whole thing.

But later, as I'm driven back home, a cold sensation spreads in my stomach. Something is lingering in my mind, like a stone I can't get out of my shoe. It all feels too good to be true, and I can't help but think that accepting this job was a mistake.

CHAPTER EIGHT

PRESENT

This time, my recurring nightmare does not end when Oliver tells me he no longer loves me and that he wants to leave. He looks me in the eye and tells me he has grown tired of keeping my secret and that he will tell everyone what I did. I'm yanked from the dream by his words, and my eyes fly open. My heart is racing, and my body is soaked with sweat. I glance at the clock next to my bed. 12:30 in the morning. After throwing cold water on my face, I leave the room to check on Mason. Like checking the doors before going to bed every night, this has become a habit every time I wake up from one of my nightmares.

The house is dark and quiet except for the perpetual creaking of the windows and grumbling in the pipes, and I tiptoe into the room, wincing whenever the floorboards squeak. I'd hate to wake him. The air shifts, becoming cool and moving quickly past my face as my eyes sweep around. His window is always slightly open, as Mason gets anxious about not having enough oxygen even though I tell him that will never happen.

Suddenly, my shoulders are tense, and my breathing halts for a second as I look around the room. I don't know why, but I feel like something has changed in here; something smells different, perhaps? But there isn't anything unusual about the scent: clean sheets and Mason's apple shampoo. The air is slightly cool, but not enough to be uncomfortable.

I'm just paranoid after the stress of the last few weeks, exhausted from thoughts of my husband being with another woman. It's no surprise that I'm struggling to keep my sanity. But what about the other times? It's not the first time since we moved into this house that I feel as if strange things are happening, like someone is watching me. But then, when you're carrying a secret, it's easy to get spooked.

As I stand in the middle of Mason's room, listening to him snuffle softly, my heartbeat slows down gradually. I listen to him breathing for a few minutes before I step over to the bed. His left hand rests on his chest, and I move it to the side so I can pull up the blanket and cover his body. I tuck it in around him, making sure it's not too tight. I hate the idea of him feeling trapped.

I sit down in a chair next to his bed for a few moments, needing to be here with him.

But when I look at the bedside table, I notice a glass.

As I do every night, I did give Mason a drink of water before bed, but I didn't bring the glass to his room and when Oliver got home late, he went straight to bed. Since Mason's unable to get himself out of bed and into his wheelchair, there's no way he could have left the room to get it. The glass was not here before when I brought him to bed.

I take a few deep breaths to calm myself, staring at the glass and trying to figure out how it could have got there. But there's no explanation. Unless Oliver got up while I was asleep and brought it to him? That must be it. I stand up, shakily, and walk back across the room. After throwing a last glance at Mason and the glass, I close the door softly behind me.

Back inside the master bedroom, I avoid waking Oliver even

though I want to ask him about the glass. He was exhausted when he got home from his fourth trip in a month, and barely said a word to me. Honestly, I'm finding it hard not to let my anger bubble up, to keep reminding myself that I need him to stay by my side. My nerves are on edge as I stand in the middle of the room, staring at his nightstand.

The phone is there, and my fingers itch to take it again and read his messages. My addiction to pain has grown stronger and, as I stare at the phone, I feel it drawing me to it like a magnet. Stepping toward the nightstand, I put my hand onto the screen to block it from lighting up too much when I remove the charging cable from the phone. Oliver could wake up at any moment and catch me in the act, and I don't want him to know I know what he's been doing. Not yet, not like this.

It's the last week of May, several weeks since I threw my pills away, and things have gone from bad to worse. To improve my chances of getting pregnant, I bought an ovulation kit and I tried to make sure that Oliver and I had sex during my most fertile days. But he has grown distant of late. I think perhaps he's been picking up on my mood, because sometimes the anger overwhelms me and I just can't be my old warm, sweet-natured self. Sometimes I feel he's just unhappy around me, often drifting off into his thoughts when he thinks I'm not watching. His travels have increased and he works late most days. And when he's home, he hardly touches me anymore. If I could just be honest about my feelings, I would say that the last thing I want is for the man who's cheating on me to even touch me. But I know that's the only way I can fall pregnant and keep my secret safe. The only way I see to make him recommit to our marriage and the promises he made to protect me.

As much as I try, I can't stop myself from taking another peek into his forbidden world. I can't think of anything but seeing what he wrote her. I stalked Jocelyn's social media accounts for three full weeks and I was convinced that she was the one having an affair with Oliver, but then I told Carmen and Dan about my suspicions and they were both skeptical.

"I know she's a big flirt," Dan had said, "and I really don't have much respect left for her after what she pulled the other day, but I don't think she would do something so dumb."

"A friend would never do something like that," Carmen added and pointed out that even though Jocelyn travels a lot, there are times Oliver is out of town and she isn't.

Even after reminding them that she had an affair with a married man before, they didn't bite, and I let it go.

I'm deeply indebted to Oliver. Without him I would not even have my freedom. Perhaps one day, I will find a way to punish him for what he's doing, to hurt him for hurting me. But for now, I need to supress my rage, to try and forgive him and make sure he stays with me.

As for Jocelyn, she means nothing to me.

I created a dummy account to follow her on Instagram. She didn't follow me back, but it's fine because I still get to see her posts. If she's the woman who's destroying my marriage, I will find out.

I sit on the cool bathroom floor with my back against the locked door. The leather on the phone's back cover smells fresh and new; he must have bought it on his trip. I curl my fingers around the warm phone and slide my thumb over the screen. The passcode is still my birthday, and that tiny fact warms my heart. Even though he's betraying me in the worst possible way, this is a little sign that deep down, he still loves me. Surely, no man would do what he did for me, not unless his love is eternal. I know it's not over between us, not yet. I still have time. I know that despite this new woman, he is still the man I fell in love with—the man who took care of me despite what I did.

The phone comes to life with a buzz, and there they are. Their stupid passionate messages, as if they're each other's teenage crushes. I grit my teeth as I read their latest texts to each other. She says she can't wait to see him again, and she misses his lips on hers. He tells her to be patient and that things will work out. My throat constricts and my chest feels like it's on fire, my entire body hurting. The agony is overwhelming.

Maybe this isn't a fling that will end with time; he's really planning to leave me for her. This can't go on. I try to pull myself together, but panic and anger rise up within me. I have to fix this somehow before our marriage falls apart completely. I can't lose him, the man I trusted with my darkest secret, the man who saved me. The fear of him exposing me is more than I can bear, and I will do everything possible to hang on to him even if the price is my self-respect.

I hurriedly turn off the phone before I can read any further, and I pull myself to my feet and stand in the dark doorway, waiting until he's sleeping soundly again. It infuriates me that he can sleep so peacefully, that he can sleep at all, while his affair is tearing me apart, destroying us. I imagine myself picking up the pillow and pressing it down over his face, and the thought gives me a little relief. But I don't want it to end like that. Part of me hates him so much, but I just can't keep hold of that hatred, not after all that we've been through together. How can I hate the man who destroyed his life for me, the man who has always been my hero? Would he even have done something like this, if it wasn't for the secret I've made him bear?

It would be too risky to return the phone to his nightstand, so I take it with me to my side. I climb under the covers and slide the phone under his pillow, and I'm hoping that when he finds it, he'll think he must have been too tired to put it on the bedside table.

In the past, I curled up to him every night, feeling safe against his body as his slow breaths went in and out like the tide. But not anymore; there's a female-shaped wall between us now. I turn my back to him and prepare to cry myself to sleep. When I feel him shifting next to me to find a comfortable position, I hold my breath and count the beats of my heart. Instead of going back to sleep, I listen to him patting the surface of his nightstand, searching for his precious phone. When he doesn't find it, he sits up in bed and yawns. Then he continues to search the bed in a more and more frantic manner. I open my eyes and continue to listen to his movements. Finally, I hear a soft sigh. Then the familiar soft blue glow lights up the room.

They chat for what feels like thirty minutes, but it may well be more or less than that: I'm unable to keep track of time when I'm so upset. When he lets out a low chuckle, my lips press together in disgust. A wave of nausea slams into me and I grit my teeth, but the bile is rushing to my throat so fast there's no way I can keep it down. I spring out of bed and run to the bathroom. My throat fills with bitter bile as I bend over the toilet bowl, gripping the edge of the counter as I retch. Once my stomach is empty of vomit and there's only a small amount of acidic green fluid dripping into the toilet bowl, my breath catches in my throat.

Could it be? I had a negative pregnancy test earlier, but could it be too early to tell? I'm not normally sick like this, even at times of extreme stress. My mind racing, I hear Oliver walk up behind me.

"Are you okay?" he asks.

If only I could believe that he really cares. I wait for him to come to me, to pull me into his arms like he used to not too long ago. When he doesn't, I wipe my mouth with the back of my hand and nod. I don't trust myself to speak yet. I flush the toilet and lean against the sink, my hands clutching onto it as I meet his gaze. He has the nerve to still have his phone in his hands and, as my gaze travels to it, he drops it into the pocket of his pajama pants.

In a rush, I suck in a deep breath and blurt out the words: "I'm pregnant, Oliver."

CHAPTER NINE

The words are out. Oliver can't unhear them, and I can't unsay them. Perhaps I should have been honest and told him it is only a suspicion, but as soon as I spoke, the words seemed true. I have been feeling weak and emotional lately, and I thought it was just the strain of his affair, my sleepless nights and my growing paranoia. But perhaps it's my body sending me signals, my hormones spiraling.

Oliver stares at me, and his facial expressions change through shock, confusion, and incredulity. Finally, I can no longer pinpoint what emotion he's showing. Is he disappointed that the pregnancy will complicate his affair, or is he excited about impending fatherhood? I used to be good at reading him, but that was before he became someone totally different from the man I married.

"What did you say?" he croaks. He sounds tortured, not at all how I would expect a man to react when his wife tells him she's pregnant with his child. I consider backpedaling and telling him it's some kind of twisted joke. But maybe he's just in shock? Maybe this will work for us, just as I planned. Maybe this will bring him back to me before I lose everything we built together. Before I end up in prison. Before I lose Mason.

"I said I'm pregnant," I repeat. My voice is low but unwavering.

He blinks several times and rubs his eyes. "But you can't— how's that possible?"

"What do you mean, how?" I wrap my arms around my body.

"You're on the pill, aren't you?"

"I am," I say, "but birth control pills are not one hundred percent effective, you know. They fail sometimes. I know we didn't plan this, but Oliver, aren't you happy? We're going to have a child, of our own."

He runs a hand across his forehead and doesn't speak for a long moment, just stares into space. And despite the churning pain in my belly, I ask him to say something—anything. But to my horror he walks out of the bathroom, walking past me as though I'm not even there. I remain in the bathroom, frozen to the spot, unable to believe what's happening. Maybe I should understand that he needs time to process the news. But I can hear him talking on the phone in a hushed tone. Her.

I'm consumed with anger. Why is he turning to her? What is he promising her? How dare he walk away from me in a moment like this?

When I compose myself enough to walk back into the bedroom, he disappears into the corridor and shuts the door. Feeling like I've been stabbed in the gut, I clench my fists and grind my teeth, careful not to scream out. In my despair, I'm ready to go after Oliver, to fling myself at him in an effort to vent the hurt raging through me, to tell him I know everything, that I'm leaving him. Something, though, some calm, self-protecting voice in my head, warns me to stop and bite my tongue. Oliver may deserve my anger, but I need to tread carefully. I need him. Most importantly, Mason needs me to make our marriage work.

I lower myself onto the bed and wait for our conversation to start, trying to clear my mind of all its thoughts. But when Oliver returns, he goes straight to the closet and pulls out his leather suitcase. Without even acknowledging me, he drops it onto the bed and, in horrified silence, I watch him pack.

"Where are you going?" I ask casually, though on the inside, I'm shaking.

"I forgot to tell you." He lowers a favorite pale-yellow shirt into the suitcase. "I'm driving to New York."

"New York? But you don't sell property there."

"I'm meeting a client who's based there in two days." He still won't meet my eyes. "Why all the questions?"

"Why all the questions? Oliver, you got home a couple of hours ago." I pick up my phone and glance at it. "You have a meeting in two days and you're leaving today... at one o'clock in the morning. Don't you think I have the right to know—?"

"I'm catching an early start because I have other important things to do in New York. I hope that answers your questions."

I don't know how else to respond. He's making it all up, and I'm overwhelmed by the coldness in his voice. Tears continue to blur my eyes as I blink them away. "What about what we just talked about... in the bathroom? What about us, Oliver?"

He ignores me, continuing to shake out his shirts and fold them neatly before placing them into the suitcase, followed by socks, ties, and underwear. I clutch my trembling knees and stare at him, unable to believe he would treat me like this. He doesn't even care that he's making a mockery of our marriage. It's too late, he's already in too deep. He's fallen in love with the other woman, and I don't mean anything to him anymore. Our family means nothing. Instead of talking to me, he occasionally picks up his phone, glancing down at it.

"Are you expecting a call?" I ask. I feel so stupid right now. Maybe I am. Maybe I have been for a long time.

"My client."

Client.

What would happen if I told him? How would he react; would he still go on the business trip knowing that I know everything?

"When will you be back?" I ask instead.

"I'm not sure yet. I have a lot of things I need to handle over there. I'll have a pretty busy schedule."

My heart lightens for a moment as I fool myself into believing that maybe he's going to end things with her face to face. Until I know more, I need to hold on to that thought. I climb back into bed and wrap the duvet around my shoulders. I turn away from him, toward the wall, to hide the tears in my eyes, and I listen as he moves around the room and his feet carry him into the closet and then into the bathroom. The toilet flushes, and water from the tap starts to run. Then he brushes his teeth and walks back out. He doesn't even have time for a shower, he's that desperate to get away from me. The suitcase is zipped shut, and the mattress sighs when he lifts it from the bed. Then I hear his footsteps as he walks to the door. No kiss. No goodbye. The door closes, and I hear his footfalls heading to the living room. When the front door bangs shut, I roll to my back and stare up at the ceiling.

I would do anything to keep our family together and make sure my secret is safe. But maybe it isn't safe anymore. It's possible that he's already too far gone with this woman, and he's falling far enough away from me that he might accidentally tell her everything. My only hope is that this isn't the case, that I can still bring him back to me before it's too late. But if he doesn't come back, what should my next step be?

When he's gone, I do a pregnancy test since I have several hidden in the bathroom. I get the results shortly thereafter.

One single line, one twist of the knife in my gut.

* * *

I wake up to the sound of Mason calling me. It's already 9 a.m., and he must be worried because I never sleep in that long. I wish I could stay in bed, to hide under the covers until the storm passes. But Mason needs a mother and I promised to be one to him. I force myself out of bed and, with my head aching and my eyes swollen, I go to his room. The glass from last night is still on his nightstand, but I don't have the energy to think about what it might mean right now.

"You look sad," Mason says, looking up at me with worry sketched across his little face. I haven't looked in the mirror, but I can imagine that my eyes are red.

"I just didn't get much sleep last night," I say, glancing out the window. The car is still in the driveway, which is strange because I thought Oliver would be driving. He must have taken a cab to the station and caught a train out of town.

I continue to make small talk with Mason as I help him brush his teeth and get dressed, and then he helps me make scrambled eggs and toast for breakfast. While he's eating, I return to my bedroom and call Carmen. She already knows that I've decided to get pregnant without Oliver knowing. Initially, she was surprised and tried to dissuade me, but she later came around. Dan gave me the idea, but I didn't tell him about it because I suspected he would feel bad and wouldn't want me to pursue it. I know he hates lying and wouldn't understand me throwing my pills away without talking to Oliver.

"I think I've made things worse," I say to Carmen, my voice cracking.

"Why, what did you do?"

"I told Oliver I'm pregnant."

"You're pregnant?" Carmen's voice rises in surprise, then

she blows out a breath. "Well, how... How did Oliver react?" she asks. Her voice is almost a whisper.

"He left." I shut my eyes and rub my forehead. "I thought I was pregnant, and he left before I did the pregnancy test, and then the result was negative. But I can't tell him that because he won't answer my calls."

For a few seconds, Carmen is silent, and when she speaks again, her voice is low and soft, full of compassion and empathy. "I'm sorry, Tess. I know how much you wanted a baby."

In need of something to hold on to, I tighten my fingers around the phone. "Yeah, I did, but I'm not sure Oliver does anymore. He just walked out on me."

"Has he told you where he's going?" Carmen asks cautiously.

"Apparently, he has a business meeting in New York. Carmen... I think he has left me." I swallow back the lump in my throat and try not to cry. "You should have seen the look in his eyes. It was as if he was looking at a stranger instead of his wife."

"Ah, crap. Tess, I'm so sorry. I'm sure he'll be back. It must have been a shock for him. Just give him some space."

"I want to believe that, but I have a bad feeling." I wipe the tears away as they leak out of my eyes.

"Mom," Mason calls from the kitchen. "The milk is spilled and my trousers are wet."

"Just a minute, sweetie." I turn my attention back to Carmen. "I need to go, Mason needs me."

"Okay, go. Call me if you need anything; I'm here for you. And look, I know it's not what you want to hear right now, but maybe this is for the best. You deserve better, Tess." Carmen's voice is gentle and light, and I know she's just trying to reassure me even though she has no idea what I really deserve. "For now, how about I come by in the evening to cheer you up; I'll bring

Dan and we can watch a movie or something, take your mind off everything."

"Please don't take this the wrong way, but I think I want to be alone with my son. He needs me right now, and I should focus on him."

"You're right. Call me if you change your mind."

I feel a pit of guilt in my stomach for shutting Carmen out. But I need time to think about what to do next. I need to do what's right for me and Mason.

After changing him, I hold up the glass I found in his room in front of him. "I found this in your room. Did Daddy bring you water last night?"

He nods, and I look at him perplexed. "Are you sure?"

He nods again. "Yes. I was sleepy, but I saw him. He was wearing a hood, and he sat with me for a long time. Can we please watch a movie later?"

I kiss him on the cheek, amused that a child can change topics so fast. "Yes, of course we can watch a movie."

I don't say it to Mason, but there just cannot be any truth to what he is saying. Oliver was exhausted when he went to bed, and he was wearing his pajamas. I don't even think he owns a sweater with a hood. Perhaps Mason has been having strange dreams, like me. But then how did the glass get in his room?

CHAPTER TEN

THREE YEARS AGO

A week after my meeting with Henry Baldwin and his son, a moving van arrives at my rental flat. The contract was signed the day after the offer was made and my belongings are packed, but I still find it hard to believe it's happening, that I will be moving into an actual mansion to take care of a cute little boy and will get paid well. The nanny agency fees will be deducted, but even then, it will still be more money than I've ever earned in my life.

After meeting Henry, I'm not so worried anymore about his formidable reputation. He really seems to like me, and I can't imagine what could possibly go wrong. But I went to bed last night with the expectation that the whole thing will be called off, as it still seems too good to be true. But Henry Baldwin is a man of his word, and apparently also a man who gets whatever he wants.

"I want you," he said last Monday, and his words have stuck with me. It feels amazing to really be wanted by someone, not pitied or ignored, but singled out by a man who can give me the home I've always longed for.

When I asked him over breakfast with his son why he chose

me for the job, he just said he had liked my photo on the
website, that he always trusts his instincts. And then Mason
sealed the deal by speaking to me even though he was shy
around strangers. Serving me coffee, pastries, and fruit, and
asking me about my life, Henry made me feel so welcome. He
didn't treat me with the condescension I'd expected from such a
wealthy man.

"I knew it would be a perfect match," he said, grinning, and
I felt my stomach flutter again, like it had when I'd first seen
him outside.

It doesn't take long for the moving crew to load my
belongings into the van, as I don't own many clothes or posses-
sions. It is just a little maisonette, with a single room that
combines the kitchen, living room, and bed, and a tiny bathroom. It often feels claustrophobic and the walls are so thin I
can hear all of my neighbors' movements. But I still feel a
pang in my heart as the early morning light bursts through the
window and paints the room with soft, warm light, illumi-
nating the tiny bedroom that was my first real home after
years of living in crowded shared apartments and filthy
bedsits. The air is a soft, white noise that muffles any sounds
that might otherwise disturb the silence. Letting my gaze fall
over each part of the room, I try to commit it all to memory, to
carry it with me after I leave. The walls are painted with a
creamy white lacquer and I found the few items of furniture
myself, in flea markets and antique shops. I felt safe here, for
the first time.

Ava Johnson, my landlord, was not pleased when I told
her I was moving out within a week, but her demeanor
changed immediately when I told her I'll pay the next two
months' rent plus a penalty fee to give her time to look for
someone else. It was Henry's idea, and he said he'd cover the
cost. The contract says I'll be living with Henry and Mason
for a trial period of three months to begin with, then we'll

extend it to a year if all parties involved are happy. If it doesn't work out, I will have enough time to find another place to live.

"Ms. Rivers, we're all done here," one of the men says, two boxes in his grip.

I thank him and look around the room one last time, thanking it silently as well. Henry offered to send a car to get me again, but I declined his offer. My old Toyota will do just fine. In a daze I get behind the wheel and follow the mover's van.

When I finally arrive at my new home, Henry meets me at the front door.

"Tess! So good to see you again. I hope you had a pleasant drive."

"It was fine, thanks. I'm really looking forward to taking care of Mason."

"Excellent." He rubs his hands together. "Come on in. I'll show you to your room."

He leads me up the stairs, down a long, narrow corridor, and into a cozy bedroom.

"I hope you like it," he says, holding the door open for me.

It is a simple but airy room, with two windows looking out across the courtyard, so I can see the forest in the distance. The walls are gray stone and my bed has a quilt made of cream, white, and beige patchwork squares.

"It's lovely," I say to him.

"I'm glad to hear it." He points to a door on the far end of the room. "That door will lead you to your own bathroom." He glances at his watch. "I'm off to a meeting. Take your time settling in and if there's anything you need, don't hesitate to ask Becca."

"Thank you so much, Mr. Bald—"

"Baldwin?" He shakes his head. "I thought we were past that. Henry, please."

"Okay, Henry, then." I can't stop the smile that spreads across my face. Calling a man as powerful and wealthy as him by his first name feels strange, and the warmth in my cheeks gives away my discomfort. "I'll remember next time."

"Good. I'll see you later. I should be able to make it to dinner. I'll arrange for your things to be brought up."

"Thank you, Henry." I pause. "Where's Mason?"

"At school. He should be back around two, and Becca has left some instructions about his routine in your room. He's really excited about you moving in."

"So am I." I peel my gaze from his. The man makes me feel like a shy little girl.

Once he is gone, I review Mason's schedule and unpack, setting my clothes and toiletries in the bathroom, and when I catch my reflection in the mirror, I stare at it. The face that stares back at me is no different from the one I've seen every day for the last thirty-four years. The same deep-set dark eyes, the same wavy brown hair, the same small nose that turns up a little at the tip, the same naturally pink lips. But today, there is some new sense of excitement carved in my features. My life has changed drastically in only a few days. On the surface it all seems perfect, but I am afraid I might do something to ruin it all.

I could end up falling in love with the father of the child I am supposed to look after. A man who would never be interested in someone like me.

"Stop it," I scold myself out loud. What the hell am I doing, thinking like that?

Done with my unpacking, I go downstairs to the kitchen in search of something to drink.

"Hey there." Becca walks in holding a basket full of laundry.

I smile at her. "Hi, Becca. It's nice to see you again."

"It's nice to have you back here, Tess." She glances around the kitchen. "After throwing this laundry into the wash I was planning to have a cup of coffee. Will you join me? It would be nice to have a little company now that Jane's gone."

"Who's Jane?" I ask.

Becca hesitates a moment as if regretting bringing up the name. She puts the basket down and opens a cupboard, pulling out two cups. "Maybe we should have that tea now."

She doesn't say a word as she prepares the tea and places mine in front of me.

"Jane was Mason's old nanny," Becca says, sipping her tea.

"Why did she leave?" I ask, curious. If she was fired, maybe I can learn from her mistakes and not do the same thing.

"She got engaged to a nice young man downtown."

"But why would she give up her job?"

"She didn't," Becca says, dropping tea bags into our cups. "She was asked to."

"But why?"

"That's not my story to tell." Becca twirls a lock of her silver hair around her finger. "The only advice I can give you is, guard that heart of yours."

"You mean—"

"Exactly." She winks.

I laugh. "I'm here for the kid, nothing else."

Becca doesn't say a word, and when the doorbell rings we both glance at the kitchen door.

"That must be Oliver. I'll get it," she says and hurries out of the kitchen, mumbling something about how frustrating it is when people keep forgetting their keys. She returns with a bearded man wearing jeans, a leather jacket, and a ponytail. He is around the same age as Henry, or maybe a little younger. The wrinkles around Becca's eyes deepen as she smiles. "You know what, I'll finish up the laundry and leave you two to get to know each other."

"Hi," Oliver says, pulling out a chair. "You must be the nanny. Henry mentioned you."

"I am. I'm Tess." I stretch out a hand and he squeezes it.

"It's a pleasure to meet you, Tess. I'm Oliver, the black sheep of the family."

He chuckles, as if it is a joke, but there is something on his face as he says it, a touch of sadness.

"You're Henry's brother?"

He raises an eyebrow. "You're on first name basis already? That was fast."

"Sorry, I... Ummm."

"Hey, I'm just teasing. I don't mean to make you uncomfortable. I apologize."

I rake a hand through my hair. "No, it's fine, really."

He shrugs off his leather jacket and drops it on the table. "Seriously though, Henry is a good man. Just don't get too close, okay?"

"I'm sorry, what—?"

He laughs. "It was a joke, Tess. I joke a lot. If you're going to stick around, you need to get used to it."

"Oh." Heat floods my cheeks again, as Oliver gets to his feet, stretches, and grabs his jacket. Then he glances at the cup in front of me. "Finish your tea in peace. I just dropped by to get some documents from Henry's office. Catch you around, Tess."

I stare at the door long after he walks out. What are both he and Becca hinting at? They seem to think I am here to do more than the job I am being paid for, and the thought makes me uneasy. It is as if they can read my mind, see the undeniable attraction I feel for Henry. But I am here for two reasons only: the beautiful home, and the paycheck.

CHAPTER ELEVEN

PRESENT

Two days after Oliver left for New York, Carmen shows up at my door, carrying a box of Oreo and peanut butter drizzle doughnuts.

"I know you want to be alone, but when you didn't turn up at the book club yesterday, I was worried."

I rub my temples and force a smile. The past twenty-four hours have been hell. I have barely eaten and I hardly slept last night as I waited for Oliver to call me. I tried reaching him several times, but my calls went unanswered. He's definitely sending a message and I don't want to understand it. I don't want to think about what this could mean for us.

"It's okay," I say and let her in. The smell of doughnuts tickles my nostrils and even though I don't have an appetite, they make my mouth water.

"Where's Mason?" Carmen asks after I close the door.

"Playing video games in his room."

I often do my best to limit screen time for Mason, but today I've been too weak to stick to the rules. We've been watching TV and eating loads of junk food, and of course he hasn't minded that at all. In fact, unlike me, he is in high spirits.

At one point I was tempted to tell him what was going on between me and Oliver, to explain why I was upset, but I couldn't bring myself to do that. I still want to do everything I can to make sure his family doesn't fall apart. I keep hoping that Oliver will come back of his own accord, that he just needs time to think it through.

Without asking, Carmen pops into Mason's room to give him a hug, and I'm grateful for that. It can't be easy for him to be trapped in the house with someone who's in such a rotten mood, and I'm sure Carmen is a breath of fresh air for him.

"Now, let's deal with those doughnuts," she tells me when we settle at the kitchen island. "Don't you dare tell me that you're not hungry. You don't need to be hungry to eat doughnuts."

I smile at her, suddenly overwhelmed with gratitude that she showed up, someone who understands what I'm going through. Carmen hands me a doughnut and I sink my teeth into it. As delicious as it had looked before, in my mouth it tastes like sweetened sand. I sigh and put it down again.

"I shouldn't have done it," I confess to my friend. "I shouldn't have lied about the pregnancy."

"You didn't lie." Carmen bites into her own doughnut, licking peanut butter glaze from her lips. "You did think you were pregnant in the moment."

"I know, but I should have waited to take a test. I wasn't thinking right."

Carmen reaches for my hand. "The best thing for you to do right now is to calm down. Everything is going to be alright."

"How? I can't even reach him to tell him the truth. He's not returning my calls and not answering them either. Maybe he knows I lied." Dread drops like a stone in the pit of my stomach, making me nauseous.

"How? He wasn't here when you took the test. I'm sure it's just because men react differently to the news of pregnancy."

"I know, but he looked so disappointed or angry. I don't even know which."

"Well, if he's going to react like that then Tess, maybe you need to really think about whether this is working out. How he's treating you... It's just not okay."

I bite into my lip. "You don't understand, Carmen. We've been through a lot together. I know this probably sounds weird, but he's a good man. And honestly, if he finds out I lied about this, I think it's going to ruin everything."

Carmen tucks a copper strand of hair behind her ear. "Okay, well, if he comes back prepared to be a father and you're really determined to make things work with him, then I have an idea. It might sound crazy at first, but just hear me out, okay?"

"I'm listening."

"Well," she says, "how about you don't tell Oliver that you're not pregnant?"

My eyes widen. "What do you mean? It's not as if I can magically make myself pregnant."

"What if you can? I mean, how about you just pretend you really are."

Confused, I tap the tips of my fingers on the surface of the kitchen island. "Carmen, I don't think I follow."

Carmen straightens up in her seat and tries again. "What I mean is, what if you pretend until you actually are pregnant?"

Laughter bubbles up my throat and spills from my lips. "How in the hell am I supposed to do that? Won't he expect to see a baby at the end of it?"

Carmen avoids my gaze as she chews on a cuticle. "He will, unless, unfortunately, the baby dies."

My mouth drops open in shock. "You can't be serious!"

"I am. I know it sounds awful, but think about what he's done to you. He's been lying constantly, for his own selfish reasons. But your lie would be to help your marriage." She pauses to prop her chin on her hand, her eyes pensive. "Maybe this will give you and Oliver time to reconnect, and then after you end it, you can try again to conceive for real. Or maybe you'll get pregnant anyway in the next few weeks, and then it won't matter."

Slowly, I process her words. "I see what you mean, but it will be hard to keep up the pretence for long. I'd have to end it very early, and what if that isn't enough time to work things through with him?"

"Well, I bet it's possible to order a fake belly online, if that's what you're worried about. Actors use them all the time."

I can't help myself from laughing nervously. "You can't be serious."

"It's up to you, honey. But I'm happy to help you, if you want me to." Carmen dabs her lips with one of the pink napkins that came with the doughnuts. Rosie's Sprinkles is written in white across it.

"Carmen, this is too much." I pause. "No. I'm not doing this," I say, giving my half-eaten doughnut another chance. This time it tastes like doughnut and melts in my mouth.

Finally, Carmen stands up and comes to me, giving me a warm hug, wrapping me in the scent of the new perfume she concocted, something with a note of vanilla. "I'm so sorry you're going through this," she whispers. "I just want to help. If you change your mind and want to leave him, I'm here for you. Or I'll help you make this pregnancy thing work. Whatever you need."

I don't know what to say, so I just hug her back and don't reply. Then I pick up my phone and pull up a photo of me and Oliver on our wedding day. It had been just the two of us and two witnesses. I think about the words Oliver told me that day, that he would take care of me, that he wanted us to be a real family. At the time, we had been living together for five months and everybody on Cherry Lane Street already thought we were married. That was what we wanted them to believe, and we finally made it legal and didn't have to keep lying anymore.

Now, despite the way he's treating me, I can't imagine a life without him. It tears me up inside to think of him right now, out there somewhere with another woman. What might he say about me, when she wins his trust?

"Wow, Tess. You looked so beautiful on your wedding day." Carmen leans in to take a closer look at the wedding photo. I was dressed in a cream lace knee-length dress and my hair was in a goddess braid on top of my head. My eyes glittered with hope and I looked so happy, but I know that inside, at that time, all I felt was darkness and fear.

I think about the idea Carmen proposed long after she leaves. Then late in the night, when Oliver still isn't home, I give her a call.

"I'll think about it," I say.

* * *

A few days later, as soon as I get back home from taking Mason to the GP for his checkup, Carmen comes round with a peach tote bag. While Mason is in his room reading a new book I just bought him, I pull Carmen into the kitchen.

"I'm not saying I'm definitely going to do it," I say in a low voice when we're sitting in the kitchen. "But maybe?"

"Okay, well, just in case, I brought you something." She picks up the bag from where she put it on the floor.

"More doughnuts?" I joke.

Carmen looks uncomfortable as she shakes her head.

"Then what is it?"

"Well, after your call the other night, I ordered some stuff online."

She glances behind her at the door, perhaps to see if Mason can see or hear us. But I know without a doubt that if he is truly absorbed in a book, he will keep on reading until forced to stop. *The Traveling Lights* is a fantasy book he's been wanting for a long time. Convinced that we're alone, she reaches into the bag and pulls out what looks like three pregnancy tests.

I hold my breath as I pick up one of the tests and peer at the little window. "This is positive."

"Yeah, positively fake."

"I can't believe people sell these things."

"You'd be surprised what you can find online." She reaches for the fake tests, but I hold on to one, still shocked at how real it looks.

What if this could work? There's no way anyone would see the test and not think it's real. Oliver definitely would.

I shake my head and put it back down. "I can't do this, can I?"

"Honey, whatever you decide, I'm there for you."

"No," I say firmly. "It's a little too freaky for me."

"Okay." Carmen drops the two tests into the bag. "But I think you should keep one of those, just in case. You need something to show Oliver if he asks, if you don't want to tell him the truth. And then you can get pregnant for real."

I groan. "I can't do this." I hand her back the test and rest my head in my hands.

"You know what you need?" Carmen says. "You need to have a little fun, to help clear your head. You hardly go out, Tess. Mason may be in a wheelchair, but there are still fun things you can do with him in town. It's not healthy for you to be holed up in here."

If only she knew how much I wanted to do that with Mason, to be out there in town, not fearing at every stage that I might somehow bump into one of them: the people who could bring my whole world crashing down around me.

"I really don't feel like going out." Partly true.

"Then how about joining in with the Big Spring Clean? It's in five days; it could be fun."

The Big Spring Clean is an event the whole town participates in, a reminder of the day a major hurricane hit Westledge in the 1980s and left a lot of destruction in its wake. A few days after the disaster, the residents came together to rebuild and clean up. Since then, the locals have carried on with the annual tradition of a day for cleaning their homes and the town's public spaces, filling their homes with flowers and their gardens with lanterns, and celebrating new beginnings with fireworks. The date is often announced a few days before it happens as it only takes place on a beautiful sunny spring day.

"I don't know, Carmen," I say, massaging my temples. I know for a fact that Oliver would not want us to participate. Events and festivals are not allowed; they could draw tourists, people who might come from the place where we used to live. But Oliver is not here, and I'm starting to feel reckless in my anger and panic.

"Please do, it would be so much fun if you joined us this year. All the book clubbies are already in except for you."

"I'll think about it," I say.

It's only after Carmen leaves that I notice she didn't pack up the third pregnancy test. I think of calling after her, to give it back, but something inside stops me. Instead, I take it to the bathroom and hide it in my tampon drawer, a place I know Oliver doesn't look.

When I look out of the window and into the garden, my eyes are drawn to the trees and bushes that line the fence separating our property from the one next door. As I blink, my gaze darts from one bush to another and I wonder if my eyes are playing tricks on me. For a fraction of a second, I thought I saw a flash of movement. Holding my breath, I wait for a figure to appear, for my fears to become real. But nothing happens.

Somebody is out there and they are coming for me, my brain

screams. They're watching and waiting to pounce on me, to destroy what Oliver and I have built. I grab the curtains and pull them closed, before sitting down in a corner with my head between my knees and trying to get my breathing under control. In, out. In, out.

CHAPTER TWELVE

I push the cart through the produce section of the Shop & Carry while Mason follows next to me in his electric wheelchair. At the front of the store, a woman with large dark-rimmed glasses stands behind the counter, a name tag pinned to her shirt: Belinda. When I wave at her, she smiles, revealing a missing front tooth, and goes back to typing something on her phone. The store, with its brushed metal countertops, scratched wooden floors, and windows that reach up to the ceiling, is a bright oasis just a short drive from our house.

The sun shines through the windows and bounces off the brightly colored fruits displayed in rows along the countertops, exhaling their sweet and sour scents into the air to entice shoppers to pick them up. It's a small shop, but it still has everything a person would need. Shelves line the walls, stocked with cans of food, boxes of cereal, diapers, and toiletries.

Oliver often insists on us doing the shopping or ordering online so I don't need to leave the house, but I feel restless and can't bear another day staying at home. It's been a whole week; a week since I heard his real voice. Ever since he's been gone, the only thing I've been listening to over and over again is his answering machine message. And his absence is no longer affecting just me: I've noticed that Mason's mood has dropped to match mine, and he's been getting more frustrated lately. He's refusing to do homework, preferring instead to paint or play games. He won't even show me any of his paintings, but last night after he'd gone to bed, I was putting away his school supplies as I do every Friday night when I found a sketch hidden between the pages of his science book.

A stick figure with a bleeding head.

I crumpled the paper into a ball and threw it in the garbage. I hate that Oliver has left us in limbo and Mason is becoming more withdrawn each day, burying himself in dark memories and fearful thoughts. I take a deep breath and bend down to his level and stroke his hair. "I know you miss your dad."

"Don't say that," Mason says through gritted teeth. "He's not my father."

My mouth falls open at the venom in his voice. I suck in a quick breath and scan our surroundings to see if anyone heard him. Five feet from us, two teenagers are lip-locked in a passionate embrace, their eyes closed. They're too obsessed with each other to hear my son's words. A woman in her mid-twenties, who's dressed as though she's about to walk into a boardroom, passes by and glances in our direction, murmuring something. I'm about to ask if she's talking to me, when I notice the wireless earphones plugging her ears. I've worked so hard to convince everyone that we're just a normal family, so nobody goes rooting into the past we've left behind. I reach for my son's hand and try to calm him down a bit before speaking again. "I know you're angry, sweetheart, but you can't say that again. We talked about this. Oliver is your father in every way that counts."

I do understand his frustration and anger: Oliver left him too. And although he doesn't ask directly where Oliver went or when he's coming back, he must still be wondering about it. He's never been away that long before.

"I'm sorry, Mommy," he whispers, and without warning his arms wrap around me. I hug him back, laying my head on top of his. When, a few steps from us, I see a mom and child pushing a cart overflowing with cleaning products, I break our embrace and cradle Mason's face between my hands so he has to look at me. "Do you want to have some fun today? How about we participate in the Big Spring Clean?"

Mason perks up, then his face falls just as quickly. "We can't. I heard him say we're not supposed to do things like that."

I ignore the ache in my heart at hearing his refusal to refer to Oliver as Dad.

"Let's make today an exception, shall we? Our house needs a nice scrub anyway. Do you think you can help me out?"

His face lights up again and he nods eagerly. "I can do that."

Mason likes to be useful, and if there's something I know he can do, I always give him the opportunity to try. As we head over to get cleaning supplies and white lanterns for decorating the front porch, I begin to get excited about the prospect of joining in with the local buzz and enjoying myself for once, not worrying about the past or the future. It would certainly be a great distraction.

As per Mason's request, almost every product we toss into our cart smells like lemon, his favorite scent. I pick out several lavender- and vanilla-scented candles for myself as well as a new broom for him to carry.

Later, in the parking lot as I'm about to help Mason into the car, I catch a glimpse of the back of a man's head out of the corner of my eye. For a second, I think it might be Oliver, but of course it's not. I want him so badly to be here that I am imagining things. He has treated me appallingly, I know. Nevertheless, I can't ignore the nagging voice that tells me that if he is as far away from me emotionally as he is physically, then he may reveal everything, and very soon my life could come crashing down around me.

When we turn into our street, excitement washes over me. Our neighbors have already started cleaning up their homes, polishing windows, sweeping porches, painting tables, and even fixing broken furniture. Hanging laundry blows wildly in the wind and the smells of cleaning detergents mingle in the air. Cleaning doesn't sound like a festival, but on this day, with everyone coming together and preparing for the party, it feels like Christmas. When Dan, who's up on his roof, sees our car, he lowers the fairy lights he's carrying and wipes his forehead with the back of his arm. I smile at him and try not to think of last year when everyone else was having fun and we stayed inside and watched a movie.

Inside the house, Mason takes the broom to his room and gets to work while I tackle the laundry and start vacuuming. Forty minutes later, he has reorganized his books by topic and color-coded them, changed his bedding, and folded all of his clean clothes and arranged them in his drawers. He has even lit one of the lavender candles I bought. His room smells fresh and clean.

I smile at him. "You did a great job."

"Thanks," he says, puffing out his chest proudly. "Can I do anything else?"

"You can help sort out the entrance hall cupboards. The shoes are all over the place."

He salutes as he leaves the room, and I smile after him. Soon after, I hear the sound of a truck coming down the road and I run to get the overflowing bags waiting in the living room. Any truck making rounds today is probably picking up things people in the neighborhood no longer need and wish to donate to local charities.

I'm standing on the porch with two large bags when I see a taxi heading in the direction of our house. I watch in surprise as the car slows to a stop and Oliver steps out of the back seat. The bags drop from my hands and I freeze in place, the desire to embrace him stifled by my fear of being rejected. My mouth is dry as I watch my husband lift his suitcase from the trunk. In front of the house next door, Monica is lowering a box at the side of the road, but her eyes are on us. I ignore her and focus on my husband. We both don't speak until we enter the house, and as soon as he sees Oliver, Mason drops the pair of shoes he's holding and wheels himself away.

"Hey, buddy," Oliver calls after him. "Won't you say hello? I missed you."

Mason keeps right on going without a backward glance until he disappears from view. Then a door is slammed shut. That's when anger bubbles up inside me, poisoning any of the relief I had felt. I fold my arms across my chest and glare at Oliver as he lowers his suitcase to the floor and reaches out a hand to me.

"Baby, I'm so sorry," he says, as I keep my arms tightly folded. His face is crumpled and he looks exhausted, and he clearly hasn't shaved since he left home. I can't quite let go of my anger, but seeing the broken face of the man I love makes tears well up in my eyes, and I find myself taking his hand before he pulls me into a tight embrace.

We've both made mistakes. And he's back now; he left her. I have my family back, and my secret is safe. He pulls me to him and we cry together. Through my sobs, I hear the music blasting in Mason's room for a while before Oliver releases me and gazes into my eyes. "I'm sorry about how I reacted when you told me about the baby. It was just... It was a shock. I needed some time to process. But I'm excited, Tess. I'm so happy."

I hold my breath. This is the moment to tell him the truth, to release myself of this burden, but I can't find the words and I don't want to break this spell.

"You are?" I ask, baffled. "I thought—"

"I know you must have thought I didn't want the baby." He shakes his head. "It's not that. I just didn't expect it to happen now. Now that I've had time to think about it, I can't wait." He lays a hand on my stomach. "I can't wait to be a father."

He sits me down in the living room. "I want to show you something. Stay here."

He fetches his suitcase, and when he pulls out a cream and white baby pullover with the words "Daddy's Little Sidekick" embroidered across its front, I start to cry again.

During the next few hours, Oliver is attentive both to me and Mason, who has finally left his room but remains withdrawn around him. When I tell Oliver about participating in the Big Spring Clean, I'm surprised when he tells me that's okay, as an exception. He even joins in the fun, helping me clean the house from top to bottom and cleaning out the yard. We give away a lot of things, including an old wheelchair Mason doesn't need anymore. When the sun starts to set and our lanterns are lit out on the front porch, our neighbors disappear into their houses to get ready for the celebration in the town square.

"It'll be nice to go out together for once," Oliver says. "Let's end the day the right way. It will mark a new beginning for us."

A new beginning: that's exactly what it is. Even though the other woman still lingers at the back of my mind, today I choose to pretend she doesn't exist. And maybe she doesn't anymore; maybe Oliver has ended things with her. Maybe our relationship is safe again, and so is my secret. Oliver hasn't been as loving as this for weeks now, and while I'm still fighting down my anger towards him, I can't help feeling relieved. Maybe he really is sorry, for everything. Hopefully, everything will be different now. Together as a family, we get into the car laden with food to share. But Oliver doesn't drive us straight to the party on the square.

"Let's cruise around a little," he says, grinning at me, then back at Mason. "Let's pretend to be tourists."

I clap my hands in forced excitement. "I love that idea."

Since moving to Westledge, I never really allowed myself the opportunity to appreciate it fully. Now, as we drive down the curved tree-lined Main Street, my eyes observe the beauty of the small town we have come to call home. The cobblestone street is lined with Victorian-style homes and quaint shops, antique boutiques, and cafes with colorful doors and vintage signs. As I take in the cozy, dimly lit surroundings, I allow myself to be happy and to forget the present for the moment. Despite all the shops and restaurants being closed for the special day, the streets are still buzzing with life that becomes even more vibrant when we finally make our way to the town square, where long tables with starched white table covers are stationed around the magnificent clock tower that stands proudly in the center of the square and is lit from within only on special occasions.

In honor of the Big Spring Clean, the houses are decorated with fairy lights, glowing lanterns, and white flower arrangements hanging from the doors. It doesn't matter what flowers are displayed in the arrangements, they only have to be white and green. I roll down my window and the sounds of laughter and marching band music, the aromas of fresh bread, buttered popcorn, and barbecued meats immediately lure us out of the car. We stay only an hour, not long enough to hear the crack of fireworks at midnight, but I leave satisfied and convinced that today is the start of many more celebrations to come. Maybe I don't always have to hide away, living in fear.

But when we arrive home, I notice that two of our lanterns are laying on their sides. The snow-white baby's breath wreath is no longer on the door but on the porch floor, its fragile petals scattered everywhere.

"Who did this?" Mason asks, agitatedly rocking his wheelchair back and forth.

We made the flower arrangement together, so he's clearly upset.

Oliver pushes a broken stem aside with his foot and unlocks the door. "Most likely it was just a bunch of kids who had nothing better to do than spoil the fun."

Mason follows him into the house, but I remain outside for a moment staring at the other houses, which have their flower arrangements still intact.

CHAPTER THIRTEEN

A few weeks later, I'm about to head to bed when I stop and turn around. I'm not sure if I already checked the doors and windows to make sure they're locked. I probably did, but I want to double-check. I flip the light switch back on and make my way down the hall toward the front door. It's locked, and so are the other doors and windows. I'm pulling the curtains in the living room window closed again, when I notice a red Beetle car drive by. I know the car and I know the owner. It's Jocelyn and, as she slows down, she's looking toward the house.

Without thinking, I walk out of the house and go and stand in front of hers. She has already parked the car and gone inside, and I watch as one by one, the lights go on upstairs. She doesn't even have the decency to close her bedroom curtains as she starts to undress, lifting her shirt off over her head and unhooking her bra. A twisted part of me comes alive and my heart is beating so fast I'm worried I might have a heart attack.

I tried so hard to give her the benefit of the doubt, but as I watch her, I know I can't keep swallowing my feelings. Nothing she or anyone says will change my mind about her. Everyone has a dark side and I'm fighting hard to keep mine at bay. But if she comes near Oliver again, I will no longer stop outside her house, I will invite myself in.

Back in my house, I lock the doors again and go and climb into bed next to my husband.

Oliver pecks my cheek. "Goodnight," he murmurs, and his breath smells like spearmint mouthwash. I wonder whether he was smoking again and is trying to cover it up.

Since the Big Spring Clean, we have been in a really good place and I can feel our marriage flourishing. He brought me a stunning bunch of red and white roses and we've been going out on dates, cooking meals together, and watching movies. We've even been making love, the best we've had in a long time and I'm still hopeful that one morning the test will show positive for real this time.

But sometimes I still lay awake at night wondering if he's grieving the end of his love affair, if he regrets ending it with her. I'm afraid they will get back together sometime, even though he thinks we're having a child. Or what if they already have?

Yet again, I can't sleep tonight so I lie in bed staring at up at the dark ceiling, thinking about her and what I'm going to do. When he starts snoring, I slide out of bed. It's late, but I need to talk to Carmen and, after checking in with Mason, I enter Oliver's office and lock the door. I'm not the kind of person who calls a friend in the middle of the night, but if I don't talk to someone, I'll go insane.

"What's going on?" she asks when she picks up. "Are you okay?"

I take a deep breath and pour out my frustration. "I'm just tired, Carmen. I can't sleep, and I'm still worried Oliver might be with this other woman. What if he still loves her?" The word stings like a bitter pill on my tongue.

"He doesn't," Carmen says. "He's at home with you, not with her."

"Barely," I respond, bitter this time.

"What are you thinking?" she asks. "It's not too late to leave him, if that's what you want to do. I'll be there for you and Mason, you know that."

"I can't leave him, Carmen. I told you, that's not an option. Not for me." I pace around the room until I stop at the window.

"Then you have to give it more time. He thinks you're carrying his child, he'll come around."

"I know, I just... sometimes I feel like I'm losing it. I—"

I feel it again, the feeling of someone's eyes on me.

As I observe a man standing across the street, my skin prickles. A hood covers his head and, with his black clothes, he fades into the shadows and I can't make out his face or much of his shape. But in my bones, I'm sure he's staring straight at me.

"Tess, are you there?" Carmen asks from the other end.

"Yeah. I have to go. I'll—let's talk tomorrow."

"Are you okay?"

"I'm fine."

It's a lie, I'm paralyzed. My breathing is shallow, and it feels like the ground beneath me is crumbling and at any second, I'll fall through it.

"Tess, you're not. You don't sound okay."

"I'll talk to you tomorrow," I repeat before ending the call.

Trying to see the person better, I press my face against the window. But it's too dark outside and I can't make him out at all. Then suddenly my heart leaps into my throat as he starts jogging down the street, and he doesn't stop until darkness completely engulfs him.

My spine tingling with a cold shiver, I back away slowly from the window. Oliver must hear about this. I don't know if he will believe me, he knows how paranoid I can be, but I have to try. I hurry back to our bedroom, thinking about what he said last time I told him I felt like someone was watching me. He told me I was imagining it and even joked that I was probably listening to too much talk about thrillers in my book club. I swallow and steel myself to fight for him to believe me. Without switching on the light, I sit next to him. He's lying on his back with his arms at his sides. The soft light from the streetlamps outside casts a faint glow into the room through our thin curtains, enough for me to see his face. The room smells of the pine-scented body lotion he applied after his shower, and for a brief moment I feel calm again. Oliver always made me feel safe.

"Oliver!" I shake him awake. As I do so, he stirs, turning around to face the other way. "What's going on?"

"Someone was standing in front of our house."

"Who?" His voice is groggy.

"I think it's the man Mason saw in his room a while ago."

Oliver turns back to face me and switches on his nightlight. "What man?"

"The person Mason saw in his room that night," I say. "I think that's who brought the glass to his room."

Oliver sits up in bed. He rubs his eyes with the back of his hand. "What are you talking about? What man? What glass?"

I sigh. I totally forgot that I didn't tell him about it. I had meant to ask him whether it had been him, as Mason said, but before I could talk to him about it, he'd left for New York.

I quickly tell him the story and he scratches the side of his head. "I still don't understand what you're talking about. Let me get this straight. Mason saw a man in his room in the middle of the night?"

"Yeah, and he said it was you, that you were wearing a hood."

"I don't remember this at all." Oliver's forehead creases. "And I don't have a hooded sweater."

"I know." I throw my hands up in the air. "But what about the person I just saw? He was staring at our house and he had a hood over his head."

Oliver gets out of bed and peers out the window. "There's no one out there."

"Not anymore," I say, desperate for him to believe me. "He ran off."

Oliver comes back to the bed and takes my hand, rubbing the back of it with his thumb. "Are you okay?" His tone tells me he's genuinely concerned.

"I'm fine, Oliver. I'm not making this up."

"Well, if you ask me, it sounds a lot like the pregnancy is stressing you out a bit."

"What about Mason, is he crazy too? He said he saw someone in his room." I'm trying not to lose my temper, but this is absurd.

"And you really believe him?" Oliver's voice sounds flat. "What if he lied?"

"But why would he do that? Why would he make something like that up?"

Oliver shrugs. "Tess, kids lie all the time. Some don't know the difference between the truth and a lie."

"Not Mason," I retort. "How could you say that about him? He wouldn't lie to me."

"I know you wouldn't think he would, but it's a fact that kids have vivid imaginations, that's all."

I yank my hands from him and stand up, frustrated that he doesn't think this is a big deal. I sit back down again. "What if they've found us and they're watching me?"

"Who?" he asks in an impatient tone.

"You know who."

"If they knew where we are and what happened, they wouldn't just watch us and stay quiet. We would know about it. You have to trust me on that. You are safe."

I stare at him for a few seconds, feeling more and more ridiculous as each second passes. "Maybe I'm just tired."

"I think you are." Before I can get up, Oliver pulls me

against him and I lay my head against his chest. "You don't have to be afraid; I promised to protect you. I'm never going to let anything happen to you."

I feel my heartbeat slowing down and, for a few minutes, I feel safe. After a while, I get back to my side of the bed and try to sleep, telling myself that the person on the street was a random man taking a nighttime stroll or stopping in the middle of a run.

I want Oliver to be right, I want it all to be in my head. But I know in my heart that one day, when I least expect it, one of them will come for me.

CHAPTER FOURTEEN

THREE YEARS AGO

One day, Henry arrives back home from a five-day business trip to Hong Kong, and he finds me sitting with Mason on his bedroom floor, searching under the bed for all the socks that kept disappearing mysteriously during the past week.

"Hello, you two," he says from the doorway.

"Daddy, you're back already," Mason shouts and jumps up to wrap his arms around his father. "I missed you so much!"

"I missed you too, big boy." Henry scoops Mason up in his arms, and they hold each other for a long time. I can't stop myself from smiling; so many emotions are contained in this one moment. Then Henry's eyes shift to me, and my heart stutters. They are a dark shade of blue and so intense it takes my breath away. I breathe in slowly, pulling Play-Doh-tinged air into my lungs. His gaze is still on me when he lowers Mason to the floor.

"I hope I'm not disturbing anything."

"Not at all," I say, getting to my feet. "I was just about to read Mason a goodnight story."

"I'd love to join you, if I may."

"Oh, sure," I say and move to the bookshelf. I ask Mason what he wants us to read and he points to one of the *Super*

Hunters comic magazines. Since I introduced them to him, he can't get enough, so I continue to supply him with the biweekly editions. While I read, Henry sits on the bed with Mason on his lap, and when I look up before moving to another paragraph, Henry's eyes lock with mine and I am the first to look away. I try to focus on the story and not Henry, but it is hard when he's so close. I now understand what Becca and Oliver had hinted at that day in the kitchen: this man has an energy about him like nothing I've ever experienced.

A month after my becoming Mason's nanny, Becca eventually revealed they had all suspected that something was going on between Henry and the last nanny, and that when she fell in love with someone else, he fired her out of jealousy. But even though I know that now, I can't stop my feelings from growing, and I find it exhausting every day to remind myself that he is my boss and I need to pull myself together.

I try to steady my voice as I continue to read, but I can't focus on any of the words.

"How about we continue tomorrow?" I close the book. Mason protests, but his father convinces him it's time for bed.

"I'll tuck him in," Henry says to me.

I nod and walk out of the room, and inside my bedroom, I close the door and lean my back against it. Even in my own space, I can still smell the sweet and spicy smoky cologne he is wearing. The soft knock on my door makes me jump.

"Tess," he says softly on the other side, "can we talk for a minute?"

When I open the door, he fills the doorway and leans against the frame.

"I just wanted you to know that I've been watching you and I think you're doing a great job with Mason. He really likes having you around."

"Thanks." I can't think of anything else to say, and I can't drag my eyes away from his.

"That's not all," he says and continues. "I also noticed that you haven't had any time for yourself. You didn't ask for a single day off in two months."

"I don't need—"

"Everybody needs a break, especially when running after such an active boy all day."

"It's my job." I smile. "And taking care of Mason doesn't feel like work."

"I'm not saying you don't love your job, but you don't have to take it to the point of exhaustion."

I don't know what to say to that. It's true that, right now, part of me really wants to close my door again and go to sleep. His eyes travel down my body to my hands, and I notice they are shaking. As my insides curl up with embarrassment, I tuck them into my armpits and out of sight.

"There has to be something you'd like to do in your free time."

I think about it for a moment. "I haven't been to the beach in a long time."

"Well, then, I guess that's what we'll do. Greenwich Point is not far from here. Let's drive there."

"Wh... what?" I sputter.

"It's simple. You want to go to the beach and I think it's a great idea. Tomorrow is Saturday and I was planning on spending the day with Mason. Why don't we take him to the beach?"

"Oh, I don't—I didn't mean..."

"No, Tess. I insist. Tomorrow after breakfast?"

Without thinking, I nod.

"Great, then I'll see you first thing in the morning."

"Okay." My voice comes out unnatural and stifled.

"Goodnight, Tess," he says and leaves my room.

I stand there for a long time, waiting for my heartbeat to return to normal. I have the whole night to think about what the beach with Henry will be like. I have to try to make sure nothing happens between us, no matter what my heart says, now that I know the kind of man he is.

* * *

I have just finished eating a fruit salad for breakfast when Henry walks into the dining room. Instead of his usual suits, he has on a nautical-inspired look—camel shorts, a navy blue and white striped Polo t-shirt, and a beige straw fedora hat. After a morning in the gym, I am still wearing my yoga pants and a t-shirt, and I am planning to change before we leave.

"Ready to go to the beach?" Henry asks after he has hugged his son.

Mason's eyes light up. "We're going to the beach? Yay! I'm so excited."

"I'll be ready in a few minutes," I tell them and go upstairs to change.

Standing in front of my wardrobe, I search for the most unflattering piece of clothing I can find. I settle on an oversized gray t-shirt hiding at the back. It is made of a heavy material, the kind you wear in the winter when it's freezing outside. I pull it over my head and complete the look with shorts and flip-flops.

"Is that your swimsuit?" Henry asks when I return downstairs.

"I didn't bring a swimsuit," I lie.

"No problem. Then we'll stop by a store and get you one."

I'm about to refuse his offer when Oliver shows up as if from thin air. He looks from me to Henry: "Going somewhere?"

"To the beach," Mason answers. "Come with us, Uncle Oliver. We can build a castle."

When Henry shoots his son a look, my rational mind steps in to shake me awake. I can't do it, I need to give myself a break away from this man and his piercing blue eyes.

"You know what?" I say to the brothers. "Why don't the three of you go? Spend some time together as a family."

Mason protests and the two men stare at me like I am growing two heads.

"Henry," I say, "you were right. I do need a day off."

"You're really not coming with us?" Henry's voice is soft, like he is genuinely disappointed.

"I'm sorry," I apologize, as I plaster a fake smile on my face. "I'm going out to meet some friends."

I don't really have friends. I've never been around anyone for long enough in my childhood, and since then I've always found it hard to open up to people and trust them. The few friends I have are really just colleagues from Little Treasures: we often met in the park when we took care of our charges, and we would complain about our employers. But since I started working for Henry, no one is answering my calls anymore. The only person who calls me from time to time is Doris, checking that everything is going okay. On one of our calls, she told me that the other girls had all been hoping to land my job and are disappointed that Henry Baldwin wanted me even though they had more experience.

"That's not fair." Mason pouts. "You said you'll come with."

"Sorry, Mason." I try to give him a hug, but he ducks away from me. I hate to disappoint him, but I know this is for the best. Henry is a convincing man, so before he can talk me out of my decision, I back out of the conversation.

"I'll see you at dinner."

Before I can change my mind, I run to my room and grab my phone and keys, and five minutes later, I'm in my car. It is a gorgeous summer day in Greenwich, and a light breeze quells the heat of the day, the sky blue and scattered with cotton candy clouds. I spend hours pretending to be a tourist, window shopping, taking pictures of the fountain at the center of town, and sitting on the bench in front of the library, reading the book

I borrowed. When the sun starts to sink like a vitamin C tablet into the horizon, I send Henry a quick message to let him know I won't make it to dinner. I eat at Tray's, a sandwich restaurant I worked at for a few months before joining Little Treasures.

When I arrive back at the house, it is after nine and I tiptoe to my room in the hope that no one will hear me. But when I open my door, Henry is sitting on my bed, staring straight at me.

When our eyes meet, anxiety turns my stomach.

"Henry," I say, still holding onto the doorknob. "What are you doing in my room?"

He stands up and walks to me, getting a little too close for comfort.

"Don't do that again," he warns.

"Do what?" I stutter, my mouth dry.

"Bail on me like that. When I make an appointment, I expect you to respect it."

While I am still reeling from his harsh tone, he leans forward and, without warning, he kisses me. And, despite myself, I wrap my arms around his neck and kiss him back.

CHAPTER FIFTEEN

PRESENT

I'm standing in front of the large bathroom mirror, naked. I scan my body in search of signs of pregnancy that are not there. My eyes move from my face down to my stomach. It is a little bloated, but it's only because lately I've been eating a lot of salty potato chips for comfort. Fortunately, the pregnancy guidebook I bought said most women only start to show between twelve and eighteen weeks, and I'm still a while away from that mark. Oliver thinks I'm between seven and eight weeks pregnant, and even though our love life has been wonderful lately, every time I take a test it is negative.

Keeping a secret is hard work, let alone two. The pressure to come up with more smaller lies to cover up the big ones is exhausting. When I pretend to have morning sickness or swallow down the prenatal vitamins I picked up at the drugstore, I feel like a fraud, and most days I wake up in a cold sweat after dreaming he found out and left me in a rage, promising to tell everyone what I did. Every day, I wrestle with my conscience over what to do next. And when he pulls away from me at night, or I see him glancing at his phone, anger gnaws at the lining of my stomach.

I stare at my reflection, trying to imagine I'm really pregnant, running my hands over my empty stomach. I'm still standing in front of the mirror when I hear a noise on the other side of the bathroom door. The door handle wobbles.

"Tess?" Oliver calls from the other side.

I grab my white bathrobe and fasten it. "Hey," I say.

"Why did you lock yourself inside?"

"I didn't realize I did." I turn on the faucet.

"Right," he replies and goes quiet.

I'm about to let him in when I hear his footsteps retreating. I splash water on my face and brush my teeth, and when I finally step out of the bathroom, Oliver eyes me suspiciously and I feel myself shrinking inwardly.

"Is everything alright? Are you feeling poorly?" he asks.

A huge knot forms in my throat, but I force myself to swallow it down before speaking. "I'm fine. Why do you ask?"

He places his hand on my wrist, gently applying pressure until I lock eyes with him. "You're acting strange."

"I'm tired. I didn't sleep too well."

"You've been having trouble sleeping for a while now, haven't you?"

I nod. "I made an appointment with the gynecologist for today to make sure everything is fine."

He pulls out his phone to check the time, glancing at it for a moment and then stuffing it back into his pocket. "What time is your appointment?"

"Noon," I say, avoiding his gaze.

Oliver scratches his head. "I don't have much planned for today, hardly any meetings." He grins at me. "I'd love to go with you to the doctor."

"Don't!" I say way too fast for my liking. "It's not necessary. You don't have to worry. I'll be fine on my own."

"I know you will be, but I'd love to hear our baby's heartbeat." He brushes some hair back from my face.

"I know you can't wait to, honey." I lean in and kiss him gently on the lips. "It's just that I don't want you to get too excited in case—"

"That will never happen to us." He puts a hand on my belly and drops it again as if burned.

"I know, but I'd rather have the first trimester behind us."

"Fine," he says. "But we need to tell him soon. It's past time."

"Who? Mason?" Blood drains from my face.

Lying to Mason is unbearable; he trusts me so much.

"Yes. Why wait, what's the problem?"

"For the same reason why I want you to wait before coming with me to the doctor."

"Tess, I don't understand why you're being so negative about this. Mason deserves to know."

When he leaves the room, I think he's going to the kitchen for breakfast, but within minutes, he wheels a sleepy Mason into our room. My blood turns cold. "What...?"

Oliver stations him next to our bed and sits down next to me.

"Mason, Mommy and I have something exciting to tell you. I... we want you to know that we're having another baby." He takes my hand in his and squeezes it again. "What do you say?" he asks Mason. "Are you excited to be a big brother?"

Mason squints as if he's trying to figure out if we're serious, glancing between the two of us. His panicked gaze rests on my face. "You can't have a baby," he says. "I don't want to be a big brother."

"Look, you're going to be an amazing big brother," Oliver continues.

"I don't want to be," Mason shouts and my heart flips. I didn't think about how he would react. I was so focused on Oliver that I never even thought about the possibility that we might have to tell Mason. And now there's no turning back unless I undo this madness. I have already planted a few seeds of doubt in Oliver's head, that some pregnancies never make it to term. A miscarriage wouldn't be too much of a surprise.

"Mason," I say then stop, recognizing all too well the anger in his eyes.

Mason wipes his mouth with the back of his hand and spins his wheelchair around. We watch as he rolls himself out of the room, and he doesn't look back as he disappears through the doorway. I turn on Oliver, the heat of rage flushing up my neck. "You shouldn't have done that. We should have waited."

"Until when? He's a part of this family. It's good for him to get used to the idea of a baby coming into our lives."

"I know, but I'm not comfortable with how you sprung it on him. You... we should have warmed him up or something."

"I really don't know what the problem is." Oliver shoots to his feet, looking hurt. "This is supposed to be a happy time for us. But I'm getting the odd feeling that you're not excited."

"Baby, this is all new to me," I say carefully. "I don't know what to think or feel. I'm just scared."

Oliver sighs and rubs his forehead with the tips of his fingers, as though trying to massage away a headache. "Exactly what are you afraid of?"

I swallow the lump in my throat and stare at my hands clasped in my lap, unable to come up with an answer. Oliver comes to kneel down in front of me and takes both my hands into his. "This is the new life we wanted, darling. You know how much I've always wanted a baby with you. Try to enjoy the journey."

When he doesn't get a response from me, he rises to his feet again. "I need to go to the office after all, I'll see you in the evening."

I watch him getting dressed. "You won't stay for breakfast?"

"I'll grab a piece of fruit on my way out."

After Oliver leaves the house, I sit Mason down for his

breakfast, and since I'm not hungry I use the time to tidy up his room for him. I'm folding the bedsheets when I come across a comic book. I frown as I read the title: *Super Hunters*. It has been a long time since I bought Mason a copy of his favorite comic, and definitely not since we moved to Westledge. The comic books remind me too much of the time when he was an active little boy, who would run and jump around, pretending to be one of the heroes in the books, and it hurts so much that he can't do those things anymore.

My legs are shaking as I walk back to the kitchen. "Mason," I say, "where did you get this?"

"I don't know," he says without looking up, and my blood turns to ice.

CHAPTER SIXTEEN

I open my eyes and reach across the bed for Oliver, but he's not there. He's been away for five days, attending a real estate summit in Wilmington. And two days before he left, Jocelyn posted in our WhatsApp group that she's going to Miami. But Oliver has been so wonderful lately, just as thoughtful and attentive as he used to be. I choose to believe that he's not lying to me again, that he's not with her. But I still have an undercurrent of doubt inside me, and it's almost a full-time job trying to keep thoughts of Jocelyn out of my mind.

I'll give it another week to see if his affair is truly over. If not, then the pregnancy clearly isn't working. And I'll have to do something else.

As soon as I've finished homeschooling Mason and he's watching a documentary on the emperor penguin for a project we're doing, I sneak to the basement. Before visiting her mother at the care home yesterday morning, Carmen dropped off a package that I ordered online to be shipped to her address, since I didn't want it to arrive while Oliver was home.

I hid it in a box filled with Christmas decorations. I pull it out and take it with me to our bedroom, careful not to be seen by Mason, before locking myself in the bathroom and sitting on the lip of the bathtub, staring at the box. The name Pink Clover is written across the front, and the model pictured on the outside looks like she's four or five months pregnant. I'm not that far along. If Oliver comes home and finds me with an abnormally big belly, he'll definitely become suspicious. Did I order the wrong size?

I open the package and pull out a plastic bag. The seal is broken and I pull out the glossy note. It's white with raised type in robin's egg blue. First, it congratulates me on the purchase, then it goes on to say that the belly is made from medical grade waterproof silicone, and that even though it will feel strange at first, once I get used to it, it will feel as if I'm really pregnant.

Blocking out any thoughts of guilt, I remove the baggy clothes I've been wearing around the house and step inside. As I slide the belly on over my own, a bump forms instantly. To my relief, it's not too big or too small, just the perfect size for a first-time mom just into their second trimester, perhaps experiencing a little bloating. It does feel strange against my skin, but when I put my hands against it, they're actually met with warmth that radiates from my body. So if Oliver decides to touch my stomach, he won't suspect a thing. I'll just have to hold off sex somehow for a few weeks before I end the fake pregnancy, or if it happens, I'll have to be extra careful.

I'll leave it on, I decide. I need to get used to wearing it before Oliver returns from his trip. I dress quickly in a pair of light-colored jeans with a t-shirt, and a gray cardigan that hangs like a waterfall across the front. In late July, the weather has warmed up, but I can pretend I'm cold, as I often am. I study my reflection in the mirror, then I bend to pick up the package. A small envelope falls out, and I turn it over in my hand, then open it. It's a fake ultrasound photo complete with my name and a date, from the last time I told Oliver I was going for a checkup.

Oliver will be back in two days and now I'll have something to show him, proof of my pregnancy. I slide the ultrasound back into the envelope and get to work tearing up the box that had the pregnant belly in it. I stuff the pieces into a plastic garbage bag, the one we keep in our laundry room for the recycling bin. I'll take it out later.

After another quick check in the mirror to make sure the belly is firmly in place, I go to the kitchen to make a snack for Mason. I'm too agitated to eat, so I make him some toast and take it to him in the living room. He barely looks up when I place the plate on the removable tray of his wheelchair, where he sometimes rests his iPad.

"Mason," I say after a moment of silence. He looks up at me with a surprised expression.

"I want you to know that I love you. You're my favorite person in the world."

"You're my person," he says back and goes back to nibbling his toast.

Ever since Oliver told him about the baby, he's been reserved again and barely makes eye contact with me, even when we're alone. I'm convinced that the reason he was so upset about a baby entering our lives is out of fear of losing me. He acted out of jealousy, and I can understand that all too well. I just need to keep assuring him that no one can ever replace him.

As I go about my daily chores, I'm aware of the fake belly pressing against my skin, and it feels too hot under the plastic. How in the world will I be able to wear it all day and all night? I could end the whole thing right now, but somehow I can't bring myself to do it, not yet. I'm afraid of breaking the spell, of Oliver being so distraught it pushes him back to the other woman.

The hours drag on and, after washing, feeding, and putting Mason to bed, I lock all the doors, checking them three times. I fall asleep reading my pregnancy guidebook.

I'm awakened from my fitful sleep by the sound of a door closing sharply. My heart starts to race as I jump out of bed and tear through the house to Mason's room. His door is slightly ajar, but he's sleeping soundly. I close the door again softly and check the other doors and all the windows. I know that they're locked because I checked them before bed. Getting back under the covers, I close my eyes and try to focus on my breathing, but I can't sleep. I lie awake for what feels like hours. When Oliver gets home, I have to beg him to believe me. Something is definitely going on here, and I need to convince him that it's not in my head. The past is catching up. I'm certain of it. How long until it grabs me by the shoulders and forces me to meet its gaze? How long until it forces me to inhale its scent of rotting graveyard flowers?

I'm about to finally fall asleep again when my phone beeps with a notification from Instagram. Jocelyn has shared a new post. I wait a minute to brace myself, then I open the app. She's pictured lying in bed next to a silver breakfast tray. Among the items on the tray is a vase with a red rose and two cups of coffee. As I read the caption, my anger bubbles up inside me and burns the back of my throat.

Life is delicious again. #someonecares #makingmemories

That's it. The truth is right in front of me, flashing like a big neon sign. The two cups of coffee prove that Jocelyn is sharing the breakfast with someone special, and her words indicate that they had not been in a good place, but now they're back together. The fact that she won't reveal his name or face means she's doing something wrong. As I scroll through the comments, I try to absorb as much as I can. One of her followers asks a question I already know the answer to: *Who's the mysterious man?*

Jocelyn has already responded: *Some things are better left to the imagination. #mystery*

Anger boiling inside of me like a volcano about to erupt, I hit reply to the last person's comment, from my fake account: *That man is my husband.*

I'm not done with Jocelyn yet. Rather than leaving it at that, I go to her profile and click on the message tab. It's important that she knows I know. My breathing is uneven as I compose a scathing message.

Keep your hands off my husband, you home-wrecking tramp. Consider this my first and last warning.

CHAPTER SEVENTEEN
THREE YEARS AGO

The morning after Henry kissed me, he strolls into the kitchen dressed in a light gray shirt and a black suit. He kisses Mason, then glances at me. "Morning, Tess," he says, accepting his cup of espresso from Becca. "Did you sleep well?"

"Sure," I reply, my voice trembling slightly.

I couldn't sleep all night thinking about what had happened between us. His gaze had driven fear into me that was quickly replaced by shock and overwhelming chemistry when he kissed me. As he downs his coffee, he eyes me over the rim. "What do you have planned for the day?"

"I was thinking of driving Mason to preschool then—"

"Why would you want to do that?" He glances at his watch. "The driver is scheduled to pick him up in half an hour."

"I want Tess to take me," Mason cries out, bouncing up and down on his seat, so excited he almost knocks his cup of milk over.

"Mason, you'll go with Bobby," Henry says. "Tess has other things to do."

"No. I want to go with Tess, please, Daddy." The little boy crosses his arms over his chest and his mouth forms a pout.

"That's enough, Mason," Henry snaps. "You will do as I say."

Mason's eyes water and he stares at Henry in shock. It is rare for his father to lose his patience with him.

"Henry," I say, stepping in to iron out the tension, "it's really not a problem. I don't have much planned for this morning."

"Yes, you do." He sighs and places his empty cup in the sink. "You have a meeting to attend."

"What meeting... where?"

"With me. I have a short virtual meeting first. After that, I need to see you in my office. Eight o'clock. Don't be late."

Yet another order from him. I know better than to argue.

"Okay," I say, nodding.

He leaves the kitchen and I hold Mason close to me, trying to soothe him. "Don't cry, Mason. Your daddy does not like it when you cry."

"But I wanted you to take me to preschool."

"I'm sorry, sweetie, but you heard what your dad said. I think he has something important to talk to me about."

I kiss his head. "I'll see you later. I'll ask your father if I can pick you up instead. Then maybe we can go to the park."

Mason wipes at his tears. "Do you promise?"

I ruffle his hair. "I promise."

"It's a deal, then." He runs off to find his backpack and when Bobby arrives to pick him up, he gives me another hug and runs off.

"That boy loves you," Becca says as she loads the dishwasher. "I've never seen him that close to anyone before. It's a shame he hasn't got a mother; it's not good for a child to grow up without one. It must be hard."

I grab a rag to wipe down the table. "Yeah, it is. I also grew up without a mother. She died when I was ten."

She doesn't need to know that my father died the same day,

that both had overdosed. She also doesn't need to know that I didn't shed one tear at their funerals.

Becca closes the dishwasher and comes to take my hand. "I'm so sorry. I wish I had known."

"It's okay. I'm okay." I take my hand away from her and wipe up a few drops of spilled milk. Then I straighten up and smile at the kind woman. "I have a meeting with Henry in ten minutes. I better go."

"You better. The boss doesn't like people being late."

I laugh. "You're right about that."

"Don't forget what I told you," Becca says when I am about to walk out of the kitchen.

When I rack my brain for what she is talking about, she sighs. "The day you arrived, I warned you to watch out for your heart."

I only smile and walk away, my cheeks hot with shame. If she only knew what had happened between me and him last night. Would she look at me differently? Would she say I told you so? Becca has been working for Henry for twelve years. If anyone knows him, it's her, so I would be lying if I said her warnings don't make me uneasy. But she has nothing to worry about; what happened last night will never happen again.

I wish I could believe my own thoughts.

When I get to Henry's office at eight o'clock sharp, I knock gently.

"Come on in, Tess," he calls from the other side of the oak door and I enter.

The office is large and masculine with a large mahogany desk. The walls are covered in shelves filled with books, two oil paintings that look like they're worth millions of dollars, and pictures of Henry with politicians and business tycoons. In one corner is a small sitting area with a leather couch and a coffee table, and a large flat-screen TV is mounted on the wall above a fireplace. The air in the room is cool, like he's turned on the air conditioning. Or maybe it's my body temperature acting wild.

Henry sits behind the desk, looking at something on his laptop, and I take a seat on the other side. "You wanted to see me," I say and he looks up.

He pushes his laptop aside and folds his hands on the desk. "I'm sorry about what happened last night."

"That's okay," I say, feeling my stomach plummet. "It was nothing."

Still holding my gaze, he runs a hand through his hair. "You must understand that I've never done anything like that before."

I wave my hand dismissively. "Don't worry about it. It's not the first time a guy—"

"I'm not apologizing for what happened," he says. "I'm just sorry for not sharing my intentions with you first."

"I'm sorry... what? You don't regret it?" I stare at him, at a loss for words.

"I only do things I want to do, Tess. That's why I'm successful in business. And when my instinct tells me to do something, I go for it. I've wanted to kiss you since the day I saw your profile photo on the nanny agency page."

My mouth drops open. "You hired me to be your child's nanny because you liked how I looked?" I'm not even sure whether to be flattered or insulted.

"No. I was looking for a nanny and I was right to hire you. You're efficient at your job and you're good for my son. But I will admit the first thing I noticed when I saw your photo was how beautiful you are."

My cheeks burn. I never thought of myself as beautiful, just average.

"Henry, do you always say what's on your mind?"

He throws his head back and laughs. "I try. Unlike many people I've met in life and business, I prefer being upfront."

"Right." I stifle a laugh. I've never met a man like Henry before. And I have never been both attracted to someone and repelled by them.

"Perhaps it's a good thing I didn't tell you I wanted to kiss you. I have a feeling I wouldn't have gotten a yes."

"Probably not," I say honestly. "But it can't happen again. I'm here to be your son's nanny. Nothing more, nothing less."

"What if I tell you I want it to happen again?" He leans over the table, his eyes locked on mine.

I feel my breath quicken and I have to lean back to keep from being drawn in by him. "You need to look for someone else to kiss. I'm your employee."

"I see." He strokes his chin. "How about taking you to lunch today? Is that off limits too?"

"I can't; I think it's best we keep things professional. Besides, I promised I'd pick up Mason from preschool. He was really upset I couldn't take him. He's my priority, after all."

"I understand," he says, leaning back in his chair and clasping his hands behind his head. "He'd really love that."

"Yes. We're going to the park after." Watching him, I am unsure if I am happy about his defeat or disappointed that he gave up so easily.

He rises from his seat and walks me to the door. "Thank you for taking the time to talk to me. It's a shame we can't have lunch together today, but tomorrow is another day. I'll make the arrangements."

"Henry, I told you I can't."

"As your boss, I give you permission to."

I let out a breath. "I'll think about it."

As I walk out of his office, I know my job is in danger. Going to lunch with him, spending time alone together would be the start of something, and it is something I don't want to begin. I go outside for air and drop into a hammock on the edge of the garden, staring up at the clear sky. Shutting my eyes, I relax in the cool breeze, trying to slow my racing heart. When I have calmed down enough to go back inside the house, I look up at the building and see Henry watching me from his office window, a phone pressed to his ear, and I suppress a shudder. His stare makes my gut twist with anxiety, but I can't deny that I am drawn toward the thrill. After a few seconds, he disappears from the window.

The rest of the day passes without incident. I take Mason to the park as promised, and, after dinner, I bathe him, read to him from the *Super Hunters* comic book I bought him, and tuck him into bed.

When I go to my room, I find an evening gown on my bed. It is made from glittering blue fabric with tightly stitched embroidery that catches the light, and a note lies on top of it with my name elegantly written across the front.

Tess, I changed my mind about lunch tomorrow. We'll be flying to New York for dinner instead. I won't take no for an answer. Please wear this. My private jet will be ready to board at 6 P.M. —H

I lay the note back down on top of the dress. I have to admit, I am flattered by his persistence and the dress really is beautiful. I can't resist trying it on, and it hugs my curves tastefully and feels like the most expensive thing I have ever worn. When I remove it, I wonder, after everything I've gone through, would it be so terrible to be made to feel like a princess for one night?

The only problem is, it doesn't stop at one dinner, or two, or even three. It doesn't stop at one kiss either, and before I know it, I have done what I told myself I wouldn't do. I have fallen in love with Henry. But it is not only his charm that wins me over in the end; it is also the fear I have buried deep in my stomach, of saying no to him.

CHAPTER EIGHTEEN

PRESENT

When Mason and I come back from a long evening walk, we turn into our street to see the light on in the living room.

I never leave the light on.

Having grown up poor, that kind of wastefulness isn't in my nature. I look down at Mason: "Honey, do you know if we left the light on?"

He tips his head back and stares at me blankly. "I don't know. Maybe."

Bringing my gaze back to the house, I try not to panic as I grip the handles of Mason's chair tightly and keep moving forward. What if it's them? What if they have finally caught up with us and are ransacking our home in hopes of finding something that would serve as evidence against me? Or maybe they're just trying to scare me? I swallow hard and a trickle of dread trails down my spine. It's not possible for someone else to be in the house unless they forced their way in. It can't be Oliver, since the car is not in the drive.

"We can't go in there," I whisper to myself just as an idea hits me.

We'll go to Carmen's house; perhaps she will let us stay the night at her place. Oliver will be back tomorrow.

Or I should brave it and call the police.

No, I can't do that. I might end up saying the wrong thing and draw attention to myself. Innocent people are nervous around the police, so what about someone who is guilty? I feel sweat trickle down my back as I push Mason's wheelchair across the road.

"Where are we going?" he asks.

"We're visiting Aunty Carmen," I say. "We haven't seen her for a few days."

"Is there a book club today? But I don't have my book."

I take another deep breath and push myself forward. "No, not today."

Since I've been in such a bad place, I couldn't get myself to go to the last few book club meetings and pretend I'm fine. Dan and Carmen are the only people I continue to meet up with occasionally for coffee and a chat. Jocelyn, who returned from Miami a day ago, is having an affair with my husband and, if I'm honest, I'm afraid to be around her. I don't think I'll be able to control myself in her presence. Her reply to my message on Instagram was a simple wink emoji that spoke more than words ever could. A few hours later, she blocked me from seeing any more of her future posts. On that fake account, anyway. Perhaps I'll set up another.

Someone calls my name and my body stiffens a little. But it's only Dan, who's standing at his front door wearing a pair of colorful pajama pants and waving at us.

"Hi, Dan," I say, and wave back, sighing with relief.

I park the wheelchair and Dan squats by Mason, holding a pizza in one hand. "Guess what?" He rubs the dimpled part of his chin. "I ordered pizza, but it's too much for one person. Amanda and Noah left this morning to visit the grandparents. If you haven't had dinner yet, you and your mom can help me finish it."

Mason shrugs and looks up at me with pleading eyes. "I want pizza," he says with a tiny smile.

I laugh, and smile at Dan. "That's kind of you. We'll be happy to."

I am desperate to get inside, somewhere safe, and I thank Dan internally for his perfect timing.

Dan grins easily. "It's no problem at all. Come right in."

He's helping me carry Mason in his wheelchair up the steps into the house when my back starts to prickle, and when we lower the wheelchair in the doorway, I turn to look back at our house. Someone is standing at the window watching us.

But the longer I look, the lighter my heart becomes. It's not a stranger in the house, it's Oliver. It's safe to go home. Suddenly, despite everything, there is nothing I want more than to be with him, the man who knows everything about me and who has always kept me safe.

"I'm really sorry, Dan, but we need to get back home."

"Oh," he says, a tinge of disappointment in his voice. "Well, okay."

"But I want pizza, Mom," Mason interjects.

"No, Mason. We'll eat at home." I turn to Dan. "Again, I'm so sorry to change the plans, I just saw that Oliver is home. I hope you enjoy the pizza."

"Don't worry about it." He squeezes my shoulder and turns to Mason. "You know what, Mace, you don't have to eat the pizza here. Give me a second." He goes back inside and comes out with a fat slice of pepperoni pizza that he hands to Mason. "Enjoy it."

When we get back to the house, Oliver is sitting on the couch watching the game and he switches off our wide-screen TV and gets up.

"You're back early," I say, my emotions torn between relief

at seeing him, and anger with him for being drawn in by Jocelyn yet again.

"I wanted to surprise you." He presses a kiss to my lips and studies my face. "You didn't tell me you were having dinner at Dan's house. I thought this week's book club meeting was yesterday."

"It was, but we didn't go... and we didn't have dinner with Dan."

Oliver looks down at Mason, who's enjoying the crust of the pizza, and ruffles his hair. Mason visibly flinches, but Oliver is used to him acting strange around him; he has never really adjusted to our new reality.

Oliver raises his eyebrows at me. "I thought I saw you leaving Dan's house just now."

"No, we just stopped by." I don't want to tell him yet that I thought someone was in the house, not in front of Mason. "Where's the car?"

"In the garage. I cleared a space." He pauses. "I have a surprise for you."

"Oh?" I say, feeling the corners of my mouth curl. Has he brought me flowers again?

"Come with me," he says, taking my hand and leading me to his office.

I come to a halt in the doorway and my heart drops to my feet. A baby crib is standing on one side of the room, where a couch had once stood.

"Surprise," he says, coming to stand behind me.

I stare at the baby bed for a long moment, saying nothing. My mouth is so dry, it's hard to get any words out. "That's... That's—"

"It is," he interrupts me. "I know you said we should wait before buying things for the baby, but I couldn't resist. Once we prepare the guest room, we can move it in there. This is temporary." He pauses. "Say something. Do you like it?"

I nod. "It's... It is beautiful."

The crib is made of oak and has a soft mattress, with embroidered white and pink flowers.

"When did you build this?"

Mason and I had been out of the house for an hour; was it enough for him to come home and assemble a crib? I know for a fact that Oliver is not very handy.

"I had it brought over already assembled." He pulls me into his arms and hugs me, then pushes me back, glancing down at my stomach.

"Looks like the baby has grown a bit."

I stiffen in his arms and heat floods to the area of my body covered by silicone. I can almost feel the sweat popping out of my skin.

I lay a hand on the tiny bump. "I know. A lot can happen in a short amount of time."

To distance myself from his prying eyes, I walk to the crib, pretending I want to take a closer look as my pulse thuds in my throat and he follows me. I'm tempted to move away again before he touches me, but it's too late. He's on his knees and his hands are on my stomach. I draw in a shaky breath and hold it as he presses his ear to my abdomen as if he's listening.

"Hey, little soldier," he says. "I know it's all comfortable in Mommy's tummy, but you'll love it out here too."

Tears prick the back of my eyes. Maybe he really has stopped things with Jocelyn, even though I'm sure she's still trying to get her claws in him. If the circumstances were different, if my pregnancy had been real, this moment would have been wonderful. We would have been celebrating the life growing inside me.

But this is all wrong. It can't end well. Oliver is so invested already, and if he ever finds out, I don't think he'll forgive me. And if he turns against me, my whole life will be over. But maybe it already is...

"I think someone was in the house," I blurt out.

He drops his hands from my stomach. "What do you mean...? Are you sure this time?"

"I heard a door banging in the middle of the night. It woke me up."

He stands again and closes the door so Mason doesn't hear our conversation.

"Babe, you have to stop driving yourself crazy like this. No one is watching you. No one came in the house. The pregnancy hormones are—"

"Not making me crazy," I counter in a cold tone. "Strange things have been happening around here. I found... I found a comic book."

"What comic book?"

"*Super Hunters*. Remember I used to buy them for Mason in—Wait," I say and hurry to the door. "I'll get it."

I rush to our bedroom and make a beeline for the closet, where I hid the magazine in my underwear drawer. I check the entire drawer, but it's not there. I search the small space again and run to the bathroom to look in the trash can.

No comic book.

When I return to the office, I'm empty-handed and feeling ridiculous. Oliver is sitting behind his desk, his hands clasped together and his face wrinkled with concern. The chair creaks as he shifts. "It's not there, is it?"

"I know I put it there, but I can't find it." My body is sweating and my pulse is racing. "I'm not lying about this."

"I didn't say you were, sweetheart," he says, coming to hug me. "But I think you're being a little paranoid. The things you're afraid of are not real. Stop looking over your shoulder. No one is after you."

I fool myself into believing him and let him pull me into a hug that stills my heart the way only he can. But then we go to bed, and he picks up his phone again.

I hear him tapping away, and my whole body is frozen. I just know it; I know what he's doing. Again.

That's it, I'm done. I've waited long enough for Oliver to end the affair, and now I will have to do it for him. I wait until he's fast asleep before I get out of bed and go to the kitchen for the apple pie dish I still haven't returned to Jocelyn.

Ten minutes later, I knock on her door.

CHAPTER NINETEEN

A few days later, I'm feeling stronger than I have in a long time. I'm even in the process of training my mind to think I'm truly pregnant, to adopt a pregnant woman's mindset. The only hard part about pretending I'm pregnant is making sure Oliver never discovers I'm on my period. I've made sure to hide my tampons carefully. The period cramps are the hardest to hide sometimes because they always hit me hard, but when Oliver catches me in pain, I just pretend the discomfort is related to the pregnancy. Since I've been wearing the bump, I've been putting him off from sex, telling him I'm too tired or feeling unwell. It won't be long before he thinks I've had a miscarriage, and then everything can get back to normal.

But can I really pull it off? If Oliver rushes me to the hospital or insists on accompanying me there afterwards, and a checkup shows I've never been pregnant, what will I do? I'm still putting it off, even though I know I have to get it over with before long.

I pull out a bread knife from the drawer and take it with me to the cutting board. Mason has been asking me about the book club for a while, so I decided to host today's meeting.

An hour before the guests arrive, Oliver finds an excuse to go out.

I sink the blade into a salmon sandwich, cutting it into triangular pieces. "You never work on Saturdays."

"I know," he says, "but I have an important meeting with a client on Monday that I want to prepare for."

"You can do it at home in the office." I pull out a bag of watercress from the crisper and place it on the chopping board. "We won't be loud. Reading is a quiet activity, after all."

"Sorry," he says, kissing me. "I need to pick up some house plans anyway. I might as well stay there and do everything else."

Carmen is the first to arrive, and while Mason is in his room, trying to decide on his next book, she helps me set up the table on the patio with the snacks and drinks.

"Has he noticed?" she whispers when I bring out the wine glasses.

"Oliver?"

"Who else?" She bites into a carrot stick. "Is he suspicious at all?"

"I don't think so." I place a hand on my belly.

"Any improvements on the marriage front?" Carmen asks. "You look a lot happier and more relaxed."

"I'm getting there. I'm just glad the affair is over." I put down the platter of sandwiches and pour myself a glass of iced tea. "Now it's just a matter of getting our marriage back to where it was before Oliver cheated."

"Well, that's really great, but how can you be so sure he's still not seeing her?"

"Call it a hunch, call it a wife's intuition or whatever, but I know it's over. I can feel it." I take a large sip from my glass and swallow the sweet, cool liquid.

Carmen nods. "Okay, I hear you. I'm just worried about you, but I'm glad you feel like you can trust him. Listen, he thinks you're at fourteen weeks now, right? So if you're thinking of doing this for a while still, you'll need to make another order for a bigger suit before too long."

Calling the fake stomach a suit is the safest way to talk about it, but it always makes me want to laugh.

"No. I think that soon enough, I'm done."

"And by that you mean..." Carmen dips her head to the side.

"Yeah. I'll end it soon."

At 2 p.m. on the dot, the doorbell rings, followed by a knock on the door. Monica and Lillian walk in at the same time and I ask them to take a seat in the living room while I get my copy of *Rebecca* from our room and check on Mason.

"Have you chosen a book yet?" I ask, poking my head through his door.

He bobs his head in a nod. "I want to read my comic book."

My heart skips a beat. "Which one?"

"*Super Hunters*. You bought it for me, remember?"

"No, I—" I shake my head. "Do you know where it is?"

"You had it last time. Can I have it back?"

It only takes one thing to send my mood spiraling. Oliver had done such a stellar job of talking me down and comforting me, convincing me that the comic book never existed, that I'm running away from shadows that are all in my imagination. I don't hear the rest of what Mason tells me.

The doorbell rings again and I let Dan and Noah enter, my mind in a haze. During the meeting, I greet my guests, serve them treats, and smile at the right time. Then I sit with my book and pretend to read even though all the words have merged into one. I only jolt to life when Lillian brings up Jocelyn's name, asking if anyone has seen or heard from her.

Dan snorts. "You know what she's like, always dashing around from place to place."

"I know," Monica says, "but usually she sends a message in the group to let us know. This time she just left without a word, and only two days after she'd come back from Miami. She hasn't posted anything on her Instagram for a while. It's not like her at all; I'm just a bit worried."

"You know what?" Carmen jumps in after meeting my eyes. "I'd bet a million dollars she's lying on a beach somewhere. Jocelyn can take care of herself."

Everyone agrees and the conversation moves on, as I relax and sink back into my thoughts.

Later on, Monica comes to sit beside me and congratulates me, her hand resting on my arm.

"For what?" I ask, perplexed.

To my horror, she presses a hand to my belly. "You don't have to hide it, darling. I'm so happy for you and Oliver."

Lillian overhears us and comes sidling up. "You sneaky mama," she quips. "No wonder you didn't come to the other meetings. You wanted to keep this little surprise all to yourself, didn't you? How did you figure it out?" she asks Monica.

"I didn't at first, she's still so tiny, but I noticed that while she was reading, she kept putting her hand on her stomach."

I did? I didn't even notice, I guess I really got into the role of a pregnant woman. Lillian pats my shoulder. "Don't worry, we won't blab. We understand how important it is to keep something like this to yourselves for a little longer."

Behind her, I watch as Carmen wheels Mason to his room. I mentioned to her that he doesn't like to hear about the baby, that he gets angry and jealous. For the next ten minutes, the women continue to talk among themselves about the joys of pregnancy and babies. I know that if I don't fake the miscarriage soon, the whole town will know.

I sigh with relief when they finally leave, including Carmen who has to go and visit her mother. Finally, only Dan and little Noah are left.

"I suspected you were pregnant for a while," he confesses, "but I didn't want to say anything in case I was wrong. But now that you've confirmed it, I guess congratulations are in order." He leans in and gives me a hug.

"Thank you," I say, with guilt rising in my stomach, "I was going to tell you—"

"Tess," he says, putting a hand on my arm, "I understand. You don't have to explain to me. I'm just happy that you're happy. I assume things are okay again with Oliver."

"Yeah, I think we're finally on the mend."

Dan's phone beeps in his pocket. "Sorry," he says as he pulls it out and glances at the screen.

When he looks up at me again, his face is pinched and something resembling fear is reflected in his eyes.

CHAPTER TWENTY

"What's wrong, Dan?" I ask, concerned. This is the first time I've seen him look so scared.

He glances at Noah's pram, which is parked in the corner of the room, as if to see if he's awake.

I put a hand on his arm. "Hey, we're friends. Tell me what's happening." I lead him to the couch because he looks like he might collapse any second.

He drops onto it and looks at me. "Remember when Jocelyn mentioned that I was in prison?"

"It's none of my business," I say quickly. "I don't need to know about it."

"It's okay, I trust you."

I smile gently and nod my head. "Yes, I remember what Jocelyn said."

Dan covers his face with his hands before dropping them again. "She was right. Five years ago, I was incarcerated for causing a fatal accident. I was on the phone with Amanda and we were arguing about something I can't remember now, but since I was distracted, I didn't notice the red light." He rakes a hand through his hair and lets out a breath. "I was lucky to survive the crash. The other driver did not... She was headed to her wedding, but she never got there because of what I did."

Dan's words hang in the air as I attempt to process what he just said. There are no words I can use to make him feel better, I know that all too well, but I must find something to say. "I'm so sorry. I had no idea. But you didn't mean to do it. You're a good man."

Dan attempts to smile, but he can't. "Thanks for saying that," he says. "But it's not that simple. I was sentenced to four years for vehicular manslaughter, but only served two as I was released early for good behavior. The family of the woman who died was furious, and I received numerous death threats. That's why Amanda and I decided to—" He pauses suddenly, buries his face in his hands, then looks up. His face is red with anguish and he is crying. "We decided to move from our home in Virginia to here. We wanted to just get away from everything so we could start over, but..." his voice trails off into nothingness.

"You're still getting threats?" I ask and he nods.

"All the time. The text message I got was from the man the bride was going to marry." He pulls out the phone and shows it to me.

Your time will come and I'll personally make you pay. I'll take away what you love most.

The words swim before my eyes as I stare at them, and I feel as if they are addressed to me. I guess Dan and I have more in common than I thought. We're both trying to get away from the past.

While I'm still thinking about what to say, Dan stands and wipes away his tears. "You know what, let's not talk about that anymore. I'll handle it." He scratches his chin and puts on a brave face. "Now let me help you clean up before Noah wakes up."

"You don't have to," I say, picking up some iced tea glasses from the coffee table. "Oliver will be back soon, he'll help."

"I know, but I want to." Refusing to take no for an answer, he follows me into the kitchen and starts clearing the dirty plates.

"Okay," I say, thinking maybe he needs something to keep his mind off the text he just received. "I appreciate your help."

Working side by side, Dan tells me about the funny moments he shares with Noah and we keep the conversation light. I understand his need to distract himself from the past, and pretend that everything is normal, that everything will be okay. As he's talking, I start wondering whether the reason he chose to be a stay-at-home dad is actually because it's hard for him to find a job with a criminal record.

Suddenly the door slams, and Oliver walks in with a foul look on his face.

"Dan," he says in a clipped tone and takes a dirty plate from him, "go on home. I'll help my wife clean up."

Dan looks like he's about to say something, but he catches something in Oliver's eyes and meekly leaves.

I shoot Oliver a look and run after him. "I'm really sorry, Dan. That was—"

"Don't worry about it, Tess. Thanks for everything." He takes Noah and walks out the door.

I return to the kitchen, fuming.

"Why did you do that, Oliver? He was just being nice."

"Let him go and be nice to someone else's wife," Oliver hisses and walks out. He takes the folders he brought with him and disappears into his office, leaving me to do the work.

CHAPTER TWENTY-ONE

THREE YEARS AGO

"The mother wants to talk to you," Becca says as soon as I walk through the door after picking up Mason from preschool.

"Whose mother?" I ask and cringe when my mind answers my own question. "What does she want?"

Becca shakes her head, her eyes wide. Henry's mother, Catherine Baldwin, pops into the house occasionally, but she never says anything to me beyond a greeting. Henry and I have been seeing each other for a month, and she must have found out.

My voice shakes slightly as I turn toward Mason. "Go upstairs and find a new puzzle for us to work on later. I need to speak with your grandmother."

Before I finish asking, he takes off.

I would have told him to go say hello to Catherine, but I don't like her treatment of him. Whenever I've seen her talking to him, she has been cold and distant. She treats him like a piece of furniture, and Becca once told me that she did not approve of his adoption, that she wanted a Baldwin heir for her son.

Becca's hand lingers on my shoulder as she whispers, "Good luck," setting my teeth on edge.

Don't jump to conclusions, I tell myself. *Maybe it's nothing.* Maybe she has just come over to introduce herself officially.

As I enter the living room, I see her sitting on the couch, her legs delicately crossed at the ankles and her face turned toward the window. Catherine is small and delicate, and she has that wealthy person's habit of holding her head up high, so that she always seems to be looking down at you. Though her curly, tawny brown hair is streaked with gray, she looks at least ten years younger than her actual age, somewhere in her late sixties. She is still fit and healthy, running daily and keeping her appearance impeccable.

She wears an elegant black dress and holds a teacup delicately with one hand, the saucer hovering underneath it in her other. She didn't see me coming, and I clear my throat to get her attention. Very slowly, as if tearing herself away from the view, she turns to face me with clear blue eyes just like Henry's. We are both about to speak when Mason appears and interrupts us.

"Tess, I can't find a puzzle that I like," he says, ignoring his grandmother the same way she often ignores him. "Can I go outside to look at the birds?"

Birdwatching is one of Mason's favorite things to do, and he would do it for hours if we let him. I put my hands on his shoulders and smile. "That sounds like a good idea." I try to disguise the trembling in my voice, but it is still audible.

Looking at his grandmother as if seeing her for the first time, Mason gives a small wave before running off.

"You're good with him," Catherine says, patting the spot next to her. "Sit down."

"Caring for him is easy." I smile, joining her on the black leather couch. "He's a lovely boy."

With an eyebrow slightly raised, she replies, "Perhaps."

Mason deserves so much better, a grandmother who dotes on him rather than treating him like an outsider.

"You wanted to talk to me?" I ask.

Catherine sets her teacup and saucer down on the coffee table and sits up even straighter.

"It has to do with your relationship with my son," she says in a clipped tone; her eyes hold mine. "Where do you think it's going?"

Her words hit me so hard that any courage I had slips away. She continues to stare at me unflinchingly. Waiting patiently for my reaction, she clasps her hands in her lap and her mouth twitches. Her eyes are so penetrating.

"Henry and I... we like each other," I say, even though I have no idea whether I am allowed to confirm our relationship. To my knowledge, he hasn't told anyone about us, leaving them to come to their own conclusions. He is not someone who is inclined to think he owes anyone an explanation.

"You like each other," Catherine says, returning the words back to me as though they are tennis balls. "A nanny and her employer, who happens to be one of the wealthiest men in the country."

Anger rises like lava in my throat. "I'm not with him for his money, if that's what you mean."

She raises an eyebrow. "Well, once this is all laid bare, that's not what everybody will think."

"Mrs. Baldwin," I say, trying to be as polite as I can despite wanting to put her in her place, "your son is a good man and I like him. And that's the only reason why—"

Catherine cuts me off. "The job you were hired for was to look after his son, not get into his bed."

I bite my tongue. "With all due respect, I don't believe it's right for us to discuss this without Henry present."

I start to get up from my seat, but she stops me with a firm hand on my shoulder.

"I disagree," she says, simply. "Now is the ideal time to discuss this matter." She pauses and takes a breath. "Once in a while, my son tends to think with his body instead of his brain.

It is, therefore, necessary that a person of reason should intervene and bring order to the situation."

The situation?

"Let me ask you again," Catherine says. "Where do you envision this so-called relationship going, Tess?"

"It's new. We don't know yet." My words sound empty and weak.

"Surely every relationship should have a destination, don't you think? Do you think you would like to marry my son at some point in the future?"

To be honest, the thought has never occurred to me. In fact, I've never really considered myself to be the marrying kind. I saw firsthand from my parents' marriage how much damage two people can do to each other when shackled together by marriage vows. But now, despite myself, I find myself wondering if things could be different, with Henry.

"Catherine," I say slowly.

"Mrs. Baldwin to you."

I take a moment to stop myself from saying something I might regret.

"Mrs. Baldwin, Henry means a lot to me. But it's early days yet and we have not talked about the future."

"You have not wondered why my son would not talk about the future with you?"

"It's early to talk about things like that," I respond. "But I know that I care about him and he cares about me."

"I know your kind, my dear." She smiles at me, her voice sweet. "My son may sometimes rescue strays from the streets, but I am not as blind as he is. My purpose in being here is to protect his reputation. What would people say if they found out he was dating his child's nanny?"

Of course. She is afraid that Henry could cause a scandal in the family. I try to say something, unsure exactly what, but she lifts her hand, her palm facing me. "And not only a nanny, but someone who grew up in a broken home with drug addict parents. If you really cared about my son, you would end this."

My stomach lurches and I shake my head in confusion.

"How? How do you know about my family?"

"I know everything about you. I know about the trailer parks and orphanages, and the foster families that never wanted you."

"You have no right." A sob tears its way up my throat, but I choke it down and cross my arms over my chest. "You have no right to look into my history."

"I have every right." She tucks a piece of hair behind her ear. "I do my research on anyone my son brings into this house. I'm protecting him as much as I'm protecting our family's reputation. You must understand, I will do absolutely anything for my family."

I lean back in my seat. "I know. And I do not intend on tainting that reputation."

I hate myself for sounding so weak in front of her, but I feel suddenly tired and defeated.

"Then you will end it," she orders. "Do the right thing and end it before it ends badly for both of you. Trust me, my son will not marry someone like you. You will end up getting hurt. Why not be the one to get out first?"

Holding her gaze, I straighten my shoulders, hoping I look more confident than I feel. "Mrs. Baldwin, I'm sorry, but I will not break things off with Henry. We do not need anyone's permission to be together. We're adults."

Her face cracks into a bitter smile. "You are naïve, that's what you are."

Her smile causes something to snap inside of me, and I lash out. "And I can tell you without a doubt that you are one of the most heartless people I have ever met."

She recoils as though I spat in her face. I know as soon as the words leave my mouth that I have overstepped, but I can't take it back and, to be honest, I don't want to. She has been so rude to me and doesn't deserve my kindness or respect.

"What did you say?" she asks, her chin trembling.

I don't repeat myself, but I don't apologize either.

A beeping sound coming from her handbag breaks the tension between us, and she looks at me for a few moments before slipping her hand into her bag, pulling out a cell phone.

"It's my son," she says, her emphasis firm and possessive.

She stands up with the phone stuck to her ear and moves to the window, her back to me.

"Hello, darling," she says, then listens. "Yes, I'm at the house. I was just having a little talk with Tess."

I wish I knew what Henry is saying on the other end, or that she would turn around so I could read the answers from her expression.

"Nothing important," she says. "We're just getting to know one another, that's all." She pauses. "By the way, darling, did I tell you that Lisa is back in town?"

She finally turns around to face me, her eyes meeting mine. "Yes, Lisa Brown. Don't tell me you have forgotten about her. She was your first love."

Rage sweeps over me and I stare back at her, refusing to break eye contact.

"I think for old times' sake, you two should get together some time to catch up. She's now a successful dentist with her own new dental practice in town."

When the call ends, Catherine walks back to the couch with a satisfied grin on her face and I feel like throwing the coffee table straight at her smug little head.

"I know you don't want to hear this," I say to her, keeping my voice low and cool, "but I want you to know that there's nothing you or anyone can do to separate me and Henry."

She waits until she has sat back down again before responding. "Are you sure about that? Well, good luck to you. You will need it, because I rather suspect this will not end well for you."

"Is that a threat?"

She laughs in that annoying, tinkling way she has. "I don't need to threaten you. Some things have a way of working themselves out." She picks up her cup of tea again and takes a sip, peering at me over the rim. "Sooner or later, my son will grow tired of you, like he grew tired of all the girls like you before. He will realize that he made a mistake."

"I'm not a mistake," I shoot back.

She simply shrugs and stands up. In the doorway, she glances back at me with a cold smile playing around her mouth and then she walks out, leaving me feeling shaken and a little chilled.

CHAPTER TWENTY-TWO

PRESENT

There's someone in the room. My eyes are closed, but I still know they are there. I can hear them breathing. Oliver continues to snore next to me, and slowly I open my eyes. I'm afraid to look at the door, to see if there is really someone there, watching us in the dark. Watching me.

Without making a sound, I move my hand in the space between us toward him, my sweaty palms brushing against the cool, wrinkled sheets. The tips of my fingers finally reach him, and I feel his body heat seconds before I touch his skin, nudging him in the ribs.

"Tess," he says sleepily. "What is it?"

My belly presses against him as I whisper, "Someone's in the room." The words are too loud in my own ears. The floorboard creaks and I stiffen at the sound as I slowly sit up and turn on the nightlight, my heart pounding.

But it's too late. He's gone.

Oliver sits up. "What is it?" he asks again.

I stare at the door, my fingernails digging into my palms. "Someone was in our room. Look, the door is open. I closed it before bed; you know I always do. Someone opened it, Oliver."

He rolls his eyes and gets out of bed, yawning as he walks through the door. I listen to him moving about the house, searching for the intruder he doesn't believe in. I can't stay in bed and do nothing, so I get up and follow him. The two of us search the house together, but find no evidence that anyone had been inside, and the doors are locked.

"You're starting to drive us both insane," Oliver says when we return to the room.

I'm not sure what to say to him anymore; I sound like a broken record even to myself. Maybe I wouldn't believe me if I were in his shoes.

"Oliver," I croak, my voice breaking as I plead with him to hear me out. "How can you know with absolute certainty that they don't know, and they aren't onto us?"

"Don't do this," he warns, climbing back under the covers. "You have to stop dwelling on the past. Focus on where you are right now."

"Easy for you to say," I respond, my pulse thumping at the base of my throat. "You're not the one they will be looking for. You are not the one who they will want revenge against, or who will be sent to prison if—"

"Stop." He cuts me off with a firm voice, then he sighs and puts a hand on my cheek. "Sweetheart, how many times do I have to reassure you that you're safe?"

"Until I believe it," I reply. "All I know is that something is going on around here. And I'm afraid that one day the police will show up at our door and take me away. What will happen to Mason?"

He withdraws his hand from me. "For the last time, you have nothing to worry about." He rubs his eyes. "We need to go to bed, Tess. It's one a.m."

"I'm sorry, but I can't." I get out of bed again and head to the kitchen.

That's when I see it: my favorite terracotta and cream mug

sitting in an empty sink. I never leave a plate or mug unwashed before we go to bed. And yet, there it is. A small pool of brown liquid rests at the bottom of the mug and my nostrils pick up the warm scent of coffee floating in the air. I lift it out of the sink and take it with me to Oliver but he barely glances at the mug before interrupting me and saying, "You need to calm down. You probably left it there and forgot."

I lower the cup to my lap and close my eyes, giving up. "I'm tired, Oliver," I say.

"Then you must stop panicking for no reason," he says.

But how do I do that? If someone broke into our house, they felt comfortable enough to sit down and drink a cup of coffee. How can that not leave anyone cold? I don't take the mug back to the kitchen, and I can feel it taunting me from the nightstand. As if nothing had happened, Oliver goes back to sleep without a care in the world while I lie awake, listening for sounds in the darkness.

I can't understand why he seems so calm. In the first few months after we moved to Westledge, we were both looking over our shoulders. He impressed on me how important it was to be careful, to keep my guard up, to trust nobody but him. But now he's dismissing what I'm certain is a very real danger, right at our doorstep: even inside our home.

I need to prepare myself for what might happen.

As I pull my phone from beneath my pillow, I open the notes app and start typing a letter to Mason, in case I get taken away from him and don't get a chance to tell him how much he means to me.

Dear Mason,

If you're reading this, I'm probably not there with you.

The purpose of this letter is not to explain to you what happened. Maybe you already know.

I just want you to know how much I love you.

Despite not being your biological mother, I consider you to be my son, and I love you more than my own life.

I stop typing and squeeze my eyes shut. I can't even bear to think about a day when I might not be in my son's future. I delete the letter and turn off the phone. I'm too exhausted to find the right words, the ones that feel right. Hopefully, I'll have more time to work it out before it's too late. I get out of bed and head to Mason's room. Climbing into his bed, I hold him tight, breathing him in, wishing this moment could be frozen in time.

About an hour later, I'm about to leave his room again when he calls out to me.

In the dark, he whispers, "Don't leave me."

Tears fill my eyes as I smile. "Never," I whisper back. "I promise."

But I know that someday soon, I may have to break that promise.

CHAPTER TWENTY-THREE

THREE YEARS AGO

As the black blindfold around my eyes falls away, I gasp at the sight of a beautiful green and gold dress spilling from the bed to the carpeted floor like a waterfall. A pair of matching silver sandals lie to the left of the dress.

"What is this?" I turn to look at Henry, who is standing back looking pleased with himself.

He closes the distance between us and pulls me close, kissing the side of my neck. "That dress would look so much better with you in it."

I sigh. "Henry, you have to stop giving me gifts. It's too much."

It has been four months since we started dating and, every chance he gets, he splurges on me with extravagant presents.

"I don't have to stop. I want to buy you nice things," he mumbles against my neck. "I want you to feel special."

"I do. I feel special without all this stuff."

"But I love spoiling you."

"I know, but you don't need to."

He encircles my waist with his hands and spins me around to face him. "Too late." He presses his lips to mine.

I pull away and glance back at the dress. "But that looks so expensive."

The dress looks even more lavish than the one he bought me to wear at our first dinner in New York.

"I don't care what it cost, you deserve the best. Come on, try it on. It looks lonely over there by itself."

I grin and walk toward the bed I now share with him. I came home one day from taking Mason to a kiddie birthday party to find my clothes had been moved to his room. Becca had even hung them up in the massive walk-in closet, one side of it reserved just for me. I told him it was too early. What would people think? Becca, his mother, and his brother already didn't approve of our relationship. But Henry quickly pointed out that it was his house and he made the rules.

Smiling at him, I pick up the sandals, and disappear into the closet where I sit on one of the chaise longues and close my eyes with my head tilted back. The air smells of Henry's expensive cologne and the faint scent of new leather shoes. I feel both overwhelmed and exhilarated. I have everything I ever wanted, the kind of life I have always dreamed of. But as happy as I am to have it all, I am also terrified. The more I have, the more I stand to lose.

I never want to lose Henry, and I definitely don't want to lose Mason, who I already love so much. But everything is moving so fast it scares me and I fear that, as fast as it started, it could end. I've experienced it all too many times in my life. A foster family picked me up from the orphanage, only to bring me back a couple of weeks, months, or years later. It never lasted, not until I was old enough to leave the orphanage to start a life of my own, where I was dependent only on myself.

"Are you okay in there?" Henry asks from the other side of the door.

"Perfect," I say, rising to my feet before taking off my clothes and sliding the dress over me, allowing the silk to cascade like water down my body from my head to my toes. The rhinestone-encrusted sandals also fit like a glove and they match the dress to perfection. As I stand in front of the lit-up mirror, I don't recognize the woman in front of me.

Everything feels so right and so wrong at the same time.

Enjoy it while it lasts, a little voice inside me says.

Following its lead, I walk to the door and slide it open, and when Henry sees me, a wide smile lights up his face. "You look perfect, like I knew you would. But let's put a little more glitter."

He moves to one side of the bed and yanks out the drawer, pulling out a red square velvet box and snapping it open to reveal a yellow citrine pear-drop pendant necklace. "Would this do?"

"It's really too much, Henry. I can't take it."

"You deserve it, my love." He lifts the necklace out of its box and puts it around my neck, and his eyes dance as he stares at me. "You're ready."

"Ready for what?" My voice is laced with confusion.

"We're invited to my mother's birthday party tonight."

My breath catches in my throat. "Tonight?"

When Oliver dropped by last week, I heard him mention his mother's birthday to Henry. They talked about a party and I just assumed I wouldn't be invited. Oliver said he didn't think he would attend, either. He and his mother never really get on, and when all three of them are together, she never hides the fact that Henry is her favorite child. Oliver never acts as though he minds, but something like that cannot leave a person unscathed. That's why his resentment extends to his brother. Every time he visits, they always end up butting heads over something or other.

"I can't just show up at the party," I say, horrified. "I'm not invited."

"Of course you are invited. She sent an invitation to both of us."

"Come on, you know as well as I do that your mother hates me. Why would she invite me to her birthday party?"

"That's not true." Henry pulls me into a hug. "She's simply annoyed that she wasn't the one who chose you for me."

"You think she has really accepted our... us being together?"

Sometimes I am not sure if I should call what we have a relationship, as Henry has still not openly announced that we are dating.

"I guess she realized how happy you make me."

I press my hands to his chest. "I still don't think I should be there. It's supposed to be a family event."

"A lot of people will be coming. I can assure you that ninety percent of them are not family. You'll be my guest."

"Are you really sure I'm invited? Can I see the invitation?"

"Very well," he says, pulling out his phone. He opens up an email he received from his mother a couple of days ago and gives it to me.

Henry, darling. As you might have heard, this year I would like to make an exception and throw a birthday bash for myself. I hope to see you and Tess there. If you have other plans, cancel them.

I give him the phone back, bemused. I find it hard to believe that she would change her mind about me so quickly.

"You heard what she said," Henry says. "If you have other plans, cancel them. My dear mother doesn't take no for an answer."

"Now I know where you got it from." I laugh. "What about Mason? Who will be here with him?"

"Don't worry about him. I already arranged a last-minute babysitter."

"I can't believe you didn't tell me!"

"It was meant to be a surprise." He kisses me on the nose. "Tonight, I want you to let go and have fun."

I bite into my lip and take a deep breath. "Okay, I'll come. But if it's really uncomfortable with your mother, I'm leaving."

He laughs. "She's not as bad as you think, you know."

Nervously, I play with the large delicate pendant that dips into the hollow of my throat. Instead of excited, I feel as if the necklace is choking me, a noose around my neck.

CHAPTER TWENTY-FOUR

Anxiety swells in my chest when we pull up to Henry's parents' mansion, which is even more luxurious than where he lives. Since it is a winter party, lit-up ice sculptures grace the front, transforming it into a winter wonderland, and expensive cars are parked around the driveway, among them a few Bentleys and Mercedes. Music from inside the house spills out to greet us.

"Ready?" Henry asks.

"Not really." This is the last place I want to be. I would much rather be reading a bedtime story to Mason and cuddling up with him until he falls asleep.

A valet opens the limo door for me and Henry winks. "It will be fun."

Tightening my wool coat around me, I wait until Henry is by my side. He looks impossibly handsome in his black dress pants and cream button-down shirt, with his hair slicked back with just the right amount of gel. The biting cold doesn't seem to bother him, and he leaves his black coat open. He gives me his arm and we walk toward the entrance.

As it's four days before Christmas, the house is decorated

with stunning garlands, berry-studded wreaths, and other festive décor. The biggest and most luxurious Christmas tree I've ever seen, dressed in silver and white ornaments and delicate lights, stands proudly in the foyer. The smell of pine permeates the air, calming my nerves a little.

Women dressed in diamonds and flowing gowns walk past us, some of them stopping to greet Henry before flicking their gazes at me. When Henry doesn't introduce me, they walk on. As soon as we have handed over our coats to the butler, Catherine hurries up to us, dressed in pearls with her cream sheath gown sprinkled with crystals. Though I don't care for her, I have to admit that she looks very elegant, with her brown hair piled on top of her head and little tendrils curling around her neck.

She hugs first Henry, then surprises me by throwing her arms around me as well. A brief hug, but a hug nonetheless, and it leaves me speechless.

"I'm so glad you could both make it. Come on inside."

We follow her through the large marble foyer into the ballroom, where flashes of light dance off the walls and chandeliers. Guests stand around in groups, sipping on champagne as they listen to the band play in a corner, and wisps of cigar smoke waft through the air, mingling with the faint smell of perfume.

"Tess, dear, you should get yourself something to drink," says Catherine, as she takes my arm and leads me away, gesturing for one of the many waiters to approach us. She reaches for a glass of champagne and presses it into my hand.

"I'm surprised you invited me," I say, unable to help myself, but she just smiles and walks away, leaving me alone with strangers.

Being surrounded by so many wealthy and beautiful people makes me feel more than a little inadequate. Even in my expensive dress, I feel like a fraud. I don't fit in here.

I'm about to go back to Henry when his father, Alexander

Baldwin, appears in front of me. His steel-gray hair and neatly trimmed beard give him a distinguished appearance, but his eyes are cold and calculating. I know he wants me out of his son's life just as much as Catherine does.

In a deep, gravelly voice, he says, "I'm surprised to see you here, Tess."

"Catherine invited me, sir," I respond, sounding more confident than I feel.

He takes a sip of his drink. "Yes, I am aware. However, considering this is a family affair, and the only employees present are those serving food and drinks, I did not expect you to attend."

"I mean no disrespect to you, sir, but I'm here as Henry's guest. He wants me to be here," I say, bristling.

"Is that so?" He chuckles. "I'm surprised my son would want that, considering someone else has his attention right now." With that, he raises his glass in a mock salute and blends into the crowd.

I clutch the stem of my champagne flute as I scan the room for Henry. When I spot him, he is talking to a beautiful woman in a teal figure-hugging dress. She has voluminous butterscotch-colored hair and teeth so white I can see them from across the room. A faint spark of jealousy warms my belly as she throws her head back, laughing at something Henry's said.

Henry looks so happy in her presence; I've never seen him laugh with such complete abandon. Even with all the music and the conversations around, I hear his laughter. Or maybe I am imagining it. I take a gulp of my champagne and make my way toward them, but Catherine appears from nowhere and gets to them first. She slides her hand in the younger woman's arm like she did with me earlier.

"Oh, you two have already found each other," I hear her say as I come nearer, and she waves me over.

"Tess, come. Let me introduce you to someone special." She pauses. "This is Lisa Brown; she went to school with Henry."

The moment she says the name, it all comes back to me. The same name she said the day she came over to ask me to leave her son. It's now all too clear why she invited me. It has nothing to do with her accepting me at all. Her plan was for me to see that I do not belong in Henry's life. Someone else does.

"It's lovely to meet you," the stunning woman says, extending a slim hand. "What's her name again?" She looks at Catherine for an answer, instead of me.

"That's Tess," Henry says.

"She's the nanny," Catherine adds.

Henry says nothing.

Without wasting any more words on me, Lisa returns to her conversation with Henry. "Your mother did mention that you now have a little boy."

"Yes." Henry laughs again. "You never thought I would be the father type, did you?"

"I'm impressed." She eyes him up and down. "Mr. Baldwin, you sure have changed over the years. I guess we have a lot of catching up to do."

"I agree," Catherine says, smiling brightly. "However, I must first make a welcome speech."

She steps away from us, weaving her way through the sea of people in the direction of a raised platform at the front of the ballroom. Watching her, I suddenly feel dizzy and light-headed, although I've barely taken two sips of the champagne. Henry has hardly even looked at me; he's too engrossed in his conversation with Lisa, his old flame.

When Catherine is ready to speak, silence fills the room. She says a few polite words to welcome her guests and thanks her husband for organizing the event.

"This evening is particularly special to me because I get to be surrounded by people whom I have not seen in quite some time." She looks across the room and I know her gaze is on Lisa. "Lisa Brown," she says. "Welcome back to town. You have grown into such a beautiful and successful woman. I still remember when Henry and you dated in school. I'm sure I am not the only one who believed you would marry one day."

I hold my breath as I look from Henry to Lisa, who lock eyes for a brief second and, to my horror, smile at each other.

"It's not too late for that," someone in the audience calls out, a voice I heard not long ago. It's Henry's father, who is standing among the people in the front.

I am done; I need to get out of here.

I brush Henry's arm and lean in, fighting back tears. "Do you mind if I leave?"

"Already?" He frowns at me. "We just got here."

"I know, but I'm not feeling well."

"Right," he says in a strained voice.

I want to ask him to leave with me, but I know he won't want to go. Not when Lisa is here. They have a lot to catch up on, after all.

"She *does* look a little pale, Henry," Lisa chips in as though she knows me. "You should let her go. I'm sure your son will be happy to have her back home."

Henry turns back to me. "I'll arrange for a car to drive you home."

"That's all right," I say quickly. "I'll call a taxi."

"Alright then," he says. "I'll see you later."

My heart crashes when he goes right back to chatting with Lisa. He doesn't even pause to ask what's wrong with me; he's too distracted to care.

I pass my champagne to a waiter, get my coat from the coat room, and stumble out of the house into the chilly night air. I can't stop the tears any longer.

"Tess," someone calls as I fumble for my phone to call a taxi, and I turn to see Oliver, leaning against a black BMW, a bottle of beer in one hand and his cell phone in the other.

Unlike the rest of the guests, he isn't dressed to the nines. His shoulder-length hair hangs on his shoulders, and he wears a pair of jeans and a woolen trench coat with the collar up. Henry or his mother must have convinced him to attend.

"Please don't say you're leaving already." He takes a sip from his bottle. "Are you crying?"

I wipe my tears quickly and shake my head. "I'm not feeling well. I should go."

"Is Henry coming with you?"

"No, he's not. I asked him to stay."

"In that case, let's get out of here," he says, opening the passenger door of his car. "I'll drive you."

"You don't have to do that. I'm calling a taxi."

"Don't be ridiculous. If Henry can't do the right thing and take care of you, I'd be happy to. I was planning to get out of here anyway. You've given me an excuse."

I nod weakly and thank him, then I get into the passenger's seat.

As soon as I enter the house, I rush to the bathroom and throw up. My body is racked with pain and I feel an unbearable emptiness. After splashing water on my face, I stare at my tear-stained, puffy reflection in the mirror. To make myself feel better, I go into Henry's closet and take one of his many silk ties, a burgundy one I know he loves.

With the tie in hand, I go downstairs and get some scissors from the kitchen drawer, then I lock myself in the downstairs bathroom. Sitting on the edge of the tub, I start hacking away at the fabric until it's a pile on the floor. The feeling of satisfaction is profound, and I hold on to it for as long as possible. But in my gut, I know that it won't last.

CHAPTER TWENTY-FIVE

PRESENT

It's a beautiful late August afternoon, the kind of day one would regret not taking advantage of. The sky is cloudless, the air warm and crisp. From the open kitchen windows, I watch singing birds soaring from branch to branch like tiny kites.

I proposed we have a family picnic in the park as a way to cheer up Oliver, who has been in a bad mood the past few days and even started smoking again secretly, hiding the smell with mint gum. To my surprise, he didn't refuse and even seemed to be excited about the idea. He's still at the office, but since it's Friday, he promised to come home early. As soon as he gets here, we'll be on our way.

I'm in the kitchen, filling the basket with sandwiches, fruit, and lemonade, when my eyes land on the sink. Even though it's no longer physically there, I still see the ghost of the coffee mug sitting at the bottom, waiting for me to find it.

Just for one day, I try hard not to think about it and what seeing it meant. I tell myself that Oliver must be right, I must have used it and forgotten about it, somehow. I have been stressed, after all. And if someday soon, everything I know and love ends, I'll regret not taking advantage of every moment I have now. Instead of looking for shadows behind my back, I need to look at the sun shining in my face.

I want Mason to have pleasant memories with me. So, I've been making a real effort to do things with him and to pay him more attention. In the last few days we've watched movies, gone for long walks, painted, and even prepared meals together. We've had some great conversations; at other times, we just sat in silence on the porch, listening to the birds singing, or enjoyed the smell of damp soil after the rain. With time, I trust that Oliver and I will get closer again, and he will get over Jocelyn. Then we can continue our life as if she never existed.

Now that she's no longer a concern, I need to proceed to the next part of the plan. Last night my period started, and this morning I was already complaining to Oliver about having stomach cramps, planting the seed before I fake the miscarriage tomorrow. I've decided to bite the bullet. I'll figure out a way to make sure it works.

I finish tightening the lid on the picnic basket and glance at my watch. Oliver said he'd leave work early and be home by 4 p.m., so we can take advantage of the last hours of sunlight. But it's already half past, and fifteen minutes ago, Mason kept asking when we're leaving, until he grew bored and retreated to his room to play with his toys. I give Oliver a call again, the third time in thirty minutes. Still no answer.

Deciding that it may be best to just get everything ready, I take the basket to the car, then go back inside to get the blanket. Before I get Mason into the car, I call Oliver a fourth time and just as I'm hanging up the phone, the front door opens. He's barely taken two steps in when I rush to meet him at the door.

He stares at me with a cold look in his eyes, his face a mask of stone, and he's holding a white envelope in his hand.

"Baby, what's wrong?" I whisper, a knot forming in my gut. "I've been calling you for the last thirty minutes. We wanted to leave at—"

He tosses his keys on the hallway table and heads to the kitchen. "I stopped by the doctor."

Feeling my cheeks paling, I run after him. "Why did you go to the doctor?" I ask. "Are you not feeling well?"

He starts laughing, his head bent over the kitchen counter, his back turned to me. His laughter is harsh and ugly. "No, I'm not ill, but apparently I'm a fool."

I shake my head. "I don't understand."

He turns around and throws the envelope at me.

My hands shake as I snatch it from the air. "What is this?"

"Read it," he spits. I've never heard him talk like this to me before.

I tear open the envelope and unfold the paper inside. My world spins and my hands shake as I scan the contents. The words are floating around on the page, and I rub at my eyes to clear my vision, to see whether what I saw is real. It is. It's all there in black and white. And it changes everything.

"Tell me, Tess, what happens when a man and his wife have unprotected sex?" His voice is low and deadly.

Still clutching the envelope, I feel as if I've been thrown into ice water. Tears well up in my eyes. "I... I..." I stutter, panic setting in. No matter how hard I try, I cannot utter even one coherent sentence.

I keep looking at the words, as if they might change their meaning, but they don't. Suddenly, my knees buckle underneath me and I feel myself falling into the closest chair.

"That's right, my love," Oliver says as if I gave him an answer. "If a man has unprotected sex with his wife, he might get her pregnant. Yet my wife is pregnant and I'm unable to father a child. The facts are all there in those test results." He steps away from the counter and paces the room before stopping in front of me. He then puts his fingers under my chin and lifts my head so I am staring at him straight in the eye. "Tell me whose it is, you cheating little whore."

CHAPTER TWENTY-SIX

THREE YEARS AGO

Catherine's birthday party isn't the last time I see Lisa. A few weeks have gone by, and now I'm watching her with Henry again. They sit inside the sunroom, enjoying breakfast together with Mason in the pale January light. As much as I hate to think it, they look like a perfect little family.

I was never a jealous person, until I met Lisa at the party. But this feeling, this is more than jealousy. It feels like poison, burning a mark on my insides. Ever since the party, everything is going wrong. The lavish gifts have stopped and Henry is no longer as attentive to me as before. I spend more time with Mason than with him. Lisa keeps showing up at random times with one excuse or other. On New Year's Eve she rang the bell and said she was in the area when she decided to drop by and wish Henry a happy New Year. Does she think I'm stupid?

Even from behind the closed glass doors, I can hear their laughter and their muffled conversations. I had no idea she was coming over today either, let alone staying for breakfast. She looks fresh in a cashmere sweater, a pair of designer jeans, and tall, black boots. Her glossy hair is pulled back in a neat bun, and her face is fresh and clear. I hate that she looks even more beautiful without makeup. I peel my gaze from her and move on to Mason. While Henry and Lisa chat with their heads too close together, he plays with a shiny new toy, a red double-decker bus. He holds it high in the air, as if it is a plane, and his mouth forms an O-shape. It has to have been a gift from her; I have never seen it before and Henry prefers to buy him books. She is obviously trying to buy my little boy's love in order to get to his father's heart.

I don't know the woman, but I hate her with every fiber of my being. No one else has ever caused me to feel such revulsion, not even my parents. The longer I watch them, the more the venom courses through my veins. I'm about to walk away when Henry spots me and comes to slide open the doors.

"You're awake," he says. There is not even a hint of guilt on his face. He doesn't seem to know that what he is doing is hurting me. Or does he just not care?

"Tess, Tess, look what Lisa gave me." Mason wriggles in his chair. "It's a London bus."

"Oh, wow! It's beautiful." I push aside my pride and hurt and put on a smile.

"I invited Lisa over for breakfast," Henry says. "Why don't you come and join us?"

I shift from one foot to the other, unsure how to respond. "I—"

"Henry," Lisa places a hand on his upper arm. "Look at the girl; surely you see that she's exhausted."

I bring my hands up behind my back and curl them into fists until my nails pierce my palms. How dare she refer to me as *the girl*? She's not much older than me.

Lisa rises from her seat and comes over to me. "Poor thing, you look so tired. It looks like you have been overworking her, Henry." She brings her well-manicured hands together and her green eyes light up as she turns to Henry. "I have an idea. How about you give Tess the day off? It's Saturday and I don't have much planned. If you like, I could step in for Tess and help you look after..." Her voice trails off.

"Mason," I say with a tiny hint of triumph.

"Actually, that sounds like a good idea," Henry says brightly. "Tess hardly takes any days off."

"Wonderful." While I fume inside, Lisa's eyes twinkle at me. Her lips part in a smile that may look genuine to Henry, but I can see right through it. "How about we spend the day on Daddy's new boat?" She winks in Mason's direction. "Would you like that?"

"That's cool," Mason says to her. "I want Tess to come with."

"No," Henry replies, his gaze on my face. "Lisa is right. Tess needs to take time off. Go on, have the day to yourself."

Is he blind? Can he really not see what she is doing, slithering like a viper into his life? The night of the party, he came home at three o'clock in the morning and I asked him about her. He said it was nice to see her again, but he reassured me that there was nothing left between them. Maybe not on his end, but definitely on hers. The day she showed up for the first time unannounced, Henry wasn't home and I kind of hinted at the fact that we were seeing each other. When he got home, she said: "Henry, you never told me you were dating the nanny. You're a man full of surprises, aren't you?" Her voice was light and breezy. Henry just smiled thinly and offered to show her the house. Before they walked away, he gave me a cold look that pierced my heart. Later, he barely looked at me as he told me he didn't want anyone knowing about us; he wanted to take it slow.

I'm not ready to step down. I know that if he keeps letting Lisa in, she will push me out and replace me. But how can I compete with a beautiful, rich, and glamorous woman like her?

"Get out of the house and have some fun," Henry says to me. "Here's some cash. Why don't you buy yourself something nice?" He hands me a wad of bills.

"Henry"—Lisa lets out a peal of laughter—"you don't have to give her money. You already pay her for babysitting."

"She's right," I say to Henry, my eyes blazing. "I have my own money." With that, I walk away to let them finish their meal, hoping Lisa will choke on something.

Half an hour later, I watch from my bedroom window as Lisa gets into her sparkling white Tesla, as elegant and perfect as she always is. Mason and Henry join her inside, and I turn away, my anger white-hot and overwhelming.

I don't know how long I've been standing there when Becca enters the room and walks up to me, handing me a tissue. "I'm sorry this is happening to you, love, but I did warn you about getting involved with that man."

"Yes, you did," I say with a bitter laugh. "I should have listened to you."

The moment Becca leaves the room, so do I, making my way directly to Henry's closet. This time, rather than cutting up just one of his ties, I shred an entire designer suit. But it doesn't give me the same satisfaction it did before. I know the only thing that will help is if Lisa disappears from our lives.

CHAPTER TWENTY-SEVEN

As far as I'm concerned, I'm still dating Henry. When other people are around, he treats me like any other employee, but when it's just the two of us, he is a completely different person and I've been pulling out all the stops to draw his attention back to me.

Tonight, I sit on the bed while he gets ready for his high school reunion. It didn't surprise me when I found out Lisa had organized and paid for it, since she has been doing everything she can to get him back. She came over a few days ago to bring him the invitation personally, and made it clear that the only people invited to the reunion were ex-classmates.

"How do I look?" he asks, wearing his tuxedo.

"Handsome as always," I say, tucking away my pain.

I want to tell him what Lisa is doing, and sometimes I try, but he never takes the bait. He continues to insist that she's just a good friend and their two families are close. Lisa's father is one of the biggest investors in Henry's father's campaign.

"I better go then," he says, walking to the door. "Lisa should be here any minute."

My eyebrows shoot up. "You're going together?"

"Yes," Henry replies, putting on his silver cuff links. "She thought it would be nice to show up together, like we did at prom."

My stomach twists into a knot. "You're going as a couple?"

"Not as a couple, no." He gazes down at me. "Tess, I know you don't like Lisa, but she's a good friend of mine."

"A good friend who wants more."

"That's ridiculous," he says, sounding weary and exasperated. "I really need to go. I'll see you later, okay?"

The moment he steps out the bedroom door, the doorbell rings. While I don't want to see her, don't want to give her the opportunity to show off her beautiful clothes and hair, I do want her to see me. But as Henry opens the door and she appears in the doorway, I lose my courage and pause halfway down the stairs. She looks stunning in a black and white cocktail dress that ends a few inches below the knee and shows off her perfectly toned legs.

"That's the same dress you wore to the prom," Henry says, with a whistle.

"Not exactly." Lisa runs her hands down the sides of her body. "I had it remade."

Henry reaches for her hand and twirls her around. "It looks exactly the same. So do you."

She beams. "How kind of you to say that."

As they flirt with each other, I stand in the middle of the staircase, wishing I could go down there and shove her back out the door.

"Hi, Tess," she says, noticing me with a cold smile, then looking back at Henry. "We better get going. As the guests of honor, we can't be late at the hotel."

"I can't believe within two weeks you got everyone to come into town for this," Henry says.

"If something means a lot to me, I make it happen," she says, taking his arm.

Before they walk out the door, Henry turns around and gives me a smile and a wink. It does nothing for me.

After a quiet dinner with Mason, I go upstairs to Henry's bedroom, which no longer feels like ours. Nothing of mine is here; I am just a guest. I lie flat on my back, staring up at the ceiling, thinking about what to do next. The idea of breaking up with Henry brings up a sharp fear I have been trying to stifle. What if not being together with him means he would not want me to be in Mason's life either? I can't walk away from Mason, I love him so much already.

The clock strikes eleven. It's been three hours and Henry is still not home. What if he has decided to spend the night with her at the hotel? The thought tortures me until I fall asleep, and I'm wakened by the door opening. I sit up expecting to see Henry, but it's Mason.

"Hey sweetie. What are you doing up?"

"I can't sleep," he says. "I had a bad nightmare."

"Come over here." I lift the comforter. "Let's cuddle a little, then I'll take you back to your room."

I still find it strange that Mason has never questioned why I moved into his father's room. Henry never even told him we were a couple. He must have figured it out on his own and accepted it, accepted me. He curls up in my arms and I rest my chin on the top of his head. We both need each other's comfort, and I wait until he's asleep before carrying him to his room. I have just returned to Henry's room when I hear the sound of a car in the driveway. Unable to stop myself, I run down the stairs and peer out the library room window. They are both in Lisa's car and their eyes are on each other. Then it happens, just as I'd feared it would. They kiss. It isn't a peck goodnight, but a full-blown kiss that leaves me breathless with jealousy. A kiss that makes me realize just how much hate I'm capable of holding inside my heart.

When I stagger away from the window, I unfurl my clenched fists and stare at the blood on my palms where my fingernails dug into the flesh. I don't feel pain from the cuts. I feel numb, and I feel determined.

CHAPTER TWENTY-EIGHT

PRESENT

"Go on, spit it out. Whose baby is it, Tess?" Oliver asks, jamming his hands into his pockets.

I'm swaying as I get to my feet finally, my knees feeling like jelly. "Oliver, it's not what you think."

I never expected it to end like this. He did tell me once that he would have loved to be a father, and I just assumed he could be one.

"What are you thinking? Are you about to lie to me like you've done for months? You have made me look like an idiot."

I bite into my lip and say nothing.

"That's why you never wanted to talk about the baby. That's why you never wanted to prepare for it. That's why you never wanted me to hear the heartbeat. The guilt was eating you alive, wasn't it?"

He's pacing now, his neck red from the rage burning through him.

"I had an illness as a child that destroyed my chances of fathering a child. I left for a few days when you told me you were pregnant; I needed time to think. But I trusted you, and before long I thought maybe the doctors had gotten it wrong, or that my body had healed. So I came back to you, and then a few days ago I did another test, just to be sure. But now I know the truth. You know how much I love you, what I did for you, what I gave up for you. And then you betray me like this."

"Oliver," I say, tears streaming down my face. I take a step toward him, but he backs away and for a moment he looks as though he's about to strike me.

"Don't do that. Don't touch me," he snaps. "I just want you to tell me the truth."

Devastated, I press my palms together. "It's not what you think. Please, listen to me."

"Not what I think?" This time it's him who comes to me, and the anger in his eyes makes me step back in fear.

"Tell me, what exactly am I supposed to think?"

I bury my hands in my hair, and try to explain, treading lightly.

"I was upset. I thought you didn't love me anymore. I thought—"

"What the hell are you talking about?"

I return to the bed and drop onto it, knowing this moment will make or break us completely. The cracks in our marriage have finally opened up wide.

"You were cheating on me," I say, not meeting his eyes. "You were having an affair. I read your messages to her and from her."

His eyes narrow as he takes a step back. It's almost like I can hear his brain whirring as he tries to work out how I found out. Even for a moment, it's satisfying to have the upper hand.

"You read my texts?" His voice is like thunder, bouncing off the walls before hitting my eardrums.

"Yes, I did," I say firmly. "I needed to know the truth. What else did you expect me to do? My husband was spending time with another woman. When you went on your many business trips, you were with her, weren't you?" I shake my head. "I can't believe you would do that to me and Mason."

"That was different; it meant nothing." The twitch in his jaw tells me that he's grinding his teeth. "How dare you go off and sleep with another man, despite all I've done for you?"

"I didn't. You don't understand." I draw in a breath, ready to explain to him that the pregnancy is not real. But he is already exploding again in a rage.

"You have no right to question me," he says. "Can you really blame me after everything I have had to go through because of you?"

"Oliver, please. Let me explain."

"I don't need to listen to any more of your lies." He grasps hold of the door handle. "You don't deserve me, Tess. You never have."

With that, he slams the door so hard that wood splinters onto the floor, before he charges out and storms down the street while I watch him from the window, hot tears streaming down my cheeks.

CHAPTER TWENTY-NINE

The front door bangs shut and my chest tightens with fear. Oliver is back and, from the sound of it, he's not in the mood to continue our conversation. My body is heavy as I get up from the kitchen island. It's ten minutes before midnight and I've been waiting for him for hours.

The man who has entered the house is not the man who left earlier. He's swaying as he stumbles through the house, and he doesn't even acknowledge my presence. As I follow him to the living room, I sniff a sharp stench of stale alcohol. He's drunk, after I had waited all evening to speak to him.

"Oliver," I say cautiously, "we need to talk about this. Let me explain everything to you."

He waves a limp hand like he's swatting away a fly. "Get the hell away from me."

He throws himself onto the couch and groans. Watching him, my stomach curls. He brings back memories, memories I want to bury forever. Memories of someone I used to know. I near him to observe him closer, to gauge how far gone he is. The knuckles of the hand dangling from the couch are bruised and caked with dried blood. Trying not to recoil from the smell of alcohol, I bend to look at his other hand. There are no bruises on it, just more dried blood. I also notice a few stains on his t-shirt.

He must have got into a fight, and I'm relieved to see that his face is free from cuts or bruises. I know he was really upset when he left the house, but he has never been aggressive before. What have I done to him? I step forward again and rest a hand on his shoulder, willing my hand not to shake. "Oliver," I say in a choked voice.

He turns his head to stare at me, his eyes glassy and unfocused. Then he closes them again. Gently, I pull off his grimy clothes so he won't overheat and drape one of the couch throws over him. There's no way I can carry a grown man to the bedroom; he'll have to spend the night in the living room. Given the wedge between us, he'll probably prefer it anyway.

I pick up his clothes and take them with me to the laundry room. The washing machine is already full of dirty laundry, and I add stain remover to get rid of the blood.

The following morning, as soon as Mason has eaten breakfast, I take him to Carmen, accepting her many offers of looking after him. Even though I'm reluctant to rouse any more anger out of Oliver, I can't postpone the conversation any longer.

"I hope it's okay," I say when she meets us at the door.

"Tess, you know it's not a problem. I love spending time with Mason." She smiles adoringly at him.

"Thanks. I'll pick him up in forty-five minutes to an hour."

"Sure, but don't worry too much about the length of time," she says. "We'll make it longer if it needs to be." She leans forward and moves her head slightly to one side, eyebrows raised. "Tess, are you alright?"

Trying not to cry, I just nod. I'm not ready yet to tell her that our plan didn't work.

"If you say so." Her eyes are still clouded by questions, but she leans back. "Take all the time you need to yourself."

As I return to the house, I can barely breathe under the weight of my own anxiety and the growing dread building up in my stomach. I come to a halt in the driveway. The car is gone and the front door is wide open. Even though I know Oliver is not home, I still look for him in the house, confused about what else to do. I call his cell, but he ignores me. He doesn't want to face the conversation, and neither do I. But there's no way around it; he needs to know what I did.

I return to Carmen's house, half an hour after I left.

"That was fast," she says when she opens the door.

"I know. I needed to take care of some errands, but it didn't take as long as I thought it would."

She rests a gentle hand on my shoulder. "Why don't you go home and get some rest? You look exhausted. Did you even sleep last night?"

I didn't, but I don't tell her that. It's hard enough to keep myself together right now, and I know if I open up to her I'll simply fall apart. "Don't worry about me. I'm fine."

"Are you sure?" She leans against the doorframe. "I really don't mind looking after Mason. You can even come for him in the evening, if you like."

"I am sure," I say. If there's anyone who can offer me comfort right now, it's Mason.

"Alright, then." She scratches her chin with a nude-colored nail. "There's actually something I wanted to talk to you about." She glances behind her, then closes the door.

I twist my wedding ring around my finger. "What's going on?"

She wraps her arms across her and her expression turns to worry. "It's about Dan. I'm not sure if you read the messages in the WhatsApp group, but no one knows where he is."

"I haven't been on my phone much. What do you mean?"

Carmen shrugs. "No one has seen him since yesterday, or have you?"

"Well, I spoke to him yesterday morning about our next writing session and he said he would get back to me by the end of the day, but he didn't."

"I also tried calling him, but no response."

"Maybe he has traveled out of town?"

"Without telling anyone? Not even Amanda knows. He didn't come home last night. She's the one asking around."

"You're right, that is strange." I tuck a lock of hair behind my ear. "Carmen, I'm sorry, I need to go. I'll check the group and let everyone know if I find out anything."

"Sure," Carmen says when I walk in to get Mason. "I'm sorry he couldn't stay longer. We were having so much fun together, weren't we, Mason?"

"Yeah," Mason says.

"Don't worry. I'll bring him again next time."

I can't promise there will be a next time. I have no idea what will happen after my conversation with Oliver. Maybe he will be angry enough to betray me, to tell the police what I did. Maybe he's already angry enough to do that.

Mason keeps glancing up at me. He knows I'm not myself. And as we enter the house, for a moment I push my own problems aside and think about Dan. Where could he be? I didn't want to tell Carmen the secret he shared with me as he might not want anyone else to know. But should I tell the police about the threats he was getting?

I call Dan's number, but his phone is switched off. I'll wait a few hours before I decide what to do. To be honest, I think Dan has probably left town for a few days to clear his head. And the last thing he'd want is for the gossips around here to find out the secret he's been hiding all this time. It sounds like things have really been getting to him lately, and I can understand the need to escape, to find somewhere to breathe.

But then something niggles at my spine. I remember the day Dan was helping me clear up the dishes. Oliver had been so upset, and it's no secret that he doesn't like the man. Could he have thought Dan was the man that got me pregnant? Could he have gone to find him last night after our fight? Is that why his hands were bloodied?

The clock continues to tick and Oliver still doesn't come home. After lunch, Randy comes over for Mason's therapy session, but I can't even use the free time to write because my mind is too scattered.

"Are you okay, Mrs. Baldwin?" he asks when I take a drink to them in the den. "It's beautiful weather, isn't it?"

"Yes, I'm fine." I say, forcing a smile. No amount of his positive attitude can get me out of my rut and make me think about anything else.

When Oliver eventually returns home an hour after Randy leaves, I'm shocked by his thunderous expression; he's even angrier than he had looked when he walked out yesterday. Instead of talking to me, he pushes past me and storms into our bedroom, and I find him sitting on the edge of the bed, his head in his hands.

"Oliver? Can we talk, please?"

Ignoring me, he leaves the room and heads to his office, and I jump when the door slams shut. I leave the room again and knock on his locked office door.

"Oliver, open up. We need to talk."

He makes me wait for five minutes before unlocking the door.

"What do you want?" As his eyes meet mine, I feel his annoyance rolling off him in waves.

"Have you seen Dan? Apparently, no one has seen him since yesterday. Everybody's worried about him," I say, entering the room and closing the door.

"I don't know why you're bothering me with this. If anyone

should know where the man is, it's you." His anger drips off each word. "You've been spending quite a lot of time with him lately."

Anger sparks then flares up inside me. "Oliver, you don't think—?"

"That you're having an affair with Dan? I've known for a while."

"That's just not true." I try to keep my voice from wavering. "What did you do, Oliver? You can tell me."

But instead of giving me an answer, he walks to the door and opens it. "Get out of my office. I've got work to do."

CHAPTER THIRTY

I drop a handful of raisins into Mason's cereal and watch a few drown in the milk, like I'm drowning in my own troubles. I blink a few times to bring me back to the present and carry the bowl to the table, where Mason is waiting. It's the third day since Dan went missing and he still hasn't been found. Oliver has shut himself in his office or been out of the house and refused to speak to me, and I've typed out message after message to him, explaining everything, but I can't bring myself to send any of them. I don't even think he'll believe me unless he sees me take off the bump in front of him. I'm terrified of how he will react when he knows I lied, even if he then believes I didn't have an affair.

I sit at the table with Mason, a boiled egg in front of me. Ignoring it, I pick up my phone and check for new updates, praying for good news. Not long ago, our group used to be fun and carefree, filled with memes and talk of books. Now, every time someone posts a comment, a new fear is launched into the forum like a torpedo. I know I should tell someone what I know, both the texts Dan received and my fears about Oliver. But I don't want to betray Dan, and I can't risk Oliver's anger exploding, not when he could so easily give everything away about me. Not when he could take Mason away.

Monica: *He's still missing, the police are involved now. This is so unlike him.*

Lillian: *OMG! What if he's lying dead somewhere?*

Carmen: *I can't believe this is happening. His family must be so worried. And he has such a small child.*

Monica: *I'm going to organize a search party soon. Jocelyn, I know you're somewhere having a good time. But maybe you could come back early, join the search?*

Jocelyn doesn't reply.

I close the app, fighting against a growing sense of dread. I can't bear to read anymore. I keep replaying the day Oliver came home to find Dan helping me, how he threw him out of our house, anger sparking in his eyes.

The sound of the front door closing sharply makes me jump.

"I'll be right back." I say to Mason, and rush out to intercept Oliver before he leaves, but by the time I reach the door, he's already hurrying down the street and I watch him until he reaches the end of the road and turns left, heading in the direction of the river. I return to the kitchen to find that Mason has finished eating and has wheeled himself out onto the patio. His eyes are closed, his face tilted toward the bright morning sun. I hesitate before putting a hand on his shoulder, and he flinches a little in response to my touch.

"Are you okay, Mace?" I ask.

His chin drops to his chest. "I want to sleep."

I wheel him around to face me. "But it's eight a.m., sweetheart. You woke up not too long ago."

"I don't feel well. I have a headache." His voice is barely above a whisper. My eyes scan his face, and there are dark circles under his eyes.

I put a hand to his forehead and sigh. "I'm sorry you're not feeling well, baby. Sure, you can go back to bed. I'll get you something for the pain."

As I walk back into the house, my heart feels heavy. Mason may not know what's happening in our home, but he senses the tension as always and he's suffering. His reaction to stress has always been to fall silent. My entire body heavy, I head to the pantry to get him pain relief tablets. I take down a glass and pour some orange juice before heading back to him. He fills his mouth with juice first before inserting the tablet between his lips.

"Better now?" I ask, my voice gentle. What a stupid question; of course he's not.

"No," he whispers.

I run my fingers through his hair and then kiss his forehead. "Then off to bed with you."

I put him to bed and climb in next to him.

"You don't have to stay with me," he says.

"I know, but I like holding you while you sleep."

I position myself behind him and put my arms around him. He immediately leans his body into my small protruding belly. A tear dripping down my cheek, I press my lips to the back of his head. I'm not sure how long we stay like this, but my entire body is stiff by the time his breathing evens out and I know he's fallen asleep. I slowly ease out of the bed and leave the room, a vice around my heart.

When I stop by Oliver's office, I'm met by the overwhelming smell of alcohol. An empty vodka bottle is lying on its side next to the desk, and drops of the liquid have dripped onto the wood. I don't really know why I'm here, what I'm looking for, but I need something, anything, that would give me the answers Oliver refuses to provide.

His desk is covered in papers and receipts that almost bury his laptop, and I push them aside and flip it open. First, I scroll through his emails hoping for something, anything. The latest is from a Benjamin Garcia sent around 10 p.m. last night.

To: Oliver Baldwin
From: Benjamin Garcia
Subject: Re: Vineyard Properties

Hi Oliver,

I'm really interested in the Vineyard Properties. Can we set up a meeting to drive down to see it? I'm unable to reach you on the phone.

Thanks. B.

I pull a strand of my hair and twist it around my finger as I scan the rest of the earlier emails. There are many emails from Benjamin Garcia, all of them regarding Vineyard Properties. I come across similar emails from clients and potential clients, including an angry one from someone named Noah Gale.

To: Oliver Baldwin
From: Noah Gale
Subject: Simply unprofessional

Your attitude is unacceptable. I tried to reach you twice in the past week to discuss the progress of my new home, and you refuse to return my calls. This is unprofessional and no way to do business.

Noah G.

I've found nothing so far that I can use.

I'm about to log out of his account when I decide to check his online browsing history. At first glance, I can find nothing more than the usual business-related search queries. However, as I look closer, I notice that he has also searched for both Daniel Dunkirk and Dan Dunkirk. The searches have been made since the day he disappeared. The search only brings up Dan's Facebook account, where there are a handful of posts between Dan and a few friends and family, including one I posted for him on his birthday. The most recent post on his wall is from Amanda, who posted about four hours ago.

Sweetheart, if you're out there, please let us know you're okay.
We're really worried about you. Call me, okay?

I close the laptop, my hands shaking. As I step out the door, my entire being is telling me that I'm right, that Oliver did something to Dan. Did he scare him away, or upset him so much while he was already vulnerable that he hurt himself? I can't stop thinking of Dan smiling as he held Noah in his arms.

Did Oliver hurt him?

Suddenly full of resolve, I realise I need to get Mason out of this house before Oliver returns. Thank God he left the car. But money could be an issue. I don't have access to Oliver's account, only a separate one he set up for me, where he sends me some money for expenses and shopping. There isn't enough in there for us to get far or stay hidden for long. But we need to get the hell out and I cannot allow the lack of money to stop us. I just can't risk having Mason around a man capable of violence. Not again.

Once we're far away from him, I'll call the police, for Dan's sake. It's risky, because I'm sure that if I betray Oliver, he will betray me. But I have to tell myself that Mason and I will be safe together, even if we're always on the run. Before I wake Mason, I pack a bag with all his necessities. Warm clothes. Shoes. Socks. A change of underwear. His medication. I stuff them into his backpack and set it by his closed door. It's only after I pack a bag for myself as well that I wake him, and he looks at me with eyes droopy with sleep.

"Is it lunch already?" he asks.

"No, baby," I say. "But we're going on a trip."

I lift him from the bed and into his wheelchair, placing his backpack in his lap.

"Where are we going?"

I wheel him out of the room. "I'll tell you all about it in the car."

We barely make it to the front door when it opens and Oliver is standing there, sweat beading on his forehead.

My heart stops. For a moment, he just stares at Mason and me, and his eyes rest on the backpack in Mason's lap.

"Where the hell do you think you're going?" he asks slowly, his voice tight.

I stand there frozen, my mind racing.

"I said: where do you think you're going?" he repeats.

I tighten my sweating hands around the wheelchair handles. "I'm taking Mason to the doctor. He's not feeling well."

"What's wrong with him?" Oliver asks.

"Headache," Mason says quickly when I hesitate.

Oliver gives me a blank stare. "Why are your bags packed?"

When I don't answer, he closes the door and crosses the space between us. Without saying a word, he takes the wheelchair from my trembling hands.

"What are you doing?" I ask as he wheels Mason away.

"I'm taking him to bed. If he doesn't feel better after a nap, I'll take him to the doctor myself."

I stare at the door, but I'm helpless to say or do anything. I could open it and leave right now. But Oliver knows I would never leave without Mason. I'm still standing on the same spot when he returns. Almost like in slow motion, I watch him stalk toward me, his eyes narrowed into slits, his jaw clenched so tight it visibly twitches. His hands are curled into tight fists by his side.

"I want you to tell me why you're sneaking around," he says. "Why you're lying to me."

"I wasn't. I wasn't lying," I mutter. "I told you. We were going to the doctor."

"I'm not stupid, Tess. I know you inside out."

I stare at him as he corners me, and I'm pushed up against the door. I thought he loved me, I thought I was safe with him. But now I only see a monster.

CHAPTER THIRTY-ONE

I feel like I'm about to fall from a great height, and I know that now I have to make a choice. Let him scare me, or confront him here and now. As soon as I make my decision, I square my shoulders and arch my neck so that I am looking him directly in the eye.

"You know what? You're right. Mason and I were leaving. It's not safe to be around you." I fold my arms across my chest, trying to keep them from shaking visibly. "I know, Oliver. I know you did something to Dan."

Oliver's eyes try to burn through me and make me abandon my courage, but I refuse to be intimidated by him.

"It's really a shame, Tess. Because I did love you. More than you deserved." He pauses to let this sink in. "I loved you so much I made sacrifices to get you here. I tried to make you feel safe, to give you everything you ever wanted." He's so close now I feel his breath on my face. "And yet, you turned around and betrayed me."

Reaching out for me, he lays a hand against my stomach. My legs won't obey my commands to move away from his touch.

I grab his arm and yank it away. "Don't touch me." The words escape before I can stop them.

He shakes his head, his cheeks burning red. "How dare you talk to me that way?" The rumbling sound of his anger hangs in the air between us.

"No, Oliver. How dare you? How dare you accuse me of having an affair when it was you who betrayed our marriage vows?" My anger is hot and fierce, burning along my spine toward my throat. "I'm sorry to disappoint you, but if you think I slept with Dan, or any man for that matter, you're wrong. I never cheated on you. If you did anything to Dan, you hurt an innocent man. And he was my friend."

"Don't play me for a fool," he yells. "Do you think I'm blind? That man was always staring at you. And then I came home one day and he was in our house, alone with you in the kitchen."

"You may find it hard to believe, but he helped me clear up. That was all it was. There's nothing between us now, nor has there ever been."

"Then how do you explain that?" He pokes his finger into my belly, disgust written all over his face. "Now that you know I can't father a child"—he inhales sharply—"How did that happen if you didn't have an affair?"

"This is fake," I whisper. "It's not real, okay? You had an affair and I didn't." The pain I've been carrying fills my eyes as I recall each message he wrote to the woman he slept with. "I did this only because I thought"—I gulp down a sob—"I thought you wanted to leave me."

He looks confused now. "What the hell are you talking about?"

"This is what I mean," I say as I lift up my baggy t-shirt. "I faked the pregnancy. It was the only way I could think of to keep you." I push on, choosing to ignore the shock in his eyes. "This is not real."

As I fold the edge of the fake bump upward to reveal my flat stomach, he takes a step back. "Why? Why would you do something like that?" he asks, his voice shaking.

"I couldn't bear to think of you with another woman." My voice is getting louder, filled with anger and hurt. It's hard to contain my tears anymore. "I didn't want you to leave me. There was too much at stake. I was so desperate, so scared."

I remove the silicone belly and send it falling to the floor between us.

Oliver stands before me, speechless. His eyes dart from my stomach to my face. He opens and closes his mouth, but nothing comes out. There is a long, tense silence between us. I've plowed through what I had to say. Now it's his turn to tell me the truth. His hands are on his hips as he glares at the prop that was supposed to save our marriage. His body is tense and his arm muscles are rigid. He looks like he's about to explode and when he lifts his head, I see both anger and hurt swimming in his eyes.

"You faked the pregnancy?" His voice is low and deep, frustrated and broken.

"Yes, I did." I wipe away the tears. "And you cheated on me. You promised to love and protect me. Then you betrayed me."

"You thought you could just manipulate me, is that it?"

"You cheated on me, Oliver. You slept with another woman. Surely you must understand that I would do anything to save us. I wanted you back." I tilt my head to the side, narrowing my eyes. "Once again, where is Dan? What did you do to him?"

His fists are clenching and unclenching, and his eyes are iced over with a murderous rage. I know the look very well; it's like a mirror reflected straight back at me.

"You want the truth?" he shoots back. "Fine. I went looking for him that day because I wanted to confront him; I was going to punch him right in his idiotic face. But I didn't find him. So, in answer to your question, I have no idea where he is."

My gaze falls to his right hand, which he has bandaged up. "Why did you come home with bloody knuckles then?" I pause. "People are starting to think Dan is dead. The police are involved now."

"What exactly are you saying to me?" He peers at me through hooded eyes. "Are you actually implying that I killed him?"

"I don't know what to think; I just want to know the truth. His family needs answers. His friends do. I do."

He's nearing me again, a bitter smirk on his face. He doesn't stop until he's standing right in front of me, crushing the silicone belly beneath his feet.

"I'm not a murderer, Tess," he says in a hoarse whisper. "Only one of us in this house is capable of murder, and we both know who that is."

CHAPTER THIRTY-TWO

THREE YEARS AGO

"I'm really sorry about this," Becca says as she packs away the last of my clothes.

Henry called her from the office to tell her to move my clothes back to my old bedroom. We are officially over, forty-eight hours after I saw him kiss Lisa. The most hurtful thing is that, up until the end, he still denied there was anything between them, that the kiss meant nothing.

"You did warn me," I say to Becca with a bitter smile, lowering myself onto my old bed, where I've been sleeping the past two days. "I feel so stupid and ashamed."

Becca sits down next to me and takes my hand, but as soon as she does so, I can't hold back the tears. She holds me until my sobs subside, then looks me in the eye. "He's the one who should be ashamed, not you. I've worked in this house for years and seen many women come and go with broken hearts. Frankly, I'm tired of it. Maybe I should throw in the towel and retire early to finally go on that tour of the country with my Harry." She pauses. "What will you do now?"

I blow my nose. "What do you mean?"

She crosses her arms over her chest. "Do you think you'll stay or do you want to leave?"

It would be easy to walk out the door and call it quits. But I won't leave Mason, and part of me also wants to stay as an act of defiance to Lisa.

"I'm not going anywhere," I tell Becca.

She squeezes my hand. "You're a brave one."

"It doesn't feel that way." I wipe away the tears. "But the reason I came here in the first place was to take care of Mason. I'm not going to stop now."

Becca pushes to her feet, her knees cracking in the process. "Don't let that woman crush your spirit, girl."

"I won't." I smile up at her, but deep inside, I am nervous about seeing Lisa again. But knowing Henry the way I do now, I'm sure her days are numbered, too. Once he tires of her, there'll be someone else to fill the void.

Becca leaves my room and I remain on the bed, staring out the window at the swaying branches outside until a knock on the door startles me. Only Becca and I are at home and instead of knocking, she usually just asks to come in. I press the heels of my hands against my eyes to dab away the rest of my tears. "Come in," I call.

The door opens and Oliver pokes his head through.

"Oliver, what are you doing here?" I ask, even though I know the answer. He comes and goes as he pleases, and has been doing so for as long as I've been here.

I once overheard a conversation between him and Henry. Apparently, the house belonged to their grandparents and they left it to Henry instead of Oliver, who is obviously bitter now and refuses to let it go. He believes he has every right to be on the property, and he often shows up when Henry isn't there. Once I saw him walking the grounds, his hands in his pockets, looking like the master of the house.

"Can I come in?" he asks.

I shrug. "Sure."

I don't mind talking to Oliver; he has always been kind to me. Yes, he is often a flirt, and I have not appreciated that especially when he knew I was dating his brother, but he's harmless. He leaves the door open and walks up to the window, then he turns around and takes a few steps toward me. "I heard what happened."

I frown at him. "What happened?"

A line appears between his brows. "You don't know?"

"Oliver, I have no idea what you're talking about."

"Then why do you look like you were crying?"

"I wasn't," I lie.

Without being invited, he comes to sit next to me on the bed. "I know about the engagement."

My heart leaps to my throat and blood rushes to my ears. "What? What engagement?"

"Crap," he says, a look of shock clouding his features. "You didn't know. Henry didn't tell you?"

"What engagement?" I ask again, my mouth dry.

"Henry and Lisa got engaged last night. I thought you knew."

I laugh bitterly and shake my head. Tears prick at my eyes as my pain swells. "No. No, he didn't mention that. You would think he would have the decency to tell me himself."

When Henry came home late the night before, he claimed to have been caught up in meetings with some new business associates. I suspected he had gone out for dinner with Lisa, but I would never have guessed that he'd gone as far as proposing.

"Did he tell you?" I ask, as if it matters.

"My mother mentioned it. Knowing her, she probably announced it to the entire town. I'm so sorry you had to hear it like this."

I avert my gaze. "Henry and I are no longer together, so he can do whatever he wants with his life."

Oliver nods. "For what it's worth, he's a jerk and it's his loss. That Lisa, she loves the look of herself more than she would ever love anyone. Have you seen how every time she comes across a mirror, she admires herself?"

Even though I'm close to breaking down, I laugh. I am grateful to Oliver for trying to make the situation less awkward and painful.

"Thank you, Oliver. I appreciate you telling me."

"Anytime." He walks over to my desk and grabs a sticky note, then writes something on it before returning to me. "That's my number," he says. "If you ever need anything, call me. Even if it's just to talk."

Even though we have formed some kind of friendship, he's mistaken if he thinks that now that Henry and I are no longer seeing each other, our friendship will evolve into a romantic one. I am certainly not in the mood for another relationship, especially with another Baldwin brother. I take the piece of paper from him and stick it to the lampshade near the bedside table. "Thank you, Oliver." I clear my throat. "Look, I'd really like to stay and talk, but I'm going to pick Mason up from preschool soon, then I'll take him on an adventure in the woods."

"That sounds like fun. Want me to join you? I could protect you from the strange man in the woods Mason keeps talking about."

I pause. The woods creep me out especially as we're so remote here, and although I sometimes go jogging there, I never go too far. It will be the first time I'm taking Mason.

"Thanks for the offer, but don't worry. We'll be fine. I'm tougher than I look."

"I can see that." He chuckles. "I can definitely see that."

When he finally gets out the door, I lock it. Then I climb under my covers. I wish I could pretend it doesn't bother me, but the engagement changes everything. Lisa will eventually move into the house to live with Henry, but can I really live with her under the same roof? I know for a fact that she will continue to be her condescending self, especially in her new role as the lady of the house. But the thing that bothers me most is the fact that, once she marries Henry, Mason will become her stepson. Of course, when Henry is around, she pretends to be fond of him. But I have noticed that whenever Henry walks away for even a few minutes, she shows no interest in the child whatsoever.

Fifteen minutes after Oliver tells me about the proposal, I receive a text message from Henry.

Mason and I are going out to lunch, so you don't need to pick him up from preschool today. —H

As the words sink in, my stomach twists. I'm sure he's taking Mason out to lunch so he can break the news to him. Maybe his new fiancée will even join them.

Later in the afternoon, I am relieved to see only Mason and Henry exiting the car. When Bobby opens the door for Mason, the little boy runs out, and his body language tells me immediately that he isn't happy about something.

He runs into my arms, sobbing. "I don't want Lisa to be my new mommy. I want Tess."

Henry looks up at me, not a shred of remorse in his eyes. "We need to talk," he says.

While Becca lures Mason to the kitchen with the promise of ice cream, I follow Henry to his office, where we sit down on opposite sides of his desk.

"I'm not sure you heard—"

"I did," I say immediately. "Congratulations, I guess."

He looks closely at me. "Tess, I'm sorry it had to end this way. You have to understand that I did not plan this."

"You know what, Henry? All I have to say to you is that I hope your son doesn't turn out to be like you, to treat people in such a disgusting way."

I know I have crossed a line. He is my boss again, and if I am not careful, he could fire me on the spot.

"I know you're hurt," he says as he clasps his hands on the table. "What we had was—"

"Meant nothing," I cut him off before he has a chance to finish. "It meant absolutely nothing to you."

"You're wrong, Tess," he says. "We did have some nice times together." His brow knits. "But it was a mistake for me to mix business with pleasure. It should never have happened."

"No, it shouldn't have," I agree, standing up. "There really isn't much more I want to say to you, Henry."

"I understand, and if you want to leave, I won't hold it against you."

"No, I'm not leaving. I signed a contract, and I'm going to live up to my end. At least now, there will be no distractions." I pause. "But please tell your future wife to stay out of my way."

I stalk out of his office and head for the kitchen.

"Banana ice cream!" Mason says when I walk in. "It's the tastiest thing in the world!"

"I'm sure it is," I say, looking at the time on my phone. "We have about forty minutes before it's time for dinner. Why don't we go for a walk in the woods?"

"Can we look for the man?" he asks.

"Sweetheart, there is no man in the woods."

"There is. I promise. I saw him. He gave me cookies."

"Okay. Maybe you can show him to me then."

"He only comes out when I'm alone. He doesn't like other people. I'm the only one who's allowed to see him."

I put a hand on his shoulder. "Promise me you'll never go in the woods alone again."

Two months ago, Mason was kicking his ball around on the lawn, when he suddenly disappeared. After nearly an hour of searching, Becca and I found him in the woods. It was the first time he told us the story of the man in the woods, and when Henry's people searched the grounds they found nobody. Mason has such an active imagination, and while it does make me uneasy, we think the man is most probably an imaginary friend.

"I promise." He licks his spoon, then gazes up at me. "But he's not only in the woods. Sometimes he hides in the bushes, and when he sees me, he waves."

When he's done with his ice cream, we put on our jackets and head out, walking side by side between the trees. We don't talk much, but it's nice to spend time alone with Mason before everything changes. But as we walk deeper into the woods, my breath gets heavier. I don't like the look of the trees, the shadows they cast, or the strange noises they make. It's so dark in the forest, and even though we are not more than fifteen minutes from the house it feels like a whole other land.

After some walking we come across a blanket with an empty packet of salt and vinegar crisps, and a squashed can of Diet Coke.

"He's been having a snack," Mason whispers. "I think he's in the trees watching us, making sure we're safe."

I can't see anyone and I'm sure the litter was just left behind by a trespasser, but I feel uneasy somehow.

"It's okay," I say, though I am not sure who I am trying to convince, Mason or myself. "Let's go back home."

Mason reaches for my hand and clutches it, and we head back to the house. My heart sinks when we find Lisa's Tesla parked up front. Next to me, Mason stops walking and hugs me.

"I don't like her," he says, his voice breaking. "Can I call you mommy instead of her?"

I crouch down in front of him, my eyes filling with tears. "Of course, sweetheart. But let's keep it our little secret, okay?"

"Okay." His eyes light up. "I have an idea. I'll only call you mommy when we're alone."

"Deal," I say, wishing I could tell him that I don't like Lisa either.

And sometimes, I fantasize about bad things happening to her.

CHAPTER THIRTY-THREE

PRESENT

A sharp pain sears my chest as I stumble away from Oliver. I close my eyes, pushing against the pain as I struggle to breathe. When I open them again, the room is spinning. I keep walking until I'm in our bedroom, but before I can close the door, he enters. I fumble with the cool handle of the window, desperate for air, and my hand slips and slides on the smooth metal, making it difficult for me to grasp it.

"Why are you running from me?" he asks behind me. "You really think you can escape what you did?"

I spin around, with terror pulsing through my veins. I can barely see him through the tears in my eyes.

"I didn't." My words come out in choking sobs and warm, salty tears are streaming down my face.

"Don't worry." He gives me a smile that chills my spine. "I'd be more than happy to refresh your memory."

"Don't!" I put up my hands to ward off the memories he's about to force on me, memories I worked so hard to repress.

When he comes toward me, I go around him and head for the door, yanking it open, but he's following me and, in my rush, I almost trip over the small table in the hallway. I am about to head to the living room when I hear the TV blaring. *The Simpsons* theme music fills the house.

Oliver must have left Mason in his wheelchair instead of putting him to bed. He must have heard it all, our heated conversation, the accusations, the secrets being spilled.

I want to protect him, but right now I don't think I can.

I change course because I can't face him, not now. And I can't stop moving. I storm down the hallway to Mason's room. Before I can shut the door, Oliver's foot wedges between the door jamb and the frame to keep it from closing. He steps into the room, shutting the door behind him, and I turn to face him, locking my arms around my abdomen in a protective gesture. "What do you want from me?" I cry out.

"We haven't really spoken about it since then, but since you've just accused me of something awful, I want you to remember that night, Tess... what you did. What you are capable of."

"I'm not." I point an angry finger at him. "You know I'm not a murderer. You know that."

"No, I don't. I'm not sure of anything anymore." He grabs me by the shoulders and looks me in the eyes, his face quivering. "I protected you all this time. I made it all go away because I didn't want to believe you were capable of that kind of violence. The truth is," he continues, "I wasn't there with you that night. Not right when it happened."

"Just leave me alone." I jerk myself away from him and race to Mason's bathroom, ready to be sick. My stomach heaves and my gut twists as I lean over the basin, but nothing comes up. I turn on the tap and cup some cold water in my hands, splashing it onto my hot face before looking up into the mirror. My face is pale and drawn, my eyes bloodshot and swollen; I look like I've been crying for days.

"You're right," he says from behind. "I did have an affair. I felt trapped. You can't imagine the pressure of carrying your burden and the secret I had to protect. It was all too much for me at times. I guess I needed an escape. Can you really blame me? Can anyone?"

"It's my fault," I say, sobbing. And it is true. It is my fault. As much as I hate to admit it, my past actions have led us to this moment in time.

"That's right, it is your fault." He puts his hand between my shoulder blades. His palm is heavy and warm through the thin cotton of my t-shirt.

I shake him off and shove past him again. He might as well be a stranger. I head into his office, still trying to get away from him, but as soon as I step inside, my eyes fall on the crib in the corner of the room. I stop in my tracks as I stare at the reminder of my lie. My desperate, stupid attempt to make everything okay. I'm about to turn back and run out the door again, but he blocks my exit with his arm.

"It's okay to remember," he says. "Remember what you did and what I did for you. What we did for each other."

"I'm not a murderer," I whisper through the tears in my throat. The palms of my hands start to itch. My body is tired, exhausted from running. Running from myself. Running from all the things I did.

He closes the door. "We both know what you really are, sweetheart. You don't have to hide your secret from me. I already know what you're hiding."

"Why are you doing this to me?"

With the last of my strength gone, I sink to the floor, the pain in my heart a frozen weight in my chest. I drop my head into my hands and cry harder. My sobs rip through me and my entire body shakes with the effort to breathe.

"You did this, Tess. You need to admit it."

I listen to him, but I can't accept any more of his words. I cover my ears, but even that doesn't shut him out. Every part of my body aches, like I'm underwater and the salt is eating away at me.

"Why are you doing this?" I ask, rocking back and forth.

"Because you lied to me." He pushes his hands into his pockets and hovers over me. "Yes, I was seeing someone else for a brief time, but you have no right questioning my actions because you were the source of the stress that plagued me every day, that pushed me into her arms."

I throw him a look of disgust. "You thought I was having an affair. Why did you care if you were doing the same thing?"

"I don't owe you anything and you owe me everything. It's as simple as that. Without me, you would be behind bars." He pauses. "Thanks to me, you're not."

"I thought you loved me."

He leans against the doorframe, his arms crossed over his chest. "Hurt people hurt people. I feel betrayed right now. Betrayed by you. After everything I did for you, you should have been faithful to me."

"I've already told you that I did nothing with Dan, and I wasn't even pregnant."

"That's right. You lied to me. But I know there was something going on between you and Dan, I saw it in your eyes. He liked you, he always did, and I know you were into him, too. For me it was different; it didn't mean anything. And sometimes a man has to do what a man has to do to be happy."

My head snaps back as if he's slapped me hard across the face. How dare he imply that men have the right to cheat and women don't?

And why is he referring to Dan in the past tense?

"I don't even know who you are anymore," I whisper to him. "Who are you, and what have you done to Dan?"

CHAPTER THIRTY-FOUR

"Tess, look," Oliver says, "we need to stop this madness. Let's forget what happened in the past few days and move on."

We're both exhausted after hours of arguing, and he's assured me he didn't do anything to Dan. He wants to make it work with me. He says I'll always be his, that he'll forgive me for wanting to leave him, and we can start over. The thing is, I'm not sure that's even what I want anymore. It's clear to me now more than ever that if I didn't have a past he's shielding me from, I wouldn't be here right now.

"Why did you do it? Why did you break my heart?"

"I already explained that to you." He massages his shoulder and rolls his head. "It wasn't because I didn't love you. I was overwhelmed, so I stepped out of line."

"But you made it sound like it was your right to cheat."

"That came out wrong." He takes my hand in his and holds it tight. My skin is itching from his touch, but I can't pull away. "I cheated and you got too close to another man. And you faked the pregnancy. So, I guess we're even. Now, how about we move past this, start over on a clean slate?"

I grind my teeth and don't respond. How can he expect me

to forget everything he said to me, all the insults he hurled at me?

He moves even closer and pulls me to him. "Tess, talk to me."

"Fine. But I need you to listen to me. Nothing happened between me and Dan. I never even considered cheating on you. Besides, where would I get the time? I'm always with Mason."

"Okay," he sighs, and his voice sounds strained. "You're right." He brings my hand to his lips and kisses it. "I should've known that you wouldn't do anything that stupid."

"I was so terrified of losing you." My chin wobbles with the words. "Especially after I thought somebody was watching me. I thought you would leave us and then—"

"I would give away your secret?"

I exhale. "I thought that since you broke our marriage vows, it would be easy for you to break another promise you made to me."

He gets up and comes to kneel in front of me. "As long as we are together, your secret is safe with me."

He leans forward and presses his forehead to mine. "We're in this together, baby."

I close my eyes, searching for the strength not to push him away. "Then don't hurt me like that again. And don't call me a murderer."

"You're right. I'm sorry. I know you're not," he says. "And I'm not one either. I didn't do anything to Dan."

"I need to go to Mason," I say finally, my limbs aching as I stand up.

He kisses me on the forehead and moves out of my way. "Should we eat lunch together as a family?"

We're no longer a family, I want to say, just two people living together out of necessity. I've been watching him carefully throughout our fight, and I've told enough lies myself to know the signs. Something in Oliver's eyes doesn't sit right with me when he denies doing anything.

I can't stop thinking about Dan, his easy laugh, his gentle smile. My fear for his safety is rising with every minute. Is he lying bruised in an alleyway somewhere after my husband beat him up? How can I love a man who would hurt my friend?

But we need each other. As Oliver said, *"As long as we are together, your secret is safe with me."*

I need him to protect my secret, and he needs me not to tell anyone what I suspect.

"If you like," I say, trying to keep my voice steady. "What would you like to eat for lunch?"

He brings a hand to my cheek and smiles. "Why don't you relax? I'll cook."

"Thanks," I say simply and walk out of the bathroom.

I find Mason sleeping in his wheelchair, probably tired out from the noise around him. I stand in front of him, watching him, my shoulders slumped forward in despair. The decisions I made were to protect him, but now I'm wondering if I did the right thing. But what's the alternative? I can't imagine him being with someone else, or anyone loving him more than I do. He's my son and we'll make it through together. I don't have the heart to wake Mason, so I switch off the TV and go back to the entrance hall to pick up the silicone belly. It's still lying where we left it, not needed anymore. I carry it with me to the bedroom, unsure what to do with it now.

I'm about to put it into the trash can when Oliver appears, and he takes the belly from my hands and studies it up close. "Are you sure you want to throw this away now?"

"Why would I keep it? You already know."

"Yes, but Mason doesn't, and you know how observant he is. You might want to give yourself time to come up with an explanation for him instead of showing up with a flat stomach."

"You're right," I say. "I'll keep wearing it for a little bit."

"I think that's best." He hands it back to me. "So, what do you want to eat for dinner?"

I hug the belly to my chest. "I really don't mind. Whatever you like."

"Then how about gnocchi with pesto sauce?"

"Sounds good." My mouth stretches into a smile, but I don't feel it inside.

It feels surreal that not long ago I was on the cusp of leaving him, and now we're talking about food.

He's about to leave me alone when he turns back. "Did you see any more strange people outside the house?"

I shake my head. "Not for a while, but I still get the feeling that someone is out there."

"I'm starting to think you might be right."

My stomach lurches. "Why? Did you see something?"

He tugs at his shirt collar. "Two days ago, while in the bathroom I thought I saw someone hiding out in the bushes in the yard. But when I went outside, there was no one there."

"Why didn't you say something?"

"I didn't want to worry you. I know what stress does to you."

Anxiety rises in my chest and heat burns my cheeks. I don't say anything, waiting for him to continue.

"I'm starting to wonder if that person has been creeping around the entire neighborhood. What if they have something to do with Dan's disappearance?" He pauses. "I swear to you, Tess. I have nothing to do with whatever happened to him."

I swallow. Could it be true? "But why? If they're after me, why would they hurt him?"

"We don't know for sure that they're actually after you." He taps a finger against his lips as he thinks. "Anyway, it's just a thought."

I'm silent as I digest what he said. My heart is lifting slightly at the thought that there could be some other explanation, even though I'm scared for Dan. "I only wish we had concrete proof that someone is out there."

Oliver scratches his beard, his eyes narrowed. "Maybe we do." His face brightens up.

"Like what?" A spark of hope lights up inside me.

"Mason might have a photo or video; he's always filming from his window. If there's something to see, there's a great chance it's on his iPad. Let's have a look at it, then we can move on from there."

He's right. Mason always carries around his iPad to take photos of birds in nature; he could have taken a photo of the person watching us without even knowing it. We bought him a camera a few months ago, but he keeps going back to his trusted tablet.

"Let me speak to him," I say to Oliver.

When I return to the living room, I find Mason awake, staring straight ahead even though he has not switched the TV back on.

"Sorry, I didn't want to wake you," I say. "Did you rest well?"

"I wasn't sleeping," he says. "I was thinking."

"About what?"

He studies my face for a long time before answering. "You were crying, Mommy. Is it because of him? He was shouting at you."

I touch his cheek with the tips of my fingers. "Honey, sometimes adults argue, just like kids do. But you don't have to worry. Everything is fine."

I glance down at his iPad. It's never too far away from him.

"Can you do me a favor?" I ask.

He raises an eyebrow in question. "Okaaay."

I point to the device. "I'd really love to see the beautiful videos and photos you've been collecting the past few days. Do you think I can have a look?"

He hesitates for a moment before handing it to me. "You need to bring it back soon."

"I will, I promise. I just want to see how good you are now."

"Okay. But I need to use the toilet."

"Sure." I put the iPad on the couch and help him out.

When we are done, I take the iPad to the bedroom, where Oliver is waiting. Together, we look through every single video and photo Mason has taken in the past month and zoom in, taking in every single detail. There are quite a lot of photos and videos, and we almost give up the search, thinking there's nothing to see, until Oliver points to the screen.

"Do you see that?" he asks, zooming in more.

I lean in closer to get a better look and there it is. Behind some bushes is a shadowy figure, half hidden, half exposed. It's too far away for us to make out the face, but the person is wearing a hood that obscures their head.

Even if I can't see their face, it's enough for me to know that I wasn't wrong, all this time. And now Oliver can see it too.

CHAPTER THIRTY-FIVE

THREE YEARS AGO

Henry doesn't waste any time. Two weeks after asking Lisa to be his wife, she moves in, and three more weeks after that, at the end of February, they fly to Hawaii to get married. Mason, who still hasn't warmed up to Lisa, stays home.

"I know why they left without him," Becca says, looking up from the dough she's kneading and lifting it up to toss it back down onto the surface, releasing even more of the yeast smell into the air. "I heard Lisa tell Henry that she was afraid he might make a scene."

I take a sip of water, let it linger in my mouth a few seconds, then swallow. "Lisa obviously doesn't care about him, and Henry's too blind to see it."

"You're right about that. Thank God you didn't leave, Tess. I feel sorry for the boy, having that woman for a mother."

He doesn't need her. He has me.

As I recall what Mason told me the day we went into the woods, a warm feeling spreads through my chest. Ever since then, he's been calling me "Mom" whenever we're alone. In my heart, I have adopted him, just as Henry had on paper. I would never let him down the way I was let down growing up.

"Will you be home for the celebration tomorrow?" Becca asks.

"What celebration?" I smack my forehead. "Oh, right. That. I'm not sure yet."

As most of their friends and relatives were unable to attend their wedding in Hawaii, Henry and Lisa have decided they will throw a celebration for them, five days after they exchanged vows. Of course, I did not receive an invitation, but I guess since I live in the house, I'm automatically invited, even if it's the last thing I want to do.

The doorbell rings and Becca looks at me. "Looks like they're back," she whispers. "There goes our peace of mind. Would you mind letting them in? I have flour on my hands."

"Sure," I say and swallow hard.

When I come to the front door, I pause to take a breath. Then I reach for the handle and push it down.

"Surprise," Lisa squeals. "Meet Mr. and Mrs. Baldwin."

In her arms she holds a large solid bronze sculpture of two horses running side by side. Probably a wedding gift since both of them love horse riding. She sighs as she lowers it onto a tall pine and marble foyer table. Henry greets me politely, then walks past carrying some of their suitcases. I mumble a greeting and turn back to Lisa, who is obviously waiting for me to respond to what she said.

"Won't you congratulate us, Tess?" she asks. Her eyes sparkle with triumph.

I paste on a fake smile. "Sure, Lisa."

"I prefer Mrs. Baldwin," she says with a sweet smile.

"Sure. Congratulations, Mrs. Baldwin," I say and leave her standing there.

"Tess," she calls after me. "Before you go, could we have a quick chat? Come with me to the sunroom."

Since she is basically my boss now, I do as I am told.

She waits for both of us to take a seat before she speaks.

"While we were away, I did some thinking. I came to the conclusion that maybe your services will no longer be needed around here."

Shock zips through me like an electric current. "Why do you say that? What about Mason?"

"There's no need for you to worry about that. We have Becca, and if it so happens that we need extra help, I'm sure we won't have trouble finding a new nanny."

"Becca already has a lot on her hands," I say. "And Mason is used to me being here. It wouldn't be good for him if I leave."

"Kids are resilient little creatures. He'll get used to it."

"Have you talked to Henry about this?"

She sucks in a breath. "Tess, I do not need to consult my husband when I make decisions about such trivial matters. He's a busy man, as you know."

"With all due respect Li... Mrs. Baldwin, caring for Mason is not a trivial matter."

Her jaw clenches. "You know what I meant."

Silence falls between us, and when it becomes too unbearable, I finally speak.

"I signed a contract, and I'm not leaving before it's ended."

When the three-month trial period ended, Henry extended our contract for two additional years instead of one. There is no way in hell I am letting Lisa push me out before the time is up.

She doesn't say anything as she leans back in her chair and watches me through her long lashes. "We'll discuss that again later. There's something else I wanted to talk about."

When I don't respond, she continues.

"As you may already be aware, we're hosting a wedding reception here at the house tomorrow afternoon."

"Yes, I am aware of that."

"Good." She smiles. "The thing is, I'm worried about you being present."

"Why is that?"

"Well, I can only imagine how hard it will be for you to watch me and Henry celebrating our marriage. If I were in your shoes, I'd be devastated."

"I'm a grown woman. I think I can handle it."

"Come on, Tess. You don't have to pretend around me. Every time Henry and I are together, I see the hurt in your eyes. I'm only doing this because I care."

"It's awfully kind of you to care, but really, I'll be fine."

She rubs her forehead for a few seconds, then drops her hand into her lap. "Actually, come to think of it, I do believe only family members and close friends are invited. Since you are neither of those, you have a get-out-free card."

I smile and get up. "Thank you for letting me know about that, Mrs. Baldwin. In that case, I'll find something else to do with my time."

The next morning, I wake up early to go for a run. The caterers and florists are already downstairs, and there are wedding flowers everywhere. I find their scent nauseating. Through the glass walls of the living room, I see Lisa in front of a white marquee talking to a man carrying a large bouquet. I peel my gaze from her and walk out the door.

I had planned on running along the bike trail, as I normally do, but I head into the forest instead. I don't want to see all the expensive cars driving toward the Baldwin residence for the wedding party. As my feet pound the dirt path, I can't help feeling frightened again, as if the woods are threatening to swallow me whole. A twig snaps behind me, and I stop and slowly turn around, expecting something or someone to emerge from behind the trees and bushes. Nobody is there. There are all sorts of animal noises though, from birds chirping to rodents rustling. Just animals. Nothing to be afraid of.

I start running again. To keep from feeling afraid, I focus

my mind on the bright sun shining through the dense leaves, and the chilly breeze. I pick up my pace and keep running until a stitch pierces my side and my knees begin to wobble. I stop then and bend over, pressing my hands to my knees and taking a deep breath. When my breathing is even again, I draw in another huge breath and when I exhale, it comes out in a scream.

I scream and scream until I'm out of breath again. When silence falls, I hear a voice. Someone must have heard my screaming. Frozen to the spot, I listen as the voice gets louder. It sounds familiar.

"Teeesss!"

I take a step forward, then another until I'm running in the direction of the voice. I run down a hill until I reach the edge of a clearing, where I see a small cottage. The few times I have come into the woods, I did see it, but I thought it was unoccupied. Now a man stands in front of it, and I lift my hand to shield my eyes from the sun so I can see better.

"Oliver?"

I am still too far for him to hear me, so I run up to him. He heard me screaming, so he asks me if I'm okay.

"I'm fine, just releasing some tension," I lie and look from him to the cottage. It's best to change the subject. "What are you doing here?"

He hesitates for a moment, probably wondering whether to believe what I said or not, then he speaks. "I live here. I was at the house a few minutes ago and Becca mentioned you went for a run. I looked everywhere for you."

"Why?" I ask, confused about why he would be living in a cottage on his brother's land when they don't really seem to get along.

"I figured it would be a tough day for you and you might need a friend."

He's wrong. The reason I came out for a run was because I wanted to be alone. But I don't tell him that.

"You really live here?"

He glances behind him. "Home sweet home. Becca also mentioned that you won't be at the party and I thought maybe we could have breakfast together."

"Thanks, Oliver, but I plan on going to the library."

"You can always do that later. I've already made the breakfast and it's too much for me to eat on my own."

The traitor that it is, my stomach rumbles. I sigh and nod. "Okay, thank you."

"Perfect. Come in then."

The cottage is cozy and simple, with a warm and homey feel. There is a small table in the middle decorated with fresh flowers, and a small kitchen to the right.

"Make yourself at home." Oliver points to a wooden stool while he pulls bacon from the fridge and heats up the pan.

"Thanks." I take a seat and lean my elbows on the table as I watch him cook for a while in silence before I scan the room.

"We used to play here as kids. It used to be my favorite place," he says, turning from the stove and following my gaze as the aroma of sizzling bacon starts to fill the room. "When my grandparents died, Henry got the house and I got the cottage."

"But that's not fair, is it?"

He shrugs. "It was payback for not doing what was expected of me. I used to be a rebellious kid, brought a lot of shame upon the family. They never forgave me for it."

"I'm so sorry to hear that, Oliver."

He smiles and says nothing as he finishes frying the strips of bacon. Finally, he places a plate of crispy bacon and another of granola and fresh fruit on the table. "Don't worry about it. I've gotten used to being an outcast."

"So, you'll stay living here?"

"I have a house downtown I bought with my own money,

but I prefer it out here in my quiet sanctuary." He sits down on the stool next to me.

Curious, I ask, "What do you do for a living?"

"I'm a real estate broker. I disappointed my parents by choosing this career path rather than join the family business."

I nod and fill my plate with food. "Thank you so much for trying to cheer me up today. I really needed it. But won't Henry be upset about you not being at his party? You are his brother."

"He won't mind at all. I'm sure he'll be relieved, actually." He picks up a mug of coffee and sips slowly. "How about you? How has it been staying in the same house as the two love birds?"

"To be completely honest, it's been hard, but every time I see Mason, he reminds me of the reason why I can't quit."

"You really love that boy, don't you?"

"So much. I'd do anything for him."

He cocks an eyebrow. "Anything?"

"Anything."

Oliver fills my mug with hot coffee. "I definitely think you'd have been a better stepmother to him than Lisa."

"Thank you for saying that. I really appreciate it."

"No need to thank me. It's the truth. That kid is lucky to have you in his life."

He smiles at me, and I feel drawn in by the kindness in his eyes. I hadn't noticed it before, but they are so dark they're nearly black; they exude warmth like the coffee in my mug. The moment our eyes meet, my stomach flips and I look away quickly, my cheeks hot. The room falls silent for a few moments as an awkward tension grows between us.

"I'm the lucky one, Oliver," I say to break the silence.

In that moment, I know that, even after the contract has expired, I am going to find a way to remain in Mason's life.

CHAPTER THIRTY-SIX

It promises to be the perfect birthday for a five-year-old. The downstairs party hall is decorated in red, yellow, and cream balloons and streamers that read "Happy Birthday," and the long table is already set up with drinks, snacks, and the chocolate and caramel cake I baked last night after everyone had gone to bed. Today is my chance to show Mason how much he means to me. The past month has been tough, trying to care for him with Lisa breathing over my shoulder and overriding almost every decision I make concerning him.

I see right through her. Since I refused to quit when she told me to, she is now dedicated to making my life at the house hell, forcing me out the door indirectly. There is always something. She cancels playdates I had arranged, tells me that the food I serve Mason is unhealthy, that I let him watch too much TV, that his room is not clean enough. It is never enough; no matter how much I do, she will find something wrong and will pick at me relentlessly.

The worst is when she shows up while Mason and I are sitting quietly together. She keeps us apart as much as she can, even though she, herself, doesn't make time for him. Not once after marrying Henry has she even read him a goodnight story or helped him with his homework.

But today, I refuse to allow the darts she throws to affect me. I decided to celebrate Mason's birthday during the week after preschool so she would be at her dental practice. When I told her about it, two weeks ago, she didn't even seem interested anyway. So, as far as I'm concerned, I can do whatever the hell I want. Since Henry is working from home today, he can attend if he chooses to.

Everything is almost ready; the only thing missing is the food. Mason had wanted a hot dog-themed birthday party, and I ordered fifty hot dogs from Sparkies, his favorite restaurant.

I check my watch. The hot dogs were supposed to be delivered before I leave to pick him up from preschool. The kids will be hungry after a long day, and I want them to eat right away.

In the kitchen, I find Becca at the island folding the birthday napkins into cute bowties, and she looks up at the sound of my footsteps. "Everything ready for the birthday boy?"

"Not quite. The hot dogs still haven't been delivered."

"Did you call Sparkies to confirm the delivery?"

"Yes, I did. This morning." I pull out my phone to check if I got a missed call from them. Nothing. "They were supposed to be here thirty minutes ago."

"Maybe they got busy with other deliveries and are running late."

"Could be." I dial the number, and my call is answered after the third ring by a cheerful woman.

"Sparkies, how may I help you?"

"Hi, I'm calling to confirm a delivery. I'm supposed to get fifty hot dogs delivered today for a party, but they haven't arrived. Has something happened?"

"Your address please."

"Sure." I give her the address and wait for her to tell me the delivery truck is on the way and will be at the house in the next few minutes.

"Just a moment please." I hear the sound of papers being shuffled and then, "I'm sorry, ma'am, but there was a mix-up in the order. It has been cancelled."

"What? But you don't understand. I need those hot dogs. It's my son's birthday."

Becca shoots me a look of confusion and I avert my gaze. I didn't mean to say that out loud.

"I understand, but there's nothing I can do. Your order has been cancelled."

Anger boils up inside me and my grip on the phone tightens. "I'm sorry but that's not acceptable. I called to confirm this morning. Can you at least tell me who cancelled my order?"

"It doesn't say. I'm really sorry about this."

"Okay, thank you." I end the call, trying to keep from hurling my phone across the room.

"What happened, Tess?" Becca asks.

I rub my eyes in frustration. "They cancelled the order."

I am leaving the house in fifteen minutes to pick up Mason, and on my way back, many of the parents of the invited kids will also be making the journey up to the house. We're not close to any local shops. How would I explain to Mason that there will be no hot dog party?

"Do you think she did it?" Becca says cautiously.

"Who did?" As soon as I say the words, it hits me. "Oh my God, Lisa."

She knew I was planning a hot dog party. Mason has said it out loud enough times. She could also have heard me make the order over the phone. Surely, she can't be that cruel. The party is not about me, it's about Mason.

"She's gone too far this time." I pick up my phone again and call her cell. I don't care if I am disturbing her at work.

"Lisa, it's me, Tess. I just got off the phone with Sparkies and they said you cancelled the hot dog order for Mason's party."

"Oh, yes," she says in her snarky voice. "I forgot to tell you about the change of plans."

"What change of plans?" I can feel my throat closing up with anger.

"There will be no party at the house. We're having it at the Trampoline Park indoor playground. I'm sure Mason will prefer that to a simple hot dog party. Besides, hot dogs are too unhealthy for you to plan a whole party around them. What message will you be sending?" Her mocking tone makes me want to reach down the line and strangle her.

I close my eyes, trying to ward off an approaching headache. "How could you do that? You knew I was planning this for weeks."

"This is not about me or you, Tess. It's about Mason."

"Exactly." I suck in a breath of air, trying to calm myself so I don't lose my temper. "He wanted to have a hot dog party. That was his wish."

"Little boys don't always know what they want. Trust me, he'll remember this party more." She pauses. "Look, Tess, I'm actually doing you a favor. You won't have to run after twenty active kids for three hours. At the Trampoline Park, babysitting is included in the price."

"I decorated the party room, Lisa. I baked a cake. What do you want me to do with that? And what do I tell the parents of the kids who were invited here?"

"Don't worry about that. It's all taken care of. I found the list of their names on the fridge. And Bobby will pick Mason up from preschool and take him straight to his surprise party. As for the decorations, pack them away, and enjoy the cake with Becca."

"I can't believe you did this." I bite down the urge to scream at her.

"It's for the best, trust me. Mason will have so much fun. Isn't that what we both want, for him to be happy?"

"I want him to be happy. You on the other hand are—"

"He's my stepson. I want the best for him," she says. "I'm sorry but I need to get back to my patients. By the way, you don't need to come to the party. There's a writing pad on Mason's bed with a list of things I need you to take care of."

She hangs up before I can say anything else and I drop the phone onto the counter.

Becca approaches me. "Are you okay?"

I turn to face her, the anger in my veins making me want to lash out. "You were right. It was her. All along, she was planning a party behind my back." I chew the inside of my cheek until I taste blood. "Mason wanted a hot dog party and he's not going to get it."

"How could she do that?" Becca's voice is soft but full of anger.

"Well, she hates me, that's why. She wants me out of this house, and she's doing everything she can to make sure she gets what she wants." I sit at the island, my head in my hands. "She's pure evil. I need to talk to Henry; his wife is getting out of control. This has to stop."

I get to my feet again and head to his office. Even though we live in the same house, we have not communicated with each other properly for a while. I wouldn't be surprised if Lisa asked him to keep a distance from me.

I knock on his office door and he asks me to enter.

"Henry," I say, "we need to talk. Can I come in?"

He looks at his watch. "What about? I have a few things to do before heading out to Mason's party."

"That's what I want to talk to you about." I take a seat without him asking me to. "I just got off the phone with Lisa. Even though she knew I was organizing a party for Mason here today, she went ahead and booked a party at the Trampoline Park."

"Oh, that." He waves his hand in dismissal. "Forget about it. Mason will have so much fun at the park, he won't even notice. Lisa said kids love it there."

"It's his birthday, Henry. He wanted a hot dog party. I've been planning this for weeks, and she sabotaged my efforts."

"Tess, I know it's hard for you to accept this, but Lisa is Mason's stepmother. She's doing what's best for him."

"That's what she keeps telling me. Don't you see: it's not about Mason. It's about getting rid of me."

"I think you're wrong. She doesn't mean it like that. You have to give her a chance."

"I can't do that, Henry, because I love your son. I love Mason like my own. Lisa doesn't care about him. She doesn't even make an effort to spend time alone with him."

"That's because you always get in the way. That's at least what she told me. And to be honest, I'm tired of seeing you two competing over Mason. I'm starting to think that maybe we should cancel your contract. You either learn to work together with my wife for my son's benefit, otherwise I'll have no choice but to let you go."

He wouldn't dare, I think, as I walk out of his office.

Lisa has managed to come between me and Henry, but I will do whatever it takes to stop her from getting between me and my son.

CHAPTER THIRTY-SEVEN

PRESENT

It's 10 a.m. I overslept. Yesterday was both physically and emotionally draining. The meltdown I had left me completely depleted. As I push myself to the edge of the bed, I feel strange somehow. My hands go to my flat stomach; no more fake little baby bump. I no longer have to pretend I'm pregnant to Oliver, which means I don't have to wear it to bed anymore, only in the daytime until I'm ready to tell Mason he will not be getting a sibling after all.

My body still heavy with exhaustion, I use the bathroom, brush my teeth, and put on the belly with sweats and a t-shirt. I throw my hair in a ponytail before heading down the hallway toward Mason's room, expecting to find him still in bed. He's unable to get out of it himself and would not allow Oliver to do it for him.

But Mason isn't there and for a split second, I panic. What if Oliver changed his mind and decided to punish me by leaving me and taking Mason with him? I hurry into the living room, and I see Oliver standing outside talking to two men in gray overalls. He's pointing to something on the outside wall, above the doors that lead out onto the patio. When he sees me, he nods to the men and walks into the house. He gives me a kiss like nothing happened yesterday, as if we're not broken.

"What's going on out there?" I ask.

"I'm installing security cameras, looking out into the garden."

"Where's Mason?" I turn to go check in the kitchen.

He stops me by putting both his hands on my shoulders. "Don't worry. I took care of him. Dressed him, brushed his teeth, and made him breakfast; he's enjoying it right now. You should go back to bed, you look tired. Mason is fine."

I scratch the back of my neck. "But how did he react—?"

"We had a little struggle, but I won in the end." He pulls my rigid body to him. "I'm sorry for letting you carry all the weight of his care. I quit too soon. I'll try even harder to bond with him. From now on, things will be different... better."

Better? I doubt it. After what went down yesterday, our marriage is irreparably damaged. The things that were said have left scars that will never heal. But after seeing the photo on Mason's iPad, I know I might need Oliver soon. He protected me before; maybe he can do it again.

One of the men comes in to confirm the position of the cameras.

Oliver squeezes my arm. "I'll be right back, baby. Stay here." He follows the man outside.

While he's gone, I occupy myself with tidying up the living room.

"Thanks for installing the cameras," I say when he returns no more than five minutes later.

"I should have done it a long time ago. I'm sorry I didn't believe you when you told me someone was roaming around the house. I want you to feel safe."

But I don't. I still can't stop thinking about Dan and Oliver. I know more than anyone the darkness people can hide, what they can be capable of. I wrap my arms around my middle, still thinking about our heated conversation. The things he said. The anger in his eyes.

"Why didn't you wake me?" I ask finally. "You know I don't like sleeping in."

"You were exhausted last night. You should really spend the day in bed. I took the day off to be there for Mason."

"No, that's fine. I've slept enough. I'll go check on him."

The truth is, I also feel uncomfortable with Oliver being around Mason now.

"Alright, but take it easy. Like I said, I'm ready to be a hands-on parent. If you need me for anything, I'm here." He kisses me on the cheek and I feel nothing.

I give him a weak smile and head to the kitchen. I find Mason sitting at the table eating his cornflakes with one hand and drawing with the other.

"Morning, Mace." I kiss his cheek. "What are you drawing?"

"Nothing," he says, turning his paper upside down.

"Come on, Mason. You know I love seeing your drawings. You're so talented."

Without saying a word, he turns the paper over again to show me, and I sit down to take a close look. It's a picture of a hooded man sitting in a chair next to a bed. He has no eyes, mouth, or anything else on his face. Another person with short, curly hair is asleep in the bed, their back turned so they're facing the wall.

My stomach clenches as I look at Mason. "Who's this?" I point to the man.

"No one," he murmurs, pulling the drawing back to himself.

I take a deep breath and try again to get him to open up. "Mason, has anyone been coming to visit you at night?"

I hold my breath, afraid of his answer.

He shakes his head. "Only in my dreams."

"Someone has been visiting you in your dreams? Do you know who it is?"

He shrugs. "He doesn't talk to me."

"Can you describe him?" I ask.

"No. It's always dark." He continues to draw, and after a few seconds, his eyes go to my stomach. I let out a sigh when he says nothing. He doesn't want to ask, and I don't want to explain.

I push back my chair. "I'll be right back, sweetheart."

I leave the kitchen and find Oliver in his office cleaning up his desk. The crib is gone and I'm grateful for that.

"I was talking to Mason," I say without entering the room completely. "He was drawing something."

"That's not unusual, is it? That's what he spends his days doing, taking photos or drawing."

"I know, but there was something strange about the drawing he showed me just now. He drew a man sitting next to a bed with someone sleeping in it."

Oliver looks up at me. "What are you saying?"

"Remember when I told you that Mason saw someone in his room wearing a hood."

"The man he thought was me?"

"Yeah," I say. "I know you think it was a dream, but I don't. I really think someone has been coming to see him in his room, Oliver."

His brows meet in the middle as he waits for me to continue. "So you really think he's not imagining it all?"

It's hard for me to take the concern on his face seriously, especially when I still remember the rage, hate, and disgust that had been etched in his features less than twenty-four hours ago. It's amazing how one face can show two different people.

"I don't think. I know. I also know someone left that glass in his room and the mug in the kitchen. You know that I always wash up every cup and plate before going to bed."

"I don't know," Oliver says. "It's easier to believe that someone might watch the house, but for them to actually—It's a little far-fetched, don't you think? No one else has a key but us, and we keep everything locked. I'm putting up cameras so we can see if someone comes into the garden, but—"

"Oliver, I know it's hard to believe, but both Mason and I can't be imagining things."

I expect him to brush it off, but I can see concern growing on his face.

"Okay," he says, coming to join me at the door. "You're right. I'll have cameras installed in the entire house. I need to make sure you and Mason are safe when I'm at work. I'll keep an eye on you."

"Thanks," I say, relieved. "I think that's a good idea."

Thank God I'm no longer keeping the secret pregnancy from him; it would have shown up on camera. I follow him to the living room and watch him give the men additional instructions before coming back to me.

After an awkward silence, he asks, "Have you heard anything new about Dan?"

"No," I say in a strained voice. "He's still missing."

And part of me is still wondering if you know where he is.

His gaze wanders to the men outside, then back at me. "After they're done, I'm going to the police. I'll show them the picture we found on Mason's iPad. I know they will be asking questions about Dan, but I need you to avoid speaking to them at all costs. You know why." He clears his throat. "I also need you and Mason to stay indoors for now. If Dan is really dead, as everyone seems to think, his killer might still be out there."

"I understand." I don't want to show him how emotional I feel about Dan's disappearance. I'm afraid to rock the boat again after it almost tipped over during our conversation last night, afraid to bring back the terrifying man I saw standing before me.

"Good." He reaches for my hand and squeezes it. "I'm back, okay? I'll never leave you again. I don't want you to be afraid of me." He pulls me into his arms. "I'm sorry about yesterday, if I scared you. Right now, we need to focus on keeping you safe. I love only you."

I don't answer him back.

Before he can get the idea of kissing me, I pull away to look into his face. "What if the cops come asking questions?" I ask.

"Don't speak to them unless I'm around."

It's dark out and I'm standing by the living room window while Mason is doing a puzzle. We still haven't talked about whether he heard Oliver and me fighting last night, and I don't bring it up. Through the glass, I watch as our neighbors walk down the street with flashlights. I know all the book club members will be among them. Carmen posted in the group earlier in the evening that there will be a search for Dan at nightfall, and everyone, except for me, said they would be there.

Jocelyn never responded, but nobody pushes her. She sent a text a few days ago saying she will be away for a while. That seemed to stop people from trying to talk to her.

The thought that Dan might really be dead causes twisted fingers of fear to tighten around my heart. He's my friend, and I desperately want to go out there and help find him. But I can't, and when Carmen called an hour ago to ask if I was coming along, I said I wasn't feeling well. I've never felt so guilty before.

"Are you okay?" Oliver asks and I jump. I didn't hear him come into the living room.

I pull him into the kitchen. "I think I should go out. Everyone is out there searching for Dan. I want to help."

A warning cloud forms in his eyes. "We talked about this. I think it's not a good idea. If Dan was harmed by the person who has been stalking you... us, you would be in danger."

"I know, but I feel so terrible."

He grabs me by the shoulders, forcing me to face him. "Tess, my priority is to keep you safe. And you need to lie low. I want you to stay indoors with Mason. If it will make you feel better, I'll go out on our behalf, okay?" He sucks in a breath. "If we both join the search, we'll have to take Mason with us, and I think it will be too distressing for him, don't you think?"

"You're right," I say, still feeling heavy and guilty.

Maybe it is for the best I stay indoors. I'm not sure I can face everyone right now. As promised, Oliver leaves the house to join the search party and Mason and I continue our puzzle. He returns two hours later, and the moment he steps through the door, his face tells me he has no good news to share with me. Dan is still missing.

CHAPTER THIRTY-EIGHT

LESS THAN TWO YEARS AGO

It's May again, a year after I moved into the Baldwin mansion, and I'm in the middle of refilling Lisa's tall glass with grenadine juice when I hear the scream. I put down the glass jar and run back into the garden. A screaming Becca is standing at the base of one of the trees, and Lisa is still laying on the lounger where I left her ten minutes ago with her earphones in and eyes closed. When Becca sees me, she points to the ground and clasps her hands over her mouth. Without seeing what's on the ground, I know.

"Mason," I scream, running to the tree. When I see his unmoving body on the ground, my skin goes cold as blood drains from my face.

Panic wells up in my throat, and I push a hand into the back pocket of my jeans for my phone. Becca doesn't need to tell me what happened. Before Lisa sent me inside to refill her drink, Mason was watching some colorful birds that had landed on the tree. Lately, he has taken to climbing trees and I warned him not to do it unless I was there. I also told Lisa that she should watch him.

I dial 911 and bend down next to Mason. He is still

conscious, but his eyes are slightly unfocused and he is whimpering.

"Nine-one-one, what's your emergency?"

"What happened?" Lisa asks, running up to us finally, her long, white bohemian chiffon kimono floating behind her. "I was sleeping. I didn't see."

I ignore her like she had ignored Mason, and focus on the phone call. "I need an ambulance. A five-year-old boy fell from a tree. He fell on his back... I think."

"Is he conscious?" the calm female voice on the other end asks.

"Tess," Lisa continues to bug me, "what happened to him?"

With tears in my eyes, I shoot her my coldest look and answer the woman. "Yes, he's conscious and breathing, but he's not talking." I wrap an arm around my middle as fear ties up my insides. "Please send someone right away. Hurry."

As I stroke Mason's cheek, he says something I can't understand. "Stay still, darling," I say to him. I don't want him to exert himself in any way.

"I understand, ma'am," the 911 woman says. "I'll have an ambulance sent right away. Tell me where you are."

I quickly give her the address and stay with Mason till the ambulance arrives and the paramedics take over. They ask me a few questions, then settle next to Mason. It is hard not to fall apart when they put an oxygen mask on his mouth and start working on him.

"It looks like he hit the ground pretty hard," the female paramedic says to her partner. "He doesn't have visible injuries, but there could be internal bleeding."

As their efforts go on, Becca tries to explain to me and the paramedics what happened. "I was bringing Mrs. Baldwin her sunscreen when I saw something fall from the tree." She wipes her eyes. "I didn't know it was—I just..."

"It's okay," I whisper to her.

"It's not," Becca says. "If I had come out a little earlier, maybe I could have stopped him climbing."

"You're not the one at fault here," I say between gritted teeth as my eyes stare at Lisa.

"You're the nanny. He was your responsibility." Lisa's expression is set firm, her eyes defiant.

"I won't let you blame me for this," I say. After six months of being blamed for her failures, I'm done. "You sent me inside to get you a drink. You promised you would watch him."

When she tries to say something, I bring out my phone again and start dialing.

"Who are you calling now?" she asks.

I don't even bother to answer her; she is in no position to question my actions. She should be the one doing what I am doing, calling for help, letting Henry know what has happened and telling him to meet us at the hospital.

As Henry's stepmother, Lisa is allowed to get in the ambulance with him. After the vehicle rushes off with lights flashing, I get into my own car.

"Drive safely," Becca calls. She knows I'm far from being okay.

At Greenwich Hospital, Lisa and I are shown into a waiting room while several doctors, nurses, and orderlies rush by us toward the operating theater. My heart sinks deeper and deeper with every passing minute. Even though I try to breathe slower, it's becoming increasingly difficult to stop my mind from racing. When it becomes apparent that Mason's status is not going to be revealed anytime soon, my chest tightens and the feeling of dizziness creeps over me, preparing me for a full-blown panic attack if the news turns out to be less than favorable.

Lisa sits down, but I can't sit still. I pace back and forth, my mind racing. What if Mason doesn't make it? While I fear for Mason's life, Lisa has the nerve to scroll through her Instagram page. In addition to her being a dentist, she's also some kind of social media influencer, who shares dental tips online.

After a fifteen-minute wait, Henry finally arrives. For the first time since I've known him, he looks unkempt. His hair looks like he's been running his hands through it, his face is tense and pale and his blue tie is crooked. As soon as she sees him, Lisa tosses the phone into her handbag and throws herself into his arms, sobbing for the first time since Mason got hurt. It baffles me that Henry is unable to see her for the snake she really is.

"It was terrible," she says into his shoulder. "She should have been there watching him, but—"

Henry pulls away from his wife and turns to me. "What happened to my son?" His voice is hard and unflinching. Before I can defend myself from the accusations I know are coming, Lisa butts in. "Henry was all alone outside while she was in the house doing God knows what."

Anger bubbles within me. "Henry, I was in the house for less than ten minutes because she sent me in. For those few minutes, she was in charge of watching Henry."

"That's not even the point," Lisa says to Henry. "We pay her to look after Mason and she failed."

"Stop." Henry's voice cracks like a whip through the small room. "I need to find out how my son's doing." He storms out.

As soon as he leaves, I turn on Lisa. "How are you going to sleep at night?"

Lisa purses her lips and moves toward the door, but I catch her shoulder. "You won't get away with this, you know. Sooner or later, Henry is going to find out what you really are. And that you don't give a damn about his son. And when he does, I'll be there to watch you burn."

"How dare you? Just because you spent five minutes in his bed doesn't give you the right to speak to me with such disrespect." She pries my fingers off her arm. "Don't waste your breath waiting for him to come back to you. It won't happen. I hope he now sees how useless you are at your job and fires you once and for all."

"You know what, Lisa? I'm not going anywhere."

"But you are," a deep voice says from behind me. "I'm sorry, Tess, but Mason wouldn't be here if you had been more attentive."

My stomach clenches. "You're firing me? Now, of all times?"

Henry drops into a chair. "After what happened today, I can no longer trust you to be there for my son anymore. I think you should go home and start packing."

"But Mason might need—"

"He's no longer your concern," he says, in a tired voice. "Lisa and I are taking over. We are his parents."

"Henry, please don't do this. Not now." My words barely make it through the tears in my throat.

"Your full-time job was to look after Mason. You failed to do that and there are consequences for your actions."

I glare at Lisa, who is all smiles. She has won, just like she said she would.

"Fine," I say, pushing back my shoulders. "If Mason needs me, call me, please." I push my way through the double doors and walk out of the hospital. It is late afternoon, but the sun is still high in the sky. I put a hand on my forehead to shield my eyes from the bright light as my eyes sweep the parking lot for my car.

Instead of going home, I drive to the park and cry in my car for two straight hours. I don't want to go home. I don't want to leave Mason with that woman. I can't bear the thought of him lying in the hospital bed in pain, without me there. When I have no more tears left, I drive around town, past shops and restaurants, and buildings that Greenwich is famous for. Local attractions like the Putnam Cottage and the Bruce Museum are nothing but a blur in my vision.

I only stop the car when I get to the Simon Cove Inn. Since I no longer have a home, I have to start thinking of getting accommodation. But I am about to get out of the car when I change my mind. What am I doing? I do have some money saved, but choosing a luxurious accommodation wouldn't be a smart move. And Henry has not exactly told me when I am expected to leave his property.

Still in the parking lot of the inn, I rest my forehead against the steering wheel when my phone beeps. A message from Henry.

Mason is awake. He wants to see you.

When I arrive at the hospital, he is in a private room in the ICU, hooked up to a bunch of machines. As soon as I enter the room, Henry stands up and leaves in a hurry. He won't even meet my eyes. I hope he is ashamed for sending me away when he knew his son would need me.

"I'm sorry," Mason murmurs when I pull up a chair. His eyes are red-rimmed and shiny. "Mommy, I'm sorry for... I shouldn't have climbed up the tree."

I swallow a sob, determined not to cry in front of him.

"It's okay, baby," I whisper, bringing my face close to his. I don't even care if anyone is in the room to hear our conversation. If Mason considers me his mother, I'm not about to reject him. Until now it has just been a private game we played, but now it means everything. "Don't worry about it. I want you to focus on getting better, okay?"

He blinks, takes a breath and closes his eyes. I kiss him on the nose and look up at the window to see Henry watching us.

If I had my way, I'd never speak to him again. But I need to know what the doctors told him. Before I can leave the room, a doctor approaches him and while they talk, I stand in the doorway, shamelessly listening to their conversation.

"Mr. Baldwin," the man in the white coat says, "I have bad news. Your son had a hard fall."

"Of course, it was a hard fall," Henry grinds the words out between his teeth. "He fell from a tree, dammit."

"Sir, I know you're upset, but unfortunately the news I have to share with you is not good. Should we take a seat somewhere?"

"I don't need to sit. Tell me what's going on. I've been waiting long enough. Give me the facts."

The doctor nods and looks down at the clipboard he's holding. "Mr. Baldwin, your son has suffered a thoracic spinal cord injury."

"What?" Henry says, in a hoarse voice. "How... What does this mean?"

"It means Mason will be paralyzed from the waist down."

I cover my mouth with my hand, but cannot hold back the sob. When I was driving around town, I had imagined what the doctor would say about Mason's injuries, but I could never have imagined something as horrible as paralysis.

"But he was in surgery for hours," Henry says, grasping at straws. "Was it for nothing?"

"No," the doctor replies. "He suffered from internal bleeding as well, but we managed to control that. But the damage is extensive."

"How extensive?" Henry yanks a handkerchief from his pocket and wipes his brow. "And what can be done about it?"

The doctor hugs the clipboard against his chest and takes a step back. "We recommend physical, occupational, and psychotherapy, but there's a good chance your son will be in a wheelchair for the rest of his life."

CHAPTER THIRTY-NINE

Walking down the hall toward Mason's room, I hear Henry hollering inside his office. Seven months after the accident, I'm still Mason's nanny. Neither Henry nor Lisa have brought up the topic of me being fired anymore. They know that Mason needs me more than ever, and in the early days he spoke to no one but me. He's still in a wheelchair, unable to move his lower body, just like the doctors said would happen. Not even his father's money can buy him what he wants most.

When the doctor told Henry that Mason could spend the rest of his life in a wheelchair, he refused to believe it. So did I. Henry would not let his son go to a rehab facility and has instead hired teams of doctors and therapists to tend to him at the house. The mansion has even been remodeled to become more wheelchair accessible, including installing an elevator. Since I take care of Mason twenty-four/seven, I have been moved to a room next to his.

The first day I arrived at the Baldwin mansion, I admired the proud building. It's now a shell of its former grandeur, elegant on the outside but inside, the building feels haunted, dark, and full of despair.

"I need to see progress. That's what I pay you for." Henry's voice bounces off the walls. "You need to start doing your job."

He is probably talking to one of the many doctors who are responsible for Mason's recovery.

I have watched them come and go. Some of them come and leave on the same day, others stay for two or three weeks. One doctor, a spinal cord injury specialist from London, stayed an entire month. Henry wanted his son to be tended to night and day, until he continually saw no progress and the doctors reduced drastically in number.

As hard as it is to see Mason in a wheelchair, I have made peace with it. I still hope and pray that one day he will surprise us all, but while we wait I will accept him just the way he is. I knock and push open the door to his room. He's sitting in his wheelchair in front of the large window, which overlooks the front of the house and the woods beyond it. He is wearing a black shirt and gray khakis, and his hair is no longer spiky as he used to like it, but neatly combed back.

"Hey, sweetheart," I say, coming to crouch next to him and trying not to see the shadows gathered under his eyes. "Are you ready for lunch?"

He shakes his head, then drops it.

I miss the boy he used to be, a happy, fun-loving kid. But the last months have changed him. He is quieter and withdrawn, and hardly talks to anyone. Although he does laugh sometimes, it's rare. As expected, Lisa never gives him the time of day, especially now that he's paralyzed. I heard her on the phone once, complaining to someone about being the stepmother to a cripple, about how she never signed up for that.

A small part of me feels sorry for her. When the accident happened, she and Henry were still in the honeymoon stage and it was pretty much stopped short. Someone should have told her that we can never choose when disaster should strike. She did promise her husband to be there in sickness and in health. She knew all along that he and Mason came as a package.

During the first few weeks she kept up appearances, pretending to care about Mason, asking how he was doing. When he never responded to her, she gave up and started keeping her distance from him as much as she could. I am often tempted to gloat about the fact that Mason rarely says a word to her, but I am desperate to hear more of his voice and I don't care who he shares it with.

But Lisa couldn't care less about him, not before the accident and not after it. When she goes to bed at night, complaining of her constant headaches, she puts in earplugs so she won't hear him screaming in the middle of the night. Of course, Lisa has other things to worry about. The tension between her and Henry is palpable lately, and I figure she wants to shut him out as much as his son.

It is no secret that she blames the child for the destruction of her fresh marriage. They argue a lot and Henry is rarely home. When he is, he sits on a stool in the home bar, drinking away his pain.

"Should I take you for a walk in the woods later?" I ask Mason. "We can drop by Uncle Oliver's. He said he'll be at the cottage today."

He nods and gives me a flicker of a smile. I still feel a little uneasy going into the woods. But it is always refreshing to get to the other side of it, where Oliver's cottage waits. Getting out of the mansion even for a minute is a breath of fresh air for both me and Mason. Instead of going to preschool, he has a tutor who comes to the house during the week, and I hate to think of him being cooped up here all the time.

"Can we go now, Mommy?" he asks.

When we are alone, he still calls me that and, as the months go by, I start feeling more like I really am his mother. He's the first person I think of when I open my eyes in the morning and the last before I close my eyes at the end of the day. It pains me to my core that his own father has turned his back on him and is ashamed to take him out in public. At the start, when there was still hope, Henry would go into Mason's room with a smile on his face, greeting him with a kiss, but now, if he even comes in, he often looks down at his son and then leaves without saying a word. So if Mason is going to experience any love and affection, it has to come from me. When he has nightmares in the middle of the night or shoves his food away in frustration, it is me who comforts him, me who wipes up the gravy and the pieces of broken plates. I don't care about the money I'm being paid. I love Mason so much that I even feel guilty taking money for doing something I'd gladly do for free.

"We can only go out after you eat something," I say. "You didn't even have any breakfast."

"I'm not hungry," he says and his eyes dare me to force him.

The stubborn look on his face reminds me so much of his father.

"You have to eat something. You need to keep up your strength."

He clenches his fists and continues to refuse food.

I wait until he looks at me, then make him an offer. "How about a slice of buttered toast?"

I have learned over the past months that persistence and patience are the keys to dealing with Mason. It can't be easy waking up and going to bed in a body that let him down.

"Just one?" he asks, finally looking at me.

"One single slice and I will leave you alone."

Now that we have reached an agreement, I wheel him to the elevator that takes us downstairs. We find Marjorie, the new housekeeper, slicing carrots for a salad. She's small and fragile-looking, with a fairy-type appearance about her. And she's pretty, which made me wonder when she walked through the door whether Henry had hired her because of her qualifications or her looks.

Two months after the accident, Becca quit her job. Although she never complained before, she finally admitted that working for Lisa was impossible, and that the woman treated her like her own personal slave. Sometimes I wish I could quit as well, walk out of the fancy doors and never look back. But I'm not going anywhere without Mason. We're in this together.

Even after months of her working at the house, I have not been able to bond with Marjorie. She doesn't understand me the way Becca did. She's also quite shy and keeps to herself, which I don't really mind. I spend most of my time with Mason anyway.

I'm putting the toast in front of Mason when the sound of something crashing makes us all jump.

"Stay here, sweetheart, and eat up. I'll be right back."

I know I should stay away from Henry, but he's scaring his son. Furious, I barge into his office to find one of his laptops on the floor and pieces of broken glass all around.

"You need to get your temper under control, Henry. You're getting out of hand. The drinking, the yelling—"

He picks up a glass of Scotch and downs the golden liquid. "How dare you come in here without knocking?"

"Mason's wellbeing is my responsibility and I will not stand by and watch you scare him."

He stands up slowly and sways toward me. I don't step back, not even when he hovers over me and breathes booze into my face.

Mason can't stand up to him, but I can.

"Do you want me to stop?" he growls. "Then tell the boy to get out of that damn wheelchair. He should walk like a normal person. And you should stop pretending he's normal."

"He *is* normal," I say between clenched teeth. "And all that boy needs right now is his father. But he's too busy blaming the world for everything."

He stumbles back at my words. "Blame," he says. "Let's talk about that. I blame you, Tess, for everything. You are the one who should be taking responsibility here. Because of you, my son will remain crippled for the rest of his life. Because of you—"

"No, Henry." I shake my head. "Deny it as much as you like, but the one person responsible for this is your wife. It's her you should be lashing out at." I walk backward toward the door. "Because of me, Mason is not even more depressed right now. I'm the only one who shows him any affection around here. I'm the one holding him together." I stop in the doorway. "You used to be such a great dad. Now you're nothing but a drunk, mean jerk."

"I'm your boss. You can't talk to me like that."

"Then fire me," I threaten and wait for a response that doesn't come. "You can't, can you? You know the truth. You know that no one can love your son as much as I do." I slam the door shut and go to Mason.

Later that night, I overhear Lisa and Henry fighting.

"You need to do something about her, Henry. And you need to do something about that boy."

I can't hear Henry's response, but Lisa's next words hit me like a punch to the gut.

"Mason is not even your real son. You adopted him whole, and now he's broken. Just give him back. That way, we'll no longer have a need for Tess either. We can start over."

CHAPTER FORTY

PRESENT

It's 9 a.m. and I've already cleaned every single room in the house, hung up the washing on the line, and spent the past three hours washing and polishing the floor. And now, all I can think about is walking out the door. I can't stay cooped up inside any longer.

The pressure of staying indoors is building in my chest, making it harder to breathe. I'm starting to feel like an inmate in an asylum. It can't be good for Mason either. Oliver wants me to lie low, but he doesn't know how it is to watch the world go by through a pane of glass. He gets to go to work every morning while we're trapped inside. He said if we need fresh air we have the garden, but it's not the same. I'm not even allowed to go to the grocery store anymore.

To hell with his orders. I grab my phone from where it sits on the dining table and take it with me to the pantry, one of the few places without cameras. The small room smells of moldy bread. I make a note to find it and toss it away. I feel like a terrible friend as I dial Carmen. I've been avoiding her calls. All the messages about Dan have been unbearable, and I've turned off my phone. She tried to come over yesterday, but Oliver was the one to open the door. He told her I wasn't feeling well and didn't want to see people.

He made it clear that he wants me to stay away from everybody until we know what happened to Dan and who's been watching us. He seems really concerned, and while I think it's a bit extreme to stop me from seeing my friend, I appreciate him trying to watch out for me. But the cameras have been up for days now, and we haven't seen any more suspicious activity. Maybe the person is finally leaving us alone.

"Hi, Carmen," I say when she picks up. "Are you home?"

"Sure. Why?"

"I was thinking maybe I could stop by for a short visit."

"Of course, you can come over. Bring Mason with you. I miss you both."

"Thanks. We'll see you in about fifteen minutes."

"Take your time. I'm not working today. See you soon."

Since Mason is already in his wheelchair, we head right out.

"Where are we going?" he asks as I wheel him out the door.

"To visit Aunty Carmen." I feel more buoyed up than I have in weeks, excited to see my friend.

"Yeah," Mason says, punching the air. "We haven't seen her for days."

"You're right about that."

As we make our way down the street, my skin is prickling. I feel as though all eyes are on me.

When we pass by her house, Monica opens her kitchen window and pokes out her head. "Hey, Tess, I haven't seen you in a while. I heard you haven't been feeling well lately. Are you and the baby okay?"

"Yes, thank you, all fine." I keep walking, my feet hitting the pavement, and I don't look back even as I hear her voice following me down the street.

"It's awful about Dan, isn't it?" Monica calls. "You two were so close. Did he say anything to you?"

I don't turn around. I pretend I don't hear her, but I feel a trickle of sweat making its way down my spine. The late August sun is blazing down and my nerves are making me over-heat. I still haven't explained to Mason that Dan is missing, hoping he will be found safe soon enough and I won't have to say a word. I hope he's too wrapped up in his imagination to have heard what Monica said.

I continue on down the street, nodding at some of the neighbors outside enjoying the late summer weather, most of them housewives or people who work from home, as they call out their greetings from porches and gardens. I greet back, but don't stop for longer conversations. Finally, we arrive at Carmen's door and, before we can ring the bell, she opens it.

"I'm so glad to see you," she says, pulling me into a tight hug, then kissing Mason on the top of his head, allowing her lips to linger a little in his hair.

"I love this little man," she says, straightening up again.

"I missed you, Aunty Carmen," Mason says, reaching up his hand to grab hers.

"And I missed you." Carmen grins. "Come on, you guys. I made chocolate muffins."

"Perfect," Mason says. "I love muffins."

"That's why I made them. Just for you. I was planning to bring them by the house."

After the muffins are gone, Carmen takes Mason out into the garden and brings out painting supplies she bought for him. Excited, he gets to work creating his next piece of art, and while he's occupied, we get a chance to talk.

"What's going on with you?" Carmen asks, leaning into me. She's whispering even though there's no way Mason can hear us. "I came over yesterday and Oliver said you were not feeling well. Is everything okay?"

"Yeah, I had a migraine; I've been so worried about Dan. But I feel much better today."

I had planned on telling her that Oliver knows I faked my pregnancy, but I find myself unable to. I'm emotionally exhausted. And thinking about that day brings up too much pain for me.

"That's good. How about the... you know?" She gestures at my stomach.

"You know what?" I lean back in my seat, ready to change the subject. "I think I'm the last person we should be talking about right now. Did you hear anything new about Dan? I feel so awful for not participating in the search."

"That's alright." She squeezes my hand. "At least Oliver came to represent you." Her face falls. "Almost a week, and we still haven't heard anything new. Apparently, he had some nasty stuff in his past, and he's been really stressed lately. We all think he felt like he had to escape, get away from everything for a bit."

I rub my forehead and my fingers come away covered in sweat. "I'm scared, Carmen. What if... he's dead?" I keep replaying the last time I spoke to Dan and it hurts so bad to think I might never hear his voice again or his laughter. When we walked past his house, I purposely avoided looking at it. It would have been too unbearable to imagine him standing in his doorway waving at us with that bright smile of his.

Carmen presses her palms against her eyes, which are red, but she isn't crying. "I know. But we can't think about that, not when we have no reason to think the worst."

"It's hard not to when he's still not back. This is so unlike him." My stomach clenches as I consider Noah's future without Dan. His love for his son is so strong that he would never leave him just like that. A wave of sadness washes over me as I recall the warmth of the little boy when I'd held him in my arms and made the decision to try and have my own child. "He has to come back, Carmen. Noah needs his father, and we need our friend."

"We will see him again," Carmen says with certainty and

takes a sip of Coke. "We need to believe there is some explanation for his disappearance."

Oliver told me he went to the police and showed them Mason's photo, and they promised to keep an eye on our street. It sounds like the police already know about Dan's past, so I don't need to say anything about what he told me. I still wonder if I should speak with the police about Oliver returning drunk with blood on his hands the night Dan disappeared, but I can't bring myself to do that. They will arrest him immediately. And if he knows I betrayed him, I'm terrified of what he will say about me. In my heart, I still desperately want to believe Oliver's story that he was involved in a bar brawl.

The grandfather clock in a corner of Carmen's living room chimes loudly. It's 10 a.m. After a long silence, Carmen glances at my stomach again, hidden under my flowing dress.

"How's it going with the... pregnancy? Have you decided yet when you're going to the next stage?"

"No, not yet." My stomach hardens. I should have known she would keep bringing it up, and I really don't want to talk about this now. Carmen has a way of getting me to open up, and I'm afraid if I tell her about our fight, I'll give away things I really shouldn't.

"I think you should do it," she says, munching on a potato chip.

"I know, but—"

My phone rings before I finish. It's Oliver.

"Sorry," I say, standing up to take the call in the kitchen.

"Where are you?" Oliver asks, a cold edge to his voice.

"I... I took Mason out for a walk. He begged me to take him out. I thought it would do him good."

I hate that I'm using Mason to get out of trouble, but Oliver had made it clear that he did not want us to get out of the house.

"Go home, now," he says, his voice hard and unflinching.

When I end the call, my hand is shaking slightly. I can't

bring myself not to do as he says. As a familiar terror sweeps through me, I return to the living room and tell Carmen that we have to go.

"So soon?" she asks.

"Yeah, I think I left something on the stove. I totally forgot."

"Alright then." She gets to her feet. "Call me later so we can finish our conversation. We are also meeting for another search party tonight. If you're feeling up to it, you should join us."

"I'll let you know," I say, making no promises.

She frowns and lays a hand on my arm. "Hey, are you alright? Your hand is shaking."

"I'm fine." I step away from her. "I'll talk to you soon, okay?"

As expected, Mason is not happy to leave so soon after we arrived. He throws a small tantrum, but when Carmen tells him he can keep the art supplies, he cheers up and allows me to wheel him out of the house.

Five minutes later, as we approach our home, I spot Oliver's car in our driveway. We find him sitting behind the wheel, waiting for us. I have no doubt that he saw us leave Carmen's house, and now he knows that I was lying about us being out for a walk. A heavy weight settles in the pit of my stomach and I try to breathe slowly. In, out. In, out. Once we're inside, he shuts the door and smiles down at Mason, then takes the wheelchair from me.

"Hey, buddy, I see you were drawing. Let me take you to my office. You can finish your masterpiece there."

My entire body is tense as I wait for him to return. When he's standing in front of me again, a thunderous expression is distorting his face.

"Hey," I say, my voice shaky. "I had no idea you were—"

Whack.

With lightning speed, his backhand has slammed against my cheek and sent me staggering backwards.

I lose my balance and stumble into the hallway cupboards,

my face stinging where he struck me. My eyes fill with tears as I meet his gaze. Inside my mouth, I taste blood.

"I told you not to leave this house."

"You have no right," I whisper, horrified. "How dare you lay a hand on me?" I'm about to say more when I look past him and see Mason. He must have left the room as soon as Oliver walked out.

For a moment, our eyes lock, then he looks down at his iPad. I feel my shoulders sag as cold fear rushes through me. My son saw Oliver hit me.

"Oliver, I—"

"What?" he asks. His hand is poised, ready to strike me again. "You have something else to say to me?"

"Yes," I say through clenched teeth. "Mason is behind you. He needs me."

Oliver drops his hand but doesn't turn to look. I pull myself together and push past him, a fake smile on my face and my cheek on fire.

The conversation between me and Oliver will have to wait. This time, it won't end well.

CHAPTER FORTY-ONE

JUST OVER ONE YEAR AGO

More than a year has passed since the accident, but Mason is still in a wheelchair. Henry is getting more and more frustrated, drinking his misery away, his temper growing worse by the minute. And Lisa's headaches are growing more and more frequent.

One night, after bringing Lisa her water and pills, I'm getting Mason's bed ready for him before fetching him from the living room downstairs when I hear something fall and break. I hurry out of the room and see Henry towering over Mason in front of the elevator.

Terrified, Mason wheels himself away, distancing himself from his father, but Henry follows. The man who was once a great dad has completely transformed into a monster. I watch as Mason comes to a halt. Closing his eyes and bunching his fists, the little boy looks like he's shrinking away in his wheelchair. I can't see the tears, but I know he's crying. It isn't the first time Henry has confronted him directly about his lack of progress.

I always intervene before he goes too far because I know how it is to live with a bully for a parent. I remember the pain all too well. Most days, Henry keeps a distance, abusing his son from across the room, barely ever touching him, never hugging him. I'm not going to sit and watch this time—he's gone too far—so I hurry toward them to put an end to it.

"Are you going to be a cripple for the rest of your life?" he growls, bringing his face close to that of the boy.

"I'm sorry, Daddy," Mason mumbles.

"Sorry for what exactly?" Henry shoots back. "For being so pathetic?"

"No," Mason says, gulping down tears.

"Then what are you sorry for?" To my horror, Henry grips Mason by the hair. "Answer me. What are you sorry for?"

"I don't know," Mason cries.

"Stop it, Henry!" I shout when I reach them. "Leave him the hell alone! Don't you see you're hurting him?" My anger is at boiling point as I seize Henry's arm and yank him away.

Henry lets go of Mason's hair and turns on me, his face contorted.

"Get out of here!" he screams at me. "Take the crippled brat with you on your way out."

Tears blur my vision as I watch the man I was once falling in love with coming undone. "You're drunk again, Henry. That's why you're not thinking straight."

"So what if I had a drink?" he says. "Why is it your business?"

"It's my business when you hurt Mason. He's your son. You don't have the right to touch him."

"What the hell do you know about being a parent?" Henry yells, his face puce and veins popping in his neck. "You don't have kids, so why don't you stay out of this?"

"I'll tell you why I know!" I shout back. "I know because you remind me of my father. I told you my childhood story once. Or are you too drunk to remember?"

"I don't give a damn about your childhood." I watch his eyes brim with anger. "I don't give a damn about you."

"Well, I couldn't give a crap how you feel about me either, Henry. I stopped caring months ago. I'm only here because of your son, and you should be ashamed of yourself for the way you treat him."

"Why don't you mind your own business?" he says, swaying from side to side. "I've had it with you."

"And I've had it with you. I will not let you touch Mason again, you hear me?"

He laughs. "My son needs the motivation to get up and walk. That's what I'm giving him. Tough love."

"That's not what he needs right now. He needs his father and not a drunken monster."

"Watch your mouth," Henry warns. In his drunken stupor, he shoots out a hand to strike me, but I move out of the way in time. He starts shouting louder, sending insults flying around us, words a child should never hear. I can sense Mason nearby, crying softly.

I'm so focused on his father that I don't hear when he comes closer and attempts to get between me and Henry.

"Get away from her," Mason shouts tearfully. "Leave my mom alone." His hands grip his father's shirt, pulling it out of the waistband, shoving and pulling him at the same time as they edge toward the stairs.

He's protecting me the way I protect him every day. But this is not his battle to fight. And yet, I watch in horror as the boy shoves his wheelchair into his father's legs, shouting and crying at the same time. Henry staggers, before his hand shoots out again, and this time he strikes his son across the side of his face. Mason's scream tears through me like a knife. Henry readies himself to strike again, but I won't let him. Never again.

I throw myself at him without thinking and shove him hard, watching as he tries to grasp the railings, but he slips and tumbles down the stairs, grunting with pain at each step until he crashes at the bottom with a hard thud. All is quiet after that.

Henry's blood is oozing from a head wound, forming a pool of scarlet around him. My frantic breathing and Mason's whimpers are the only sounds that break the silence. It all happened so quickly. Having no idea what else to do, I grab the wheelchair handles and wheel Mason away.

"Is Daddy dead, Mommy?" Mason asks, trying to look back at the stairs. I say nothing as I wheel him into the closest room, which is one of the upstairs bathrooms. I need to shield Mason as best I can from what has happened. He has already seen and experienced enough trauma. As much as I want to stay and comfort him, and tell him everything will be fine, I need to go down there and find out. Nausea rises inside me at the thought of going down to see Henry, lying in a pool of his own blood.

Mason starts crying again and shaking all over. "Mommy, my head hurts." He winces as he touches the side of his head, where Henry hit him.s

"I know, baby." I cry as I try to kiss away his hurt. Then I take his face between my hands. "I need you to stay here. There's something I need to do."

When I go down to the foyer, I find Henry still in the same spot, unmoving. More blood has flowed from his wound. Panicking more and more by the second, I drop to my knees next to him. I can't see him breathing, and a sob escapes me as my mind takes me back to the day I met him for the first time, before the betrayal and the pain. He was so full of life then.

I sit there on the floor beside him, stunned and afraid. Henry is dead. I've killed him, and if the police come, they'll know it was me. I won't ask Mason to lie for me, and he saw me push him. It was self-defense, but the Baldwins and Lisa's family are powerful, and I know that if they bring in their hotshot lawyers, I will have no chance.

I didn't want him dead. I only wanted him to stop. Everything I did was for Mason.

Do something, I order myself. But what?

I could leave right now, get into my car and drive off. But doing that would make me seem instantly guilty. And what about Mason? Rising to my feet, I force myself to move from the spot and go to get my phone. I need to call someone who cares. The only person I can think of is Oliver. He is Henry's brother and my decision could backfire, but he has always been so kind to me and we've been growing close in recent months. I need someone else to think and act for me, someone to tell me what to do because my brain is frozen, unable to think straight.

"Something terrible happened," I say, my voice trembling as I press the phone to my ear and slump against the wall.

"Tess, what's wrong? Are you alright?" His voice croaks as though he's been sleeping.

"No," I say. "I don't know. I need help."

"Okay. Tell me what happened."

"Henry's dead," I mutter.

"What?" His voice sounds shrill now.

I wipe at my tears and try again. "He's dead, Oliver. I killed him."

"I don't understand. My brother's dead?"

His brother. They didn't have a close relationship, and got on each other's nerves, but when all is said and done, they were brothers. And I've robbed him of many more years together. Maybe I shouldn't have called him. What if he doesn't believe me? What if he calls the cops?

"Tess, where's Henry now?" Oliver asks cautiously.

"On the floor. I pushed him, and he fell down the stairs. He's all twisted, and there's so much blood coming from his head." As I speak, I watch Henry lying there, still unmoving, his legs bent in an unnatural angle. I turn away again, nauseated by the blood. I can't believe that only a few minutes ago I had heard his voice. And now it's trapped inside his throat, never to be heard again. I killed the man I used to love.

There's a long silence on the line.

"Tess, where's Lisa?" Oliver breaks through my thoughts. "Did she see what you did?"

"She's in bed. She had a migraine again, she didn't see. Oh my God, Oliver. I don't know what to do."

"You need to calm down," he urges. "Listen to me carefully. I need you to take Mason to bed and then wait for me. Make sure Lisa doesn't come downstairs."

"Should I call the police or nine-one-one? I'm scared."

"Don't do anything. I'm at the cottage. I'll be there in ten minutes."

Before Oliver arrives, I wheel Mason to his room, but my hands are shaking too much for me to lift him from his wheelchair and into his bed just yet. He's still in shock and doesn't say a word as I hand him his oversized stuffed dog, Bo, before I kiss him and rush out the room to meet Oliver downstairs. As soon as Oliver sees me and I fill him in, he tells me to go upstairs to bed while he goes to look at his brother and after what seems like forever, I hear sirens getting closer and then voices downstairs. I fully expect him to turn me in. But the hours go by, and the voices fade away. He comes up to my room, and what he says takes my breath away.

"It was an accident, Tess. Henry came home drunk. He tried to climb the stairs but he fell and hit his head, and died. Lisa doesn't know yet; she's fast asleep, dosed up on pills. We'll tell her in the morning."

"But—"

"But nothing. You were in bed. You didn't see what happened."

In the days after, that is the story he feeds everyone, including his mother.

Nobody ever gets to tell Lisa because she died that same night. An overdose. Oliver and his family assume that she overheard the paramedics pronounce Henry dead, and unable to go on without the man she loved, she ended her life.

In addition to lying about how Henry died, Oliver also convinces his parents that the news should stay out of the press to avoid bringing shame to the family and to safeguard Henry's reputation. The week of the funeral, which I'm not invited to because it's just for family, I pack my bags, ready to leave the Baldwin mansion. Catherine made it clear my services are no longer needed. And the way she looked at me sent shivers down my spine.

When I overheard Catherine and Alexander Baldwin saying they were going to put Mason in an orphanage, I was devastated. I begged Oliver to adopt the boy and hire me to take care of him. I had already moved into Oliver's house downtown because I had nowhere else to go.

"I like that idea," Oliver says to me after thinking about it for a week. "I'll offer to adopt Mason. But I don't need to hire you, Tess. Me, you, and Mason will get out of this town and start fresh somewhere else." He takes hold of my hand and pulls me in to a tight hug.

"Where will we go?" I ask.

"Somewhere where no one knows who we are." We pull apart and he smiles down at me. "Trust me, Tess. You want to be far away from here now. We need to start again."

Just like that, I'm sold on the plan, never thinking I might one day regret my decision or that Catherine's parting shot the day I moved out of Henry's mansion would accompany me into my new life:

I know what you did to my son. One day, I'll prove it, and I'll take away everything that you love.

CHAPTER FORTY-TWO

PRESENT

My shaking hands sink into the warm soap suds until they come into contact with the dishes underneath. As I lift one out to scrub it clean, I tilt my head back and peer out the window. Rainwater streaks the glass and distorts my reflection, making me look like a ghost. Since my world has literally fallen apart, I feel like a ghost, too: empty and hollow inside, dead.

A few hours have passed since Oliver turned me into a battered wife and my face is aching from his cruel touch. He apologized soon after, went out and brought me two beautiful roses, their thorns poking through the cellophane, before going back to work. He told me it was a mistake, that he had been so overwrought with worry for me and had not been thinking straight. I told him what he wanted to hear—that I understand and that I forgive him.

He's a fool to believe a word I said. It's clearer now than ever that I need to leave him. The fact that Mason saw him lay a hand on me is a wake-up call. The fear on his face had been identical to what I saw etched in his features the night I killed his father. Now I know: Oliver has the same violent tendencies his brother had. But in a way he's even worse, since he was sober when he struck me. I know it'll happen again, and I need to leave before it's too late. I wish I had left him immediately after his outburst, but I was in shock and I was terrified of what he might do to me or Mason.

I know that if I walk out on him, he could reveal my secret. He helped to cover up what I did, but he can just play dumb and pretend he never knew, that I only just confessed to him. Who wouldn't believe an upstanding man like him?

But as scary as it is to go, staying doesn't feel like an option right now. I've fought long and hard not to rock the boat, but I have no choice but to jump into the water and take the risk, even if it means my secret could come out into the open. Protecting Mason from him is my top priority now.

By the time I've washed, dried and put away the dishes, I've come to a decision. I need to escape and go off-grid with Mason. We'll find a place to hide, somewhere Oliver can never find us. I don't know where that safe haven is, but it doesn't have to be one particular place. If we have to keep moving for a while in order to stay safe, so be it. All I know is that I'll never forgive myself if something happens to Mason and I could have done something to protect him. I will have to ask Carmen to lend me some cash, and I'll find a way to repay her once we find a place to land.

While Mason is in his room listening to an audiobook with headphones, I walk around the house, trying to figure out a way to escape without being seen. It feels impossible with all the cameras set up, and I wonder now if maybe those cameras were not only meant for intruders. Oliver is at the office, but he said he watches the cameras while he's at work, to make sure Mason and I are okay. And if he sees me leaving the house, he will drive back immediately.

I grab my phone from our bed and take it with me to the bathroom. As far as I know, there are no cameras installed in our bathroom. But how can I really be sure? I don't trust Oliver anymore.

I dial Carmen's number, nervous butterflies fluttering in my stomach and sweat pooling into my armpits. As I wait for her to pick up, my hands tremble. Outside, the rain pitter-patters against my window and I hear cars speeding through the wet streets. Carmen answers on the fourth ring.

"Hello," I say. My voice comes out hoarse, like I've been screaming for hours. "Can you help me?"

"Sure, what's going on?" Her voice is filled with concern. "Are you okay?"

"No, I'm not." I choke back tears and shake my head. "I'm scared."

"What happened? Did something happen between you and Oliver?"

I take a deep breath. "Yes, Carmen. He hurt me."

Right now, she does not need to know the exact order of events. I'll explain it all later.

Carmen gasps. "What do you mean? Did he put his hands on you?"

When I don't answer, she lets out a harsh breath. "Oh, my God, I'm so sorry, Tess. I didn't think something like that would happen."

"Me neither. But I need to go. I need to leave him; it's not safe for me here. It's not safe for Mason; Oliver is dangerous. And Carmen, I think he might have done something to Dan."

Carmen is quiet for a long time and when she speaks, her voice is quivering. "How can I help?"

"I need money and a car. We need to get out of town. I promise I will find a way to pay you back."

"When do you plan on leaving?"

I drop onto the closed toilet bowl. "As soon as possible, today."

Silence again. "Okay," she says finally. "I'll help you. Is Oliver at home with you right now?"

"No, he's at work. But we need to be careful. There are cameras everywhere and if he sees us leaving, he'll come home." I swallow hard. "I don't know what he will do to me. He warned me not to leave the house."

"Then we have to be careful," Carmen says. "And we have to move fast. Pack only whatever is absolutely necessary. I'll meet you outside your house in half an hour. Is that enough time for you to get ready? I'm driving back from seeing my mother, so I can't come sooner."

Half an hour feels like a lifetime, but it's not like I have other options.

I nod even though she can't see me. "Thank you so much for this." I sniffle. "Thank you."

Oliver calls me soon after I end my call with Carmen.

"How about we go to dinner tonight?" he asks.

"Why?" My voice cracks from the weight of the single word. "You said I shouldn't leave the house."

"I know that, silly," he says, his voice husky with emotion. "But I'll be with you. You'll be safe."

I tighten my fingers around the phone and grit my teeth. After what he did, how can he think we're still a family? But the truth is, we never were, and I'm only seeing it now.

"What time will you be home?" I ask casually.

"Around six, I think. Can you be ready by then?"

"Yes," I lie. "We'll be waiting for you."

"Good," he says. "I won't come into the house, so remember to activate the alarm. And, Tess?"

"Yes," I whisper, my mouth dry.

"Everything is going to be fine. I promise you that. I'll take good care of you."

The same promise he made before we left Connecticut, the same promise he broke and pulverized. I will not stick around to find out if he will make things right. As usual, it takes a long time to get Mason dressed, even more so now that I am paralysed with fear. As I pull a t-shirt down over his head and shove some things into a suitcase, trying to keep out of sight of the cameras, he doesn't even ask me where we're going, and I'm glad for it. I'm sure he knows; he's a smart boy. Once I settle him into his wheelchair, I roll it into the doorway of the kitchen and grab his medication, stuffing the drugs into the big pocket at the back of the wheelchair.

The sound of a car pulling up into the driveway makes me stand up straighter, frozen, listening. Has Carmen already arrived? I check my watch. Still fifteen minutes left until she planned to be here. I run into the living room and glance out the window.

My heart stops.

It's Oliver, and the expression on his face tells me he's far from happy. Panicking, I head for the backdoor but it's locked and I have no idea where the key is. In the distance, I hear the sound of the key turning in the lock of the front door. Next to me, my little boy starts to cry, and I push him into the kitchen.

"Don't be afraid, sweetheart," I say to him, biting back my own tears. "Everything is going to be fine. I promise you that. But you need to stay here." I kiss his forehead and close the kitchen door on my way out.

Feeling like I'm about to pass out, I watch as Oliver locks the front door behind him and removes the key, dropping it into his pocket. His hair and clothes are damp from the rain. My pulse quickens and adrenaline shoots through my body, but before I have a chance to speak or act, he charges toward me. I step back, but he's too fast. He grabs me by the shoulders and pushes me against the wall. Air shoots from my lips in a dry gasp. His hands encircle my neck, pressing until I can feel my pulse beating against his fingers.

"What did you think you were doing?" he hisses, the smell of alcohol hitting me in the face. "Haven't you learned from last time?"

I can't answer; he's blocking the words from coming out. This is where it ends. I try to fight back, but I'm no match for his strength. He punches me in the stomach, and I double over. Gasping for air, I try to kick him, but he's too close. He grabs my head and slams it against the wall, and blood fills my mouth.

The world starts fading to black, but I pull myself out of the darkness. I need to stay here for Mason. I have to keep fighting.

CHAPTER FORTY-THREE

I'm desperate to get air in my lungs. In, out. In, out.

But I can't breathe.

I'm running out of time.

As Oliver's hands continue to tighten around my throat, my head is ringing and I try to blink my eyes into focus. The oxygen feeding my lungs is being cut off and the world is becoming a blur. But in the midst of it all, my mind takes me back to the past.

In a flash, I remember his face that night, kind, sympathetic. I remember his words when he told me that he'd make it look like an accident to protect me. I hear his words so clearly in my mind, as though the past has merged into the present.

Then I remember something I had blocked out.

Before I'd obeyed Oliver's order to go upstairs, I'd looked down at Henry for the last time. I hadn't wanted to, but when you try not to see something, your eyes automatically go to it. My gaze had followed his arm, stretched out next to his body, and lingered on his left hand. I'd seen a twitch. I replay that split-second moment in my head, trying to make sense of it. Back then, I'd convinced myself that what I'd seen was an illusion. My head had been spinning so fast that everything looked like it was in motion. But now, as I force my eyes to stay open, I'm not so sure anymore. What if what I saw was real? What if it was a movement, however slight? I can hear the blood rushing through my veins and my heart is racing, beating so fast it sounds like a sledgehammer is hitting the walls of my chest.

What if Henry was alive?

Oliver's hands tighten around my neck even more as I struggle to breathe.

What if I didn't kill him?

As all kinds of conflicting thoughts race through my mind, I fight and struggle to pull my head from Oliver's hands, but he's too strong.

What if I didn't kill Henry?

The words repeat in my mind as I start to lose consciousness, but I can't let go of the hope that has emerged, no matter how faint. Finally, Oliver loosens his hold on me, just enough to taunt me. I suck in air and when I exhale, it carries with it the words on my mind. "He... Henry was... He was alive."

Oliver's eyes narrow to slits, his lips fall slightly open, then his face twists into an expression of surprise. I've got my answer.

"You don't know what you're talking about." As he says the words, he starts to strangle me again. I try to squirm away, but he squeezes my neck tighter, cutting off the flow of oxygen to my brain.

The memories in my head start to die, one by one, until there's almost nothing left. But when I start to black out, he suddenly releases me and stumbles back. I slump forward, gasping and coughing blood. My hands go to my neck, touching the bruised area. It hurts to swallow. It hurts even more to breathe. My head is still spinning, and my throat feels like it's on fire, but I can't let go of what I know to be true. Henry was alive then. I didn't imagine it; the movement was real. What if I was wrong all this time? What if Henry is still alive somehow? What if he's the person who's been sneaking into the house?

Another even more terrifying thought sneaks into my shattered mind. What if he's not alive? I lift my head and look at the man I married. I've never for a second thought he was capable of this kind of violence. His face is red as he paces the small entrance hall. Oh my God. I swallow hard through my aching throat, and fresh tears burst to my eyes.

"You killed him, didn't you?" I wrap a hand around my neck like a brace in a failed attempt to lessen the damage done to my throat. "He wasn't dead."

Oliver's damp rubber soles squeak as he moves toward me. Everything is happening both in slow motion and at full speed. Before I can gather up my strength, he grabs my hair and pulls me up so that my face is level with his. His eyes as they look into mine are cloudy and unfocused with alcohol. "He would have died anyway. You had done a pretty good job on him already."

His words send a shiver racing through me. I need to keep talking, to get all the answers out of him.

"You're a monster," I manage to say between sobs. I hear the quiver in my voice, but I can't stop it. "You made me believe that I killed him. But you are the one who—"

"I did what I had to do," he says in a hoarse, raspy voice. His words are like poison as they leave his lips. "I rescued you and put him out of his misery. If he had woken up and told the cops what happened, you would have ended up in prison."

"Maybe not," I whisper, using all my might to shove him away from me. "Mason was there, he saw what happened. He was my witness."

Oliver stumbles back and comes for me again. I try to escape from him, running into the living room and toward the patio doors. But before I can open them, he yanks me back by the hair. I swivel around and my elbow meets the side of his face. He growls, grabbing his cheek. This time when he comes for me, he sends me falling to the floor, flat on my back. Then he's over me, his hands around my neck again, his weight crushing me.

"I can do it again, you know," he warns. "It gets easier each time."

"You killed him." Tears are pouring into my throat now.

Oliver killed his own brother. I'm innocent.

"You're right," he smirks. "But no one will ever know now, will they?"

Alarm bells go off in my head. It's over. I'm going to die.

But I have a reason to live, to push through. Mason. I protected him up to this point; how can I give up now? I use all my strength to try and push Oliver away. When I don't succeed, I bunch up my fists and pummel his chest and face. He punches me in the face and pain slices through me. Before I can get back my energy, he grabs one of the cushions on the couch. I scream, but the sound is low and strangled. Maybe Mason will hear me and call for help somehow.

"It didn't have to end this way," Oliver says as he brings the cushion down on my face.

I turn my head away, and open my mouth for air to flood in before the doors to my lungs are shut. I kick some more, determined to fight to the end, terrified about what he will do to Mason if I'm no longer here.

"I wanted you," he spits the words out. "The first day I met you, I was in love. I warned him to stay away from you, but he needed to prove to me that he could have anything he set his eyes on." A teardrop falls from his eyes and lands on my forehead. "He took you, even though he knew I had feelings for you." The bitterness, anger, and resentment in his voice is palpable.

I get it now. In his new life, Oliver had not only wanted what his brother had, he wanted to be like him. He has been leading the life of a successful businessman, going from one business trip to another, wearing suits even though he once told me he hates them, and ditching his ponytail to fit the role. He brings the cushion back to my face and presses down on it until his words become smothered.

"I didn't want Mason either. Who wants to take care of a cripple? I only did it for you. Things would have been so much simpler without him. But since Henry left him a nice chunk of money in his will, I didn't have to spend my own money on him."

I fight against the darkness that is fast encroaching on my mind. I'm not giving up, I want to live. I start to drift away, sinking into the darkness that's calling me.

Before I can disappear, I hear a thunking sound. Then the pressure on my head releases. A loud groan, then Oliver's weight is off me.

The cushion is snatched off my face and I come face-to-face with Carmen.

"Help me restrain him," she says and moves out of view.

Gasping and wheezing, I roll over to my side in time to see Oliver lying on the floor, clutching his head, blood seeping through his fingers. Carmen must have hit him over the head with something. He's barely able to get up, but he still tries. His eyes are wide and wild, his face smeared with blood. His lids flutter for a few seconds then he focuses on me. "You don't know what you're doing," he hisses. "You'll regret... You'll regret this."

"Shut up." Carmen kicks him in the head and pleads with me to help her again. I push through my pain and lack of energy, and together we wrestle him back to the ground and roll him to his stomach. His body is heavy, but bring two determined women together and they can accomplish anything.

Carmen uses Oliver's own tie to restrain his hands together behind his back and sits on him while I fetch a scarf for his legs. When I return, I lift my foot and bring it down on his head. He gasps loudly as the air leaves his lungs in a rush. Carmen says nothing.

The sounds of him in agony are satisfying. I can smell him now, and it's a combination of blood and urine. I almost want to laugh as a mix of blood and vomit trickles from his mouth onto the floor. He's almost unrecognizable. His face is swollen, his eyes bruised and bloodshot. I almost feel sorry for him. Almost.

While Carmen binds his legs, I move onto his back, aligning my knees with his spine. I can feel the anger and hatred coursing through me, making my whole body shake. I stay put as she digs for her phone in her jeans pocket to call the cops. I watch as she raises the phone to her ear. Even though she had surprised me with her strength just now, I can see the fear in her eyes.

It's only when we're waiting for the police that I begin to wonder how she got into the house.

The doors were all locked.

CHAPTER FORTY-FOUR

Now that Oliver is bound and helpless, I go to find Mason. He had not come out of the kitchen the entire time, and I'm guessing it's less to do with the orders I gave him and more to do with his fear of Oliver.

"Hey, sweetie," I say, pulling him into a hug that almost lifts him from his wheelchair. "It's alright now. Don't be scared."

For a while, we hold on to each other without talking and I feel safer than I have in days. When I let him go, he studies my face, then lifts a hand to my bruises, but barely touches them with the tip of his fingers, afraid to hurt me. I take hold of his hand and squeeze it tight. "You don't have to worry about me. I'm fine. And you are going to be okay. I'll never let anyone hurt you again."

As though he doesn't believe me about Oliver, he cranes his head to look past me, his eyes wide as he searches the doorway. It kills me inside to see him as afraid of his uncle as he had been of his father.

I turn him to look at me again. "He can't hurt us anymore, do you hear me? We're safe now."

He bobs his head in a nod and sniffles.

"I'll make you some nice hot chocolate. It will make you feel better."

Since my hands are still shaking, I almost spill hot milk on myself. Mason doesn't notice; he's still wordlessly staring at the door. When I hand him the drink, he gives me a faint smile and I tell him again that I'll come back to him soon.

Happy that he's safe even if shaken, I return to the living room, where Carmen is kneeling next to Oliver, filling his ears with insults. He's still too weak to move or speak. When she sees me, she stands up and hurries to my side. "There's something I need to tell you," she says, choking up.

"How did you get into the house?" I interrupt.

She pulls me down onto the couch as if we're about to have a long conversation, and averts her gaze from mine when she speaks. "I have a key."

I frown. "How's that possible? I didn't give you one."

"I know. I'm sorry." She drops her head. "I took one of your spare keys and had a copy made."

"You did what?" I sit motionless for a moment, stunned. "I don't understand."

She takes my hands and squeezes them. "I'm so sorry, Tess. I'm sorry about a lot of things." A tear rolls down her cheek and I follow the trail to her chin.

I slide my hands from hers and cross them against my stomach. "What are you talking about?" I glance over at Oliver on the floor and then back at her. "Why would you be sorry? You saved my life."

"It's the least I could do since I brought you into this mess."

"You mean the fake pregnancy?"

"More than that." She clasps her hands in her lap and stares at them. She's about to explain when we hear the screams of sirens in the distance. Oliver must have heard them too because he's writhing on the floor now, trying and failing to get away. He's also attempting to say something, but the words coming out of his mouth are broken pieces that make no sense. I've already heard everything I needed to hear from him. The rest, he can tell the cops.

"I'm Mason's mother," Carmen blurts out.

My head snaps back in shock as her words hit me like a bag of bricks. I'm sure she must have said that wrong.

My mouth opens and closes at the confusion raging inside me. "You—what?"

She looks up at me again, meeting my gaze. "Mason is my son. The reason I copied your key is so I can come and go. I just wanted to be close to him."

"It was you?"

She lets out a raspy sigh. "I wanted to be near him. I wanted him back. And to be honest, I wanted to scare you a bit. I've been so jealous of you, Tess."

My mouth is dry. There's so much I want to ask, but I don't know where to start.

"You've been sneaking into our home, in disguise? You stalked us?"

She nods, fresh tears pouring down her cheeks. "I didn't want to only see Mason during the book club meetings or when we met up."

"Please tell me you're joking." I press the heel of my palm against my forehead. "This can't be happening."

"I—Please, let me... let me explain." Her words come out broken, as if she's unsure if I'll want to hear the story she's about to tell me.

To be honest, I'm not sure I do either. I shoot to my feet and glare down at her. "Go ahead, please," I say, my voice hard. "Tell me what's going on."

She licks her bottom lip and exhales. "I was a sex worker and Henry Baldwin was my client. I got pregnant and I wanted to keep the baby, but he said he would raise the child. He wanted an heir."

"But Mason was adopted," I say, breathless.

"That's what Henry told everyone. He wanted to avoid a scandal. If it came out that he had fathered a child with a sex worker, it would have been bad for his family, especially for his father who is in politics."

I glance at the closed kitchen door, making sure Mason hasn't come out to listen. I stare back at Carmen.

"I don't believe you," I whisper. "I don't."

"It's true, Tess." She pauses. "Henry gave me a lot of money to give him the child."

"He bought your silence?"

Her shoulders slump forward. "I couldn't say no. It was more money than I could have ever imagined having. I didn't have to work anymore."

I sink back onto the couch, feeling faint. "So, you gave him Mason and—"

"I left town." She swallows loud and wipes her tears. "But not for long. With the money, I could do whatever I liked, but I regretted giving my son away. So, I watched him from a distance. I saw you taking care of him. I saw Henry's wife and mother ignoring him."

"You spied on us?" Another memory suddenly comes back to me. "Mason said he saw a man in the woods."

"It was me. I wore a man's clothes and made sure my head was covered; I didn't want him to be able to describe me to Henry. I just needed to know that my son was being well taken care of." Her voice is low now, broken. "But I had to be careful because Henry had told me if he ever saw me again, he would destroy me."

I can't believe what I'm hearing. My head is spinning and my stomach feels like it's ready to throw up everything I've eaten so far today. Deceit and betrayal are like two bitter pills on my tongue, and I'm not sure I can swallow them. "And you followed us here?"

She nods. "When I found out Henry was dead, I wondered what would happen to Mason. I watched you and Oliver take him away, and I found out where his new office was located. That's how I found out where you were."

"And that's why you moved into this neighborhood not long after we did." I cover my face with my hands, then drop them again in my lap. "You said you came to Westledge to be close to your mother's nursing home. That was a lie?"

"My mother died when I was a child." She closes her eyes and shakes her head, biting into her bottom lip. "I'm so sorry, Tess. I should have told you a long time ago. I hurt you so much and all you wanted to do was protect my son. But please understand that I did what I needed to do in order to be in his life. I just didn't see any other way."

"You could have come to me." I blink away my own tears. "You could have told me."

She drops her head into her hands and weeps. "I wasn't thinking straight. All I knew was that I wanted your life."

"My life?" A fresh wave of shock crashes into my gut.

She lifts her head. "I wanted to be the one able to take care of my son."

"So you lied to me? Pretended to be my friend?" I can't keep the hurt out of my voice. "I trusted you."

I feel like a complete fool now. And that's exactly what I am. If I have to be honest, there were times I wondered why Carmen was going to such lengths to help me out. I'd never had a friend like her before.

"What else are you hiding? Do you even have a dead husband? Is everything you told me a complete lie?"

Before she can say anything more, the doorbell rings. The cops have arrived. When I walk past Oliver, he finally finds the ability to speak.

"Don't do anything stupid," he says. His voice is weak and raspy, but his words are still menacing.

"I've done a lot of stupid things in my life," I retort. "This won't be one of them. I'll make sure you go to prison where you belong."

"They won't believe you, you know." He coughs out blood. "About what happened to Henry. My family is powerful. You will go down for it."

I glare down at him. "I don't care about your threats anymore, Oliver. I won't allow you to manipulate me, not anymore. After what you did to me, and what I think you did to Dan, I think the cops will believe me."

As I walk away from him I feel numb, inside and out, even with the pain coursing through my body. I need to explain to the police what happened, then I need a moment to take it all in, to digest everything Carmen said.

Two uniformed officers are standing outside on the doorstep.

"I'm Sherriff Jack Russ," one of them says, a man with not a scrap of hair on his head. "We received an emergency call from this address. Is everyone alright? Are you okay, ma'am?" He tries to peer past my shoulder.

"I am now," I say, even though I'm not sure about that. I may be just about alright physically, but emotionally I feel as though I've been trampled on by a pack of elephants.

"Your name, please," the officer says when I usher them inside.

"Tess. My name is Tess Baldwin." For the first time in a long time, I'm not afraid of the police. I'm more than ready to share my truth. The two officers are here to protect me, not to take me away. But Oliver needs to pay for what he did. He needs to spend the rest of his life behind bars. I swiftly explain to the officers what happened, and they rush into the house ready to restrain my husband. When they see him on the ground, helpless, they look at both me and Carmen in surprise. We've already done the work for them.

An hour after the police take Oliver away, I receive a call from the sheriff.

"Mrs. Baldwin, I'm calling to let you know that your husband has confessed to killing Dan Dunkirk."

And not long after, I receive more news. Dan's body has been found in the nearby river, trapped under an abandoned boat.

CHAPTER FORTY-FIVE

When the police took Oliver away, I asked Carmen to leave. I needed to be alone to process what she told me. Three hours have passed since she told me she's Mason's mother, and I'm ready to talk. I don't think I have much choice in the matter. The pain will be too much to bear, but I need to face it. The news about Dan hit me hard, too, and I'm not sure I have any tears left in my body.

Carmen will be here any minute. Thankfully, Mason is having a nap, exhausted from everything that happened earlier. While I wait for the woman who claims to be his mother to arrive, I keep myself occupied by looking through Oliver's phone, which fell out onto the floor during our struggle. I scroll through his recent calls absently, and suddenly my stomach lurches. The affair was never over.

My hands are shaking as I press on *Her*. The phone rings only once before it's cut off, and a part of me is relieved. It won't be long before Oliver is no longer part of my life. So why do I even care? Still, I click on the name again, but this time I don't call. Instead, I read out the single digits that make up her phone number. I grab my own phone and search for the same number in my contacts.

When the doorbell rings, I jolt upright and push Oliver's phone into my pocket, and when I open the front door, I find Carmen shifting from one foot to the other, obviously nervous about the conversation we're about to have.

"Let's stay in the kitchen," I say, my voice devoid of any emotion.

I grab a bottle of water from the fridge and hand it to her.

"Thanks," she says and lowers it to the table. Her mouth starts to twitch, and I watch as a tear slides down her cheek. I clench my jaw, trying to control my emotions. I'm conflicted about how to feel about her, furious that she lied to me all this time, but also grateful that she saved my life. If she had not had a key to our house, Oliver could have killed me. But it's still hard for me to believe that all along it was my best friend sneaking into our house and frightening me so much.

After a long stretch of awkward silence, I reach for Mason's iPad and open it to the photo of the person in the garden. "Is this you?"

She nods, and bites into her bottom lip. "Tess, I never wanted to give my son away. Henry forced me to. And when he died, I didn't think I could ever get him back, not after his uncle adopted him, not after I'd signed away the right to be his mother."

Sharp pain slices through my gut as I think of the prospect of Mason being taken away from me. If he really is Carmen's son, I'll have no right to keep him. I've tried so hard to keep him in my life, and now I'm about to lose him. How can I keep him when his mother is perfectly capable of taking care of him herself?

"I'm really sorry, Tess," Carmen continues. "I feel terrible for what I did to you." Her face is rumpled by pain and her cheeks are stained by tears. She keeps wiping them away, but they won't stop running. "You have every right to hate me."

"Are you really Mason's mother?" My voice is a fragile squeak.

"I promise you that I am." She pulls something from her pocket, unfolds it, then slides it across the table toward me. "Please, look. You'll see that I'm telling you the truth." It's a photo of a newborn baby. "I took this before Henry took Mason away."

The photo is yellowed and crumpled, and it's starting to come apart like a wet piece of paper. I take a ragged breath before I gaze down at the baby, and back at her. I see Mason's gray eyes staring back at me, and his scraps of auburn hair.

She may have given him away in exchange for money, but nothing will change the fact that she's the woman who had carried him for nine months, the one who went through the pain of bringing him into the world. If there were a way to measure love, would hers weigh more than mine? Would hers be more intense because she's Mason's biological mother?

All this time, I raised Mason as though he was my own son. I washed him and dressed him. I comforted him when he was scared. I protected him as best I could. He called me mom. How could I have known that, only a few blocks away, the woman who gave birth to him was waiting to take him away? How could I have known that it was only a matter of time before she tore us apart?

I pick up the photo next and press it to my chest, holding it there as if it can make the aches in my chest go away. I lower it again and press my finger to the surface. The baby's face is peaceful and soft, his eyes closed, a tiny smile on his lips. A lump the size of a fist rises to my throat.

I push the photo away from me. Overcome with emotion, I clench my fists on the table and swallow the tears lodged in my throat, trying to contain my anger and pain, trying not to think about the future ahead, a life without my borrowed son.

Carmen lays her hands flat on the table and sighs. "I wanted to be a part of his life. I wanted to be the one to see him every day, watch him grow. It killed me to see you have it all, to have to say goodbye to Mason after my brief moments with him, while you got to take care of him all the time."

"Is that why you had an affair with my husband? Because you wanted to take over my life?" My words are bitter and harsh. It feels as though a volcano is erupting inside of me, threatening to explode my entire being, shattering everything I thought was real. Her skin goes pale. She doesn't need to say a word; the answers are written all over her face.

I pull out Oliver's phone and slide it toward her. It's open to her contact details. The same number I have saved on my phone.

"How could you do that? I confided in you about my marriage, and all along you were the one sleeping with my husband?" My fingers flutter to my throat, brushing against the bruises on my neck where Oliver had grabbed me. I can still feel the grip of his hands around my neck. It's hard to believe that he could have killed me today.

Finally, my tears break free, I can no longer hold them back. They stream down my cheeks and drip onto the table. How could I have been so stupid? How could I have thought it was Jocelyn; how did I not see that my closest friend was having an affair with my husband?

An hour ago, I found receipts in Oliver's office that proved that most times when he said he was out of town, he wasn't. He was staying at the Jade Hill Hotel in the town square. The days Carmen claimed to be visiting her mother or even running errands in town, she probably went to be with him.

I now understand the reason why Oliver wanted me to leave the book club. It was all because of her. He was scared that she would talk, that the truth would come out into the open. Carmen doesn't pick up the phone, doesn't even look at the screen. Her eyes are on mine, pleading for forgiveness.

"I did it for Mason. I wanted to be a mother to my son, can't you understand that? I know I went about it the wrong way. I wasn't thinking straight." Her lips tremble as she wipes her eyes with the back of her hand. "I thought I would seduce Oliver and we would raise Mason together. I made sure he didn't save my name on your phone, I didn't want you to see any calls from me coming up."

"I see," I say. "When you helped me fake my pregnancy, did you know he was impotent?"

She nods. "He wouldn't leave you for me, and you wouldn't leave him. So when you told him you were pregnant I thought he'd think you were cheating. But he thought he was somehow cured. I couldn't tell him I knew about the fake pregnancy, because he'd never forgive me for my involvement. So I dropped little hints, suggestions that maybe you were also going around behind his back. But he was so happy at the thought of being a father that he didn't want to listen to me and he ended it with me for a long while. I guess he believed me in the end, and when he got another test and found out the baby couldn't be his, he suspected Dan." She picks up her bottle of water, unscrews the cap, and raises it to her lips to take a swig. "If you'd faked a miscarriage before he'd realized the baby couldn't be his, I was going to record a conversation between us with you telling me about it. I was sure he'd be so angry that you'd manipulated him and put him through pain like that, that it would be the final straw. And after what you'd done, he'd never believe you if you said I was involved."

I bring my hands together and start to clap. "An excellent plan. Maybe you two would have been good together. So, why did you do it? Why did you attack him to save me?"

She flattened her palms against her chest. "You have to

understand, Tess. He wasn't the man I thought he was. I didn't know he was violent. Not until you called me today. After the call, I remembered the day you hurried home so suddenly after you spoke to him on the phone. You looked terrified."

In the silence that follows, neither of us speaks. I'm afraid to ask about what comes next, afraid to hear what I know she will say. Everything is out in the open now. I no longer have the right to keep Mason.

"Tess, I don't want to take Mason away from you, not anymore," she says finally as though reading my mind. "I know that you love him and he needs you. I saw you comforting him before the police arrived, and I just knew in my heart that there had to be another way."

I pause for a moment, my mind racing. "What are you saying?"

"I think... maybe, if you like, he could have two mothers that love him." She reaches across the table and squeezes my hand. "Maybe one day you'll find a way to forgive me and we can co-parent him. But if you're not interested, I understand."

I nod, choking back tears. "Thank you for that offer. I'll think about it."

Before Carmen leaves, she hands me an envelope. "I'm sorry I took this when I came into your house," she says. "But please know that I don't blame you for what you did. I would have done the same thing."

After she leaves, I watch her through the window. As she walks down the street, I see her pull out what looks like a packet of cigarettes from her jeans and she lights one. I had no idea until now that she's a smoker. She and Oliver probably used to smoke together.

I'm still holding the thick envelope, afraid to look inside, but I decide to go and check on Mason first because I have the sudden urge to be near him. In the silence of his room, I watch him sleeping, unaware that his life is about to change. I reach out and caress his cheek, my throat constricting, tears flowing down my face. I want to freeze time, to stay here with him forever.

I love him and I want to keep him all to myself.

He opens his eyes and they focus on my face. "Mom," he says.

I don't answer because he can no longer call me that.

Once back in the kitchen, I muster up the courage to open the envelope and remove a stack of papers. My heart begins to race as soon as I read the first sentence on the first page. In my hands I'm holding my novel, a fictionalized account of my life over the past three years. I had hidden it in a drawer in my room, after printing it off to read through one day. Even with the changes in characters and settings, some of the events remain the same. There are only two chapters left to write, and anyone who knows me will know the truth about what happened if they read it. I was never going to publish it; I just needed to find a way to process what happened to me.

As I flip through the pages in search of one particular paragraph, I can barely breathe. The passage I'm looking at has a note written in the margin.

Your secret is safe with me, but you might want to get rid of this.

Carmen knows.

She knows about the bottle of water I brought to Lisa with her sleeping pills and pain meds that night. And the lethal concentration of crushed pills it contained.

EPILOGUE

ONE YEAR LATER

On March 16, the kitchen of my new cottage is filled with light from the setting sun. The light streams in through the windows, painting the cabinets and appliances in a warm glow. The oven is on, and the smell of baking cake wafts through the room. I wipe my hands on the kitchen towel before going to open the door. I'm not expecting anyone, so it's a pleasant surprise to see Carmen standing on the porch behind Mason's wheelchair.

"Surprise," Mason shouts.

Every time I hear excitement in his voice, my chest flutters with joy. It will take a while for me to get used to the sound of his unfiltered laughter. In the last year he has made remarkable progress, flourishing in Oliver's absence. I ruffle his hair and look up at Carmen. "What are you guys doing here? It's Tuesday. I thought you were coming on Friday."

Up until now, I've been having Mason over to stay on most weekends.

"We didn't want you to be alone for your birthday," Mason chimes in. "Can I stay, please?"

Carmen shrugs and smiles. There's no hint of sadness

behind her eyes. She loves that Mason feels close to the both of us.

"That's really sweet of you." I open the door wider to let them enter.

"Are you sure it's okay?" I ask Carmen as Mason wheels himself into the kitchen.

"Of course, it's okay. You know that. In fact, I was thinking that maybe we should revisit our arrangement. Mason could come over more often than just on some weekends."

"You mean that?" I clasp my hands under my chin, tears stinging the backs of my eyes.

"Stop getting all teary on me," Carmen says and guides me to the kitchen.

Mason has parked his wheelchair in front of the oven. "Is that your birthday cake?"

"Yep," I say.

He frowns. "Were you planning to celebrate by yourself?"

"Why not? But since you're here, we'll celebrate together."

For the longest time, I've been putting others before myself. As much as I love Mason and don't regret a thing I did for him, sometimes it feels good to have my life back, to focus on me for a change. It was tough at first, but I'm slowly getting used to it. This is my first birthday since Oliver was arrested and I want it to symbolize a new beginning for me.

It took a while for me to forgive Carmen for what she did, but in the end, I understood her, just as, after reading my story, she understood why I did what I did to Lisa. We are more alike than I wanted to admit, both hurt and manipulated by powerful people. And we both did the things we did out of love for Mason.

In the end, it all turned out perfectly. With Oliver, Mason's former legal guardian, in prison, and his family wanting nothing to do with the son of a sex worker, it wasn't hard to transfer the parental rights to Carmen.

"Mom," Mason says to me. I'm honored that he still calls me that. "You two are boring. Can I play games in my room?"

"Go ahead," I say and he disappears through the doorway.

"How is he doing at school?" I ask Carmen.

Three months after Oliver went to jail, we moved to Wilmington. We wanted to get away from the town's fury and gossip about my husband being a murderer, and give Mason a new life. Mason has been attending a school for kids with special needs, as both Carmen and I decided it would do him good to be surrounded by other children. I've been working in a local café, and Carmen gave me enough money to buy a little place of my own.

Carmen plucks a grape from the fruit basket and pops it into her mouth. "He's doing great. At our last meeting, Mrs. Young said he's adjusting really well and the other kids love him." She leans against the kitchen counter and her expression grows serious. "How about you? How do you feel now that it's all over?"

"Relieved," I say. "I'm ready to move on with my life."

Oliver's second trial has finally come to a close. His family never showed up; they distanced themselves completely, I guess to protect their reputation. The first trial was easy, since there was plenty of evidence to prove he murdered Dan. But when it came to being found guilty for the murder of his brother, he pinned the crime on me, as he promised he would.

That was until they put Mason on the stand. At first, I thought he would simply talk about how his father was attacking him that night, and how I stepped between them, but to my horror, the questioning took on an unexpected turn. Mason told the court that he saw Oliver smashing his father's head into the floor. Oliver had not seen him sitting in his wheelchair in the hallway near the top of the stairs.

The revelation shocked me to the core.

I was worried that the questioning would send Mason down

a dark path, but for some reason, it seemed to have opened him up more. He started seeing a psychologist, who helped him process what had happened. Now I understand why he never wanted Oliver to be involved in his daily care, why he was quiet around him. He was scared of his uncle. He knew before I did what he was capable of.

My plan from the beginning was to protect him and, in turn, he ended up protecting me. Because of him, I'm a free woman, and I will do everything possible to make the most of my freedom while Oliver is locked away for life, unable to hurt another human being.

While Carmen and I chat, the doorbell rings.

"Don't get up," she says. "I'll get it."

She leaves the kitchen before I can protest.

A few minutes later, she comes back with Mason behind her and in her hands she holds a large, white box. She puts it on the table in front of me and winks.

As I read the words on the box, my eyes fill with tears.

Sparkies Hot Dogs.

Carmen puts a hand on my shoulder. "Mason said you might like a hot dog party."

Mason grins and wheels himself toward me. "I did. It was my idea. Happy birthday, Mom."

Laughing and crying at the same time, I reach for my son and hug him.

"I have an idea," I say when we pull apart. "It's been raining all week, but today is so sunny. We should take advantage of it. Why don't we go out for ice cream before eating the hot dogs? Not too far from here is a great ice cream shop. What do you think?"

Mason gives me the thumbs up. "Sounds like a plan."

Thirty minutes later, Carmen and I are sitting on a bench throwing breadcrumbs to the ducks in the lake while Mason wheels himself off to get his second ice cream. For a few minutes we share stories about Dan, and talk about how he left a hole in our lives. Then Carmen crosses her legs and scoots closer to me.

"Have you heard the latest news from Westledge?" she asks.

I crease my eyebrows in confusion. "Which news? I hope it's good."

Westledge left a bitter taste in my mouth, so I try my best not to think about it when I can avoid it.

"Jocelyn announced her engagement to Oscar Davenport on all of her social media accounts yesterday."

I gasp, and my mouth falls open in astonishment. "*The* Oscar Davenport, the mayor of Westledge?"

"You got that right."

"But isn't he at least twenty years older than her, and married?"

"Twenty-five. His wife left him after she found out that he bought Jocelyn an apartment in New York, their love nest for the past year. That's where she was, by the way, when she went off the radar around the time Dan went missing. I guess the wife did him a favor by leaving, so he proposed."

I now understand why Jocelyn never posted a picture of her man on social media. It still blows my mind that I thought she was cheating on Oliver. When I sent her the message on Instagram from my fake account, she probably thought it was the mayor's wife.

Carmen stops talking when I don't respond and smacks her forehead. "I of all people don't have the right to judge anyone. I'm guilty of the same thing."

I squeeze her hand. "It doesn't matter what happened in the past. You know I forgive you."

On the evening I returned Jocelyn's dish to her, she denied having an affair with Oliver, but I didn't believe her. And when she was gone the next day, I assumed that she was going to hide her shame, afraid I would tell everyone. Even though I have forgiven Carmen, it still blows my mind to think it was her all along.

Carmen and I end the conversation when we hear Mason's wheelchair squeak. Each of his hands is holding a cone.

"Here," he says as he presses the ten dollar bill I gave him into my hand.

I look at his face and then at the ice creams. "How did you pay for those?"

"I didn't. Grandma paid for it. She said to give you this." He holds out one of the ice cream cones, blood-red strawberry with a cherry on top. "And she said she'll see you soon."

A LETTER FROM L.G. DAVIS

Dear reader,

I'm grateful and honored that you chose to read *Liar Liar*. Writing it was challenging at times, but it was also an incredible experience, and I hope you enjoyed reading it. If you wish to read more of my work in the future, I'd like to invite you to sign up at the link below.

This will ensure that you don't miss any of my upcoming book releases. The email address you provide will never be shared, and you can unsubscribe at any time.

www.bookouture.com/l-g-davis

I hope you had a good time hanging out with Tess, Mason, Carmen, and the other characters. I also hope that the fictional town of Westledge felt like a real place and that you would have loved to attend the Cherry Lane Book Club meetings or to take part in the Big Spring Clean festival.

If you enjoyed the journey, please consider posting a review. I'd love to hear your thoughts about the book, and your feedback would encourage other readers to give *Liar Liar* or some of my other books a chance. I appreciate you taking the time in advance.

There's nothing I love more than hearing from my readers. If you'd like to get in touch, you can reach me on my Facebook page, Instagram, Twitter, or my website. Feel free to contact me at any time.

Thank you again for reading.

Much love,

Liz xxx

http://www.author-lgdavis.com

 facebook.com/LGDavisBooks

twitter.com/LGDavisAuthor

instagram.com/LGDavisAuthor

ACKNOWLEDGMENTS

Firstly, I would like to thank my fantastic editor, Rhianna Louise. Rhianna, working with you from the birth of the idea for this book to the final draft has been a true pleasure. I greatly appreciate your feedback and incredible attention to detail. Thanks for being supportive, helpful, and kind throughout this journey. We had so much fun bringing this book to life, and I'm thankful to you for helping me make it the best book it could be.

Thank you also to the rest of the team at Bookouture for all you did to ensure this book's success and for your ongoing support. You guys are amazing.

This book was written under challenging circumstances and could not have happened without the support of my wonderful family.

Toye, I can't tell you enough how grateful I am for having you as my husband. When I doubt myself and my writing ability, you listen to my fears and hold my hand. I couldn't ask for a more supportive and loving partner. I love you so much.

Thank you also to my beautiful children, who are my biggest fans and motivators. Dear Dara and Simon, you make me feel like the best storyteller ever. You both give me such joy and pride, and I am blessed to be your mother.

Last but not least, I want to thank my readers. I want to thank those of you who have been reading my books for years, for your continued interest in my work, and also those who are new to my writing.

Dear reader, whether you purchased this book, borrowed it, or received it as a gift from someone, I appreciate you for taking the time to read it, and I look forward to bringing you more books in the future.

CPSIA information can be obtained
at www.ICGtesting.com
Printed in the USA
LVHW111929210822
726495LV00004B/442